5PM

A NOVEL

By
CHRIS HEINICKE

First edition COPYRIGHT © 2015 Chris Heinicke
Second edition COPYRIGHT © 2020 Chris Heinicke and KC Stories
5PM
By Chris Heinicke
ISBN-13: 978-0-9946382-6-7

Cover Photo by Mark Holzigal, Photographer
Cover Design by Rebecca Berto, Berto Designs
Additional Cover Art by Kate Reedwood (second edition)

Manuscript Services (first edition)—Editing & Interior Design by
Rogena Mitchell-Jones, Literary Editor www.rogenamitchell.com

Editing and Interior design services (second edition) provided by Kate
Reedwood and KC Stories www.LegacyHunter.space

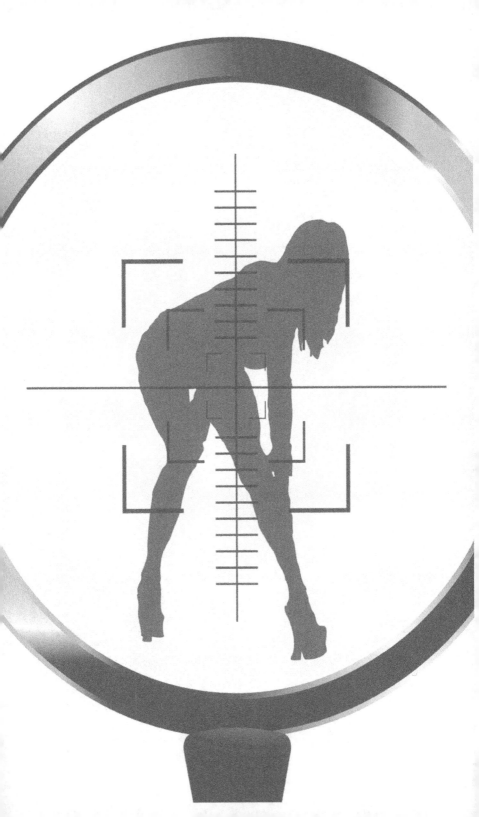

TABLE OF CONTENTS

To my dear wife, Glenda, and my three children, Ethan, Krystal, and Siobhan— whose love, support, and belief in me helped make this novel possible.

ACKNOWLEDGEMENTS AND ABOUT THIS EDITION

WRITING HAS BEEN a labor of love for me for some years now, a passion that started in school, but went into hibernation until 2006. It took me the best part of eight years to get my first book to the stage where I was ready to find a publisher, and while I was awaiting word from them, I started a new project during NaNoWriMo in 2014. This presented many challenges, given my full-time job status, and my third child arriving in the world just three months prior. But I took every spare moment I had and went to work on a book originally started in 2007 as a short story.

I completed NaNoWriMo, and a couple of weeks later, the first draft of 5PM was born. With the support of my wife, Glenda, and the editing skills of Rogena Mitchell Jones, and a brilliant cover design from Rebecca Wellwood (nee, Berto), my debut book was unleashed to the world as a self-published novel in 2014.

This 2020 edition is the result of my desire to review and address issues I had with the main character, Terry. After six years, I have grown as a writer, and I felt 5PM could use some revisions to broaden it into the book I always envisioned. With over 20k words added and a completely fresh edit, while Terry remains a flawed protagonist for most of

CHRIS HEINICKE

the story, I believe the motivations for his actions are now deeper and the story flows with greater suspense and fluidity.

A very special thank you to my friend and writing partner, Kate Reedwood, for her assistance with the revisions and editing work, which has helped bring this second edition of 5PM to life. I know our friendship and writing partnership will endure for years to come as we build our book list with our new joint venture, KC Stories.

Special thanks as well to Sarah Thorne, Chris Desmarais, and Tracey Hayer-Roberts for their assistance in beta reading this edition, and my assistant Nicole Ulery, for keeping me organized with the business side of self-publishing and helping with the monthly newsletters for KC Stories.

I also have many friends inside and outside the writing community who have been of great support over the years: Kate Annabel, Sharon Wood, Bianca Lloyd, Kat Booker, Laura Hunter, Barb Mawby, Donna Moy, Leesa Barrell, Lee Herring, Alex James, Lauren Dawes, Tracy Joyce, Jarrod Elvin, Ash and Skyla Madi, Dionne Lister, Rebecca Nolan, Mark Holzigal, Rose-Marie Haddow, Allison Cosgrove, Kylie Cosgrove, Daniel Sullivan, Kerry Radford, Suzanne Gangarosa, Cathy Dionne, Pat Viglione, the members of The Legacy Hunter Guild fan group, Andy Gasson (who also owns the excellent second-hand book shop, Magpie Books), and many, many more.

I would also like to give a special shout out to my father Malcolm Crocker, as well as his partner Sue, with whom I am building a very special father-son relationship after having been estranged for 35+ years. Thanks for coming back into my life and supporting my writing career.

CHAPTER 1

DAY 9

ALL MY LIFE, I never imagined the hiding place I used for my porno mags as a teenager would be the same place I'd be hiding in as an adult. Yet, here I am, huddled beneath a musty wool blanket, which my dearly departed grandmother made for me when I was a snotty-nosed little brat, trying not to think or breathe or do anything that might accelerate my inevitable end.

Down here, beneath a trapdoor in my childhood bedroom, the stench of rot fills my nostrils, and I hate to think how many animals have pissed here in the more than twenty years since I left home.

My nose stings from the dust that coats everything. I need to sneeze so badly my eyes are watering. But I dare not. Any sound will give away my location to the person stalking me.

I know my hunter is close. As they walk from one room to another, the clicking of their heels against the wooden floorboards draws nearer. Slow, measured steps. The sound of approaching doom echoes throughout the house louder than any shouted threat, and it encompasses a menace my heart understands. It's racing as if trying to escape my chest. But escape is not an option for me. Not now.

I should give myself up. Forgo the suspense. It's just a matter of time before I'm found. But I cling to each second of freedom like a drowning man gasping for breath. I could plead for my life. Offer money, lots of money. Cry and yell that I'm sorry and that I'll do everything to right the wrongs I've committed—if I'm just given one more chance. But I'm certain I'll end up dead anyway. This hunter possesses a heart colder than the steel pistol they carry. My words won't matter. And I don't deserve mercy even if it was offered. I've had this coming to me, and I know it.

Every few moments, the footsteps cease. I imagine my predator being thorough. Carefully scouring every nook and cranny of each room. Looking for me.

As the silence lengthens, I peek from beneath the blanket. Dust-filled beams of sunlight spill through the cracks between the old timber floorboards. My back burns from lying against the cement floor. Has the hunter abandoned the hunt? Is it safe to move?

The footsteps start again, echoing louder as they move faster down the hallway and into the room next to the one I cower beneath. I shut my eyes, willing myself not to move. The clicking of heels on wood has become the measure of my existence, counting down the moments I have left.

I deserve death. I know this.

My sins have led me to this point. I have hurt those I love more than they have me. I should surrender and embrace the punishment I deserve. I have lied, and I have cheated. Caused so much damage to so many people in the last week that a quick death would be too easy. I created this mess. I brought this on myself. I chose it with every decision I made.

But I am a coward. I cling to the hope that maybe, just maybe, there is some way to avoid this looming finality.

As the echoes of the hunter's steps come to a halt in the hallway leading to my room, I hold my breath. I'm trapped like an animal, lying injured beneath the shadows of this house. I have no weapons. If I'm found, I am dead.

Silence lingers like an uninvited party guest, lasting much longer this time. The hunter knows I'm here; they're toying with me. If the goal is to make sure I'm paralyzed with fear, they've achieved it.

Heavy heels clunk against the old timber boards. The sound is loud now, so loud, and as the volume climbs, my fear climbs with it, thundering through my veins.

I've chosen the wrong place to hide. I realize it now as the heavy footsteps contact the floorboards of my room and pass across it.

Back in the days when this room was my bedroom, this crawlspace was a secret place. The trapdoor was hidden by the throw rug I used to place over it.

But that time is past. This room is no longer my room. The rug is long gone, and the floorboards are clear of dust where I pressed on their edges to pop the hidden door panels free.

Stopping directly above me, my pursuer lets out a chuckle.

The hunter knocks on the wooden floor and easily finds the not-so-hidden edge of the trapdoor. I squeeze my eyes shut tight. This is it. My heart beats so fast, it feels like it's trying to escape the cage of my ribs and run away without the rest of me. I'm covered in sweat and goosebumps, and no longer sure the scent of piss belongs to the animals that once lived in this space.

Someone is breathing softly...and it's not me. As it's yanked open, the trapdoor creaks, the sound almost deafening in the still air. I try to turn away. My watery eyes aren't ready to filter the harshness of the sunlight, but it doesn't matter now. The game is up. I have reached the last few heartbeats of my life.

Here we are, face to face; me and my inevitable end. As the blanket is snatched from my grasp, I stare at my killer and the polished long-barreled pistol pointed at my head. I close my eyes. The blast will tear apart my skull. But at least death will be quick.

CHAPTER 2

DAY 1

THE ALARM RIPS me from a peaceful slumber. A classic rock tune, which jarringly reminds me it's Monday morning, and I need to face the working week.

I groan and slap the alarm into silence. Wasn't it just Friday? The weekend seems to take forever to come around and then flies past, especially when I spend at least half of it at open inspections or being present at property auctions.

This one wasn't all bad, though. I made a couple of big sales on Saturday, and my wife was in a rare frisky mood when she woke up on Sunday. Not that I'm complaining. With two children, we have little time for intimacy in the mornings. Or opportunity for it any other time, actually. And we have to keep the noise down. And be quick about it. And Talissa is usually too tired to really enjoy it like we used to. And maybe I am too. But, not only did we enjoy sex on Sunday, we also managed to get back to sleep for another hour before my five-year-old daughter came in and jumped on us.

Talissa opens her green eyes and smiles at me. I swear she's just as beautiful as the first time I saw her twelve years ago. Before I knew her, I'd been with many women, but she was the first to awaken my heart and not just my cock.

With her wavy, black hair hanging loose and long down her back, she looked like an agent of the devil sent to seduce me to my personal–and very exquisite—version of hell. I wanted to commit every sin with her that night, every sin she could tempt me into. Little did I know, however, how very skilled she was at being a temptress. My she-devil played it cool and sophisticated, interested, yet aloof, which only served to intensify my hunger for her. By not sleeping with me on the night we met, I found I desired her more each day. Waiting was a more exquisite pleasure, built upon long talks, light touches, and learning the taste of our desire through increasingly reckless kisses.

When the first time arrived, after several dates, it was well worth the wait and we were both more than ready. I still remember the two of us lying completely naked on the picnic rug just a few feet from the lake, basking in the moonlight as if we were a pair of horny teenagers without a care in the world. I would have died happy that night.

She still has that red silk dress she wore on that fateful night—the one that accentuates her curves. It hangs covered in the closet, but maybe I can convince her to wear it for me again soon.

"Good morning, handsome," she says to me

now, her voice slightly husky with sleepiness.

"Good morning, beautiful," I say and smile.

If I'm to face a Monday morning with any degree of enthusiasm, I need a shower and some strong coffee, and I know she does too. I lean to kiss her, but she turns her face as she glances at the time, and my lips grace her cheek instead.

"Shower first," she says and blows me a kiss, waving me in the direction of the bathroom. She wrinkles her nose as she frowns. "Urgh. Another damn Monday."

I nod and drag my tired ass out of bed and head to the en suite, letting her have a few more moments of rest. I should have known better than to kiss her before either of us has had coffee, especially on a Monday.

Sunday had been truly exceptional.

As I pass by, I catch sight of my blue eyes in the bathroom mirror and pause. For a man on the cusp of forty, I guess I haven't aged badly when I compare myself to other guys within my age bracket. I puff out my chest, patting my belly as I suck it in. Apart from a few extra pounds around the waist, and a fine speckling of grey hairs amongst the short black mass, I look much like the man who walked down the aisle with his wife ten years ago. I've never been a gym junkie, but my genetics have given me broad shoulders and strong arms. I grin, admiring how the money I've spent at the dentists over the years has paid off. This gesture also shows my wrinkles, but, if anything, they accentuate the chiseled features on my lightly-tanned face.

"Stop ogling yourself and get in the shower, Mr. James Bond," my wife calls from the bed. "You'll pass out if you keep holding your breath."

With a whoosh, the breath escapes my lungs and my belly falls back into place, which is definitely not the same place it was when I was twenty. But I guess everything changes with time.

Ignoring the mirror, I start the shower and do as my she-devil wishes.

* * * * *

THE BREAKFAST RITUAL is pretty much the same every day. I flick the espresso machine into gear and let it work its magic, and while I await my caffeine fix, I prepare breakfast for the children.

Now freshly showered and dressed in casual pants and a top, Talissa finds me in the kitchen spreading avocado on the toast and plants a quick kiss on my cheek. She appreciates this small gesture of help with the kids as it allows her a few more minutes to prepare for her day job as a dental assistant. Isaac is seven years old and is picked up by the school bus a few minutes before I leave for work, while our daughter, Matilda, usually goes to daycare or is looked after by a babysitter until my wife gets home in the early afternoon.

It wouldn't be a normal morning if we didn't have to constantly remind one or both of our children they need to keep moving, but we rarely need to raise our voices at them. They're great kids, and I owe it to Talissa mostly as I always seem to be out early in the day and back around dinnertime, then working a lot at home each night plus also going around to various properties on the weekend.

I don't see my family as much as I'd like to, but the money's good. I can afford to give them the things they like. Swimming and dance class for the kids, and, for Talissa, the visits to her favorite spa and the alone time she needs when she craves it. And I do get a lot back from what I put in at the office. My career is on the upswing.

Life is great.

* * * * *

I ARRIVE AT the main branch of Phelps Brothers Real Estate in downtown San Francisco a good ten minutes early. It gives me time to pump a third cup of coffee into my system and get my mind in the game. The real estate business is tough and brutal at times. If you want the bigger commissions, you need to wring as much money as you can from the buyers. Sometimes, you need to know when to urge your sellers to settle on a price much lower than they want because a property sitting on the market for more than three months in this area is considered dead weight, and no one wants to waste their time on something you can't move.

Roger Ballusk opens the door to the staff room and stops a couple of feet from me with the biggest grin I've seen on him in years. He was the best man at my wedding and was there on that fateful night when I met Talissa. I think he might have been slightly envious of me then, but he did take home Talissa's friend, who had also been easy on the eyes. He's still a bachelor, and as he likes the freedom that being single gives him, I see little chance of it changing anytime soon.

"Do I want to know what that shit-eating grin is about?" I ask, not bothering to wrestle away the look of amusement on my face.

"I've come across the best thing ever on the internet. You have got to check it out."

"You been downloading goat porn again?"

"Haha, real funny. You still recycling old material?"

Although he has a history of saying he's found the best thing ever, and then it turns out to be yet another kinky porn site, I can't help wondering what the hell he's found. Okay, yes, I'm as guilty as the next guy for having the odd look at a bit of female nudity on the internet, but Roger's one hell of a perverted bastard whose eyes have seen some really fucked up shit—things I wouldn't dare to even think about. Except he keeps forcing me to as he can't ever keep it to himself. And as his best friend, I'm kind of obligated to listen and look.

"Okay, out with it," I say, knowing he'll be on at me all day if I don't.

"There's this new chat game called 3DDreamChat. It's like an internet chat room except you take on the form of an animated character. You can be anything and anybody you want to be, and you can buy some real cool shit, and even get into kinky stuff with the hottest chicks."

I raise my eyebrows. "What? Are you twelve years old? You could be chatting to a pantless, hairy, sixty-year-old man for all you know. Come on, just get back into better shape and get out there again with real women."

"I'm pretty good at picking the females from the males. You get to learn how to spot the fakes from the real ones over time."

"How long have you been on this thing?" I give him a side-eye glance. I'm sure I know the answer already as he's pretty much addicted to the internet.

"Never mind that. Go on. Just have a look at it for me. Type in 3DDreamChat on your computer tonight and look me up, and I'll guide you through it. My name's RogerU69."

I can't prevent a laugh from escaping at the username he's chosen, but I nod to get him to drop it and move on. It works, for now at least, as he focusses on grabbing a coffee. But I know that tomorrow morning, and every day after, he'll be back at me about it until I check out his new favorite obsession and tell him what I think.

As the door opens, I look toward the newcomer who enters. The only female real estate agent in our branch, Kate Wilkens, is confident, and as usual, well dressed. She has one of those faces where it's hard to tell her age, but I guess her to be somewhere in her early thirties as she's been working at Phelps for nearly as long as Roger and me.

She smiles at me in that lingering way she always does, and I swear if I weren't married, she would try to have more than friendship with me. But even if I were single, I still wouldn't find her attractive. It's not the red hair or the extra pounds she carries; she's just totally, mind-numbingly boring to talk to, and, other than real estate, I can't think of a single thing we have in common. I'm sure she's told me a lot about herself, but my mind flies to a distant world as soon as she starts to discuss anything more than our job.

"Good morning," I say in response to her smile. As usual, her make-up looks like a garden trowel has been used to apply it. She would do better to ease up on it, I think, to help her with her professional image, but she moves a lot of properties, so maybe she knows what she's doing.

"Morning, Terry. Did you have a good weekend?"

I flash my client-winning smile. "You could say that. I'm sure the boss will mention the Clydesdale Estate sale I closed on Saturday during the morning brief."

"You lucky bastard," Roger says. "Good run of sales, hot wife, perfect kids, what more could you want?"

The door opens and our fourth agent enters saying, "Maybe Phelps retiring and allowing this branch to be run in my more than capable hands." George Marshall heads straight for the urn to fix himself a hot coffee. A well-dressed man of about thirty, his short dark hair is perfectly held in place with enough greasy hair product to lubricate the engines of a jet fighter squadron. He takes a long sip of the hot dark liquid before saying good morning to everyone.

George is a pleasant enough guy, but his arrogance can get on my nerves. I know he's great at his job. I just wish he didn't need to tell everyone else all the time. And I don't understand why so many women find his brand of confidence attractive, but they do. He always has one or two girls flirting around him, usually the office interns when we have them during the summer. The fact he bats for the other team doesn't seem to matter. The girls still treat him like a god anyway.

We take our seats at the meeting table. The four of us make up the engine of this real estate machine. While Phelps thinks he's the one who keeps the wheels spinning, I personally think he's just a name on a billboard, riding the riptides our work produces. Right on cue, he walks in at precisely one minute before nine o'clock.

"Good morning," Phelps says. We all respond with a simple 'morning,' which is the catalyst for him to start the Monday morning brief. He doesn't grab a coffee. He's one of those rare types who don't need a caffeine kick-start. I don't trust those types. Anyone who can launch themselves into the day without any kind of caffeine trigger doesn't seem human to me.

"First of all, congratulations to Terry for closing two big deals over the weekend. Either one of them would have been outstanding in itself, but to close the Clydesdale Estate property *and* the Regent Parade second-level townhouse is something we should all admire." It's a rare moment of recognition where Phelps almost sounds like he genuinely appreciates my work. And why not? I just brought in a hefty commission for the brokerage.

Everyone in the room claps, and while I appreciate the recognition, I'm feeling oddly irritated by it. Maybe it's because it's a Monday. Maybe I haven't had enough coffee yet. But I can't help wishing we could just move on to the next order of business.

Phelps continues with his reports and other drivel, and I let my mind wander to other things.

Talissa in that red dress. Curvy and hot. When was the last time she wore it?

I try to think of an exact moment but can't. Probably sometime in the last ten years. Probably the last time we had a date night. Probably before the kids came along. Probably...

Fuck it. I could really just go back to sleep right now. Anything's better than Phelps's droning voice. I need a new challenge. A new property to sell.

"Terry, you with me?"

"Yes?" I nod at my boss, realizing I haven't heard a word he's said for at least five minutes.

He frowns. "Good. Because in two days' time, we'll be bringing on a temp to help us with all these new properties coming our way. I'm not sure who it is yet, and it all depends who the agency sends us, but I know you could all do with a little less workload." He looks pointedly at me. I glance at the others. What the hell does he know? I'm not overworked. I love the challenge of closing the deal.

Kate groans and takes a big swallow from the

mug in front of her.

"Look, Kate, I know you're worried about Terry here catching your yearly sales, but I know how many hours you put in a week, and you need to let go of some of your workload."

"I'm fine," Kate says. "I don't need any help from a temp. Not like I have a family or even a man of my own to occupy my time."

She looks at me when she says, 'man of her own.' Damn, she needs to find someone else before I have to let her down hard. Why the hell doesn't she try Roger? He's single. Or fawn over George like every other female on the planet?

"Go look in the mirror, Kate. You have big enough bags under your eyes to pack for a two-month holiday. This isn't negotiable." Phelps looks around the room. "And that goes for all of you."

Five minutes later, the brief ends, and the five of us head to our own offices. I have a list of people to call, the top priority being a Mrs. Pellmont, a recent widow with a two-story mansion for sale. With a potential two-million-dollar price tag at stake, I have to make sure I nail it.

The day moves along slowly, and it seems to take forever for five p.m. to come along.

* * * * *

I GET HOME an hour after I leave the office, feeling like I've achieved a minor victory in securing a meeting with Mrs. Pellmont for the following Friday. She sounded pleasant enough over the phone and quite enthusiastic about my pitch. If I can sell the place for the right price, the commission alone will pay for Matilda's private school fees all through grade school.

As usual, dinner's ready not long after I get home. Not only is she beautiful, but Talissa is an amazing cook who never fails to satisfy my taste buds, and tonight is no exception.

We eat at the dinner table for every meal. No TV or anything else to tear our attention away from being a family unit. It's enough of a struggle to get Isaac to eat anything other than chicken nuggets. We can certainly do without the lure of cartoons or whatever it might be he watches during the hours between coming home from school and having dinner.

Each of us takes a turn in talking about our day. Then the kids have their baths, and we read to them for fifteen minutes before it's time for them to go to bed. Talissa and I usually wind down with a glass or two of wine while relaxing in front of the TV. Tonight is interrupted by Isaac calling out to his mother. He's not well, so she takes him into our bed and asks if I mind if she goes to bed early. I smile and say it's okay and head to my home office.

* * * * *

SITTING AT MY computer, I study the business plan I have written up so far. It looks pretty basic, and, not for the first time, I wonder whether I should just be satisfied with working at Phelps Brothers. I'm earning a decent salary, and if I go out on my own, I could risk everything.

Sure, Phelps is a pompous, superficial dickhead who would sell his own family for a quick buck, but there are much worse bosses out there who I could be working for. If he even gets a sniff I'm trying to pull clients away to start my own real estate business, I'm as good as dead in the water in this industry.

But a change of pace seems worth the risk at times. Stable income and security versus the excitement of being my own boss. The wins and losses would be my sole responsibility to manage.

The idea gives me more of a thrill than it should, considering I have a family to provide for in the balance. Talissa's job couldn't keep us afloat if I failed.

She and the children rely on me.

So, I can't then, can I? I can't take the risk.

Disappointment wraps around me like a weight that I can't shake as I realize that it's true. I can't take the risk for my family's sake. Which means I'll be working for Phelps or someone like him for forever. And the idea of that is...what?

A great opportunity I should be grateful for.

A slow death from monotony and boredom.

But if I was alone without responsibility, would I take the risk?

I push that idea immediately aside. Flatten it. Bury it. I don't like where my thoughts are taking me or the feelings they are inspiring. I love my family and that's final. Just like I love my job. I'm just irritated by this fucking monotonous Monday.

I need to get out of this depressed mood. Find something to occupy my mind that has nothing to do with real estate or life.

I shake my head to clear it as I push back in my chair. The home screen of my desktop computer stares back at me and, unexpectedly, I smile.

What was the ridiculous 3D chat program Roger was talking about? 3DD something or other? Probably anime porn or something weird that he'd like. Not my bag, but if nothing else, it should be good for a laugh.

And Roger will just bug me about it tomorrow to see if I logged on or not so I might as well check it out now.

It doesn't take long to find and download the software for 3DDreamChat, and I restart the PC to enable it to run properly. I grab a pair of 3D glasses from the livingroom, and another glass of wine, and start the new program. I have to pick a name and design my avatar, and quickly learn the glasses aren't required. Apparently, it's not the immersion type 3D, but rather a virtual environment you can interact with through character chatting. My avatar of choice is a blond surfer, and I use very little imagination and just call him Terry25 from the choices offered. The number seems to indicate an age or date or something, but who the hell needs to know my real age anyway?

I must admit, my avatar looks much more handsome than me. The graphics are almost lifelike. The textures and lighting are amazing. It doesn't look like a cartoon, but rather a realistic-looking world. Someone spent a lot of time and money making this game. I'd expected it to be cheesy, considering Rogers taste in seedy porn, but instead, I'm impressed.

It takes me a few minutes of clicking my mouse at various places within the gaming window, but I find a shop where I can get free stuff, including a decent wardrobe of clothes and a few accessories. I chuckle as I realize I'm spending more time deciding what to wear as an avatar than in the real world, but there are literally hundreds of different styles of board shorts here versus the five identical suits and shirts I own, which are hanging in my bedroom closet.

Now properly accessorized, I stare at the screen. Where the hell do I go now?

There's a prompt box on part of the screen where I can type avatar names to search for friends. I type in Roger's sleazy screen name, RogerU69, not expecting him to be online. I should have known better. We both appear a few seconds later in a small reception room, which contains two sofas; one has his avatar seated upon it and the other, my own. A speech balloon appears onscreen.

RogerU69: "I didn't expect to find you here tonight; I thought it might take a couple nights to spark your curiosity. But hey, thanks for coming, buddy. You should step into my bachelor pad."

He sends an invite to join him in 'Roger's

Heavenly Pad' via an envelope appearing in the middle of the animated scene.

I take a deep breath while I think about whether or not to accept. So far, this place has seemed pretty decent. Classy graphics and no crowds of creepers. Of course, that will likely change in a chat room called 'Roger's Heavenly Pad.' But I suppose if it's too weird, I can leave at any time. I just hope this isn't some kind of set up by Roger and I'll be surrounded by sex-hungry starfish as soon as I hit the accept button.

It's not like he hasn't set me up for weird shit before for a laugh.

I shake my head and accept his invite.

"What the hell's the worst that can happen?"

The software has a delay as it loads the graphics for 'Roger's Heavenly Pad', giving me time to second guess whether I've made the right decision. But as the chat room renders in front of me, I grin.

Roger is as I might have expected him to be, his avatar shirtless and sitting in a hot tub with two female avatars. Another two females are standing to the left of the tub, engrossed in the heated kiss they are sharing.

Not surprisingly, all four female avatars are topless and beautifully crafted, and I can't help wondering how far removed they are from their real-life counterparts. They could look completely different. Or even be males. I'd never know.

A brunette with the screen name of Brandy4U ends the kiss she's enjoying and looks at me, then at Roger.

Brandy4U: "Mmm, you've brought some fresh meat for us."

The blonde she was kissing, named CupcakeMary, breaks away from Brandy4U and walks toward my avatar.

CupcakeMary: "He looks delicious."

She waves at me and smiles.

CupcakeMary: "You should come join us, Terry."

The animations are spectacular—the boobs of the topless women sway and bounce in a natural manner, and I find it hard not to stare. Which means it's time I make my farewell. Fantasy or not, I can't be a part of this any longer.

Terry25: "Sorry ladies, I just came here to have a look at this chat program and say 'hi' to Rog. I'm a married man."

One of the women in the hot tub bounces in the water, making her boobs jiggle. She grins, noticing me watching.

SweetSindy24: "I'm married, too. Do you think it stops me from having fun?"

This is all wrong. Surely, there must be something else to do in this program. The chat window with Roger is still open, and I message him there directly.

Terry25: "Hey, sorry, but I need to leave your orgy room. Without sounding like a party pooper, I can't get into what's going on in there. Have a great night."

RogerU69: "Oh, come on, Terry. None of this is real. It's all pretend. Live a little, just like you did when we were younger."

Terry25: "That was different. I had nothing to keep me grounded and, yeah, okay, I did enjoy getting some action as often as I wanted. But that was with real women. Not this fantasy shit. Besides, I have Talissa. You have fun running around pretending to fuck hotties who are probably two-headed trolls in real life."

RogerU69: "No need for that, Terry. Well, I'll see you at work. I know you're not getting any tonight anyway. Otherwise, you wouldn't be here."

I frown. Mostly because he's right. I'm not getting any action tonight. Or any night soon. But just because Talissa and I might not have sex as often as before we had kids, it doesn't mean I go around looking elsewhere for some action. I mean, I'm not blind. I notice a beautiful woman when I see one, but it ends there.

I swallow the last of my glass of wine and exit Roger's bachelor pad. The program pops me into a blues bar where a menu opens on the screen with a list of suggested drinks and songs. A sweet slide guitar accompanies a deep voice singing a song called 'Scotch on the Rocks' about a train coming from another town, but not bringing the singer's lover back. The song is good, my kind of music, but I turn down the volume on my speakers before anyone wakes, and then search the virtual room for the nearest exit. Did I click the wrong button when I left Roger's place? I thought I was leaving the game. But this seems to be a new meeting area.

The room is dimly lit, with only a few tables and chairs visible, and no exit sign pointing me in the direction I need. Five other avatars are in the room, listening to the music. A blonde woman, calling herself BluesGirl88, approaches me as I stand there uncertain what to do next. How can I leave if there's no exit?

BluesGirl88 looks immaculate in a little black dress that barely covers her upper thighs. Her mouth moves, but instead of texting, her voice comes over the speakers of my PC. I turn the volume up just enough that I can hear her more clearly against the background music playing.

BluesGirl88: "I said, welcome to my club."

Her voice is husky, reminding me of Talissa's when she's feeling sexy, and I find myself wanting to hear more. I don't have a microphone to use with the computer, so I continue typing,

Terry25: "Whoever you have playing in this club, I hope they have a CD I can buy."

She laughs.

BluesGirl88: "CD? Who buys those things anymore? But, yes, you can buy their music online. Are you having a drink?"

She raises the glass in her hand with a nod at me. I assume she prefers just to talk out loud than type. It is quicker, I'll admit.

Terry25: "I've just finished my third glass of red. I think that'll do me for tonight."

My head is feeling a bit light already. But it's a pleasant buzz at the end of a crazy day.

BluesGirl88: "There's no limits in here. Isn't there something you want to celebrate?"

I look at her then at my empty glass. I suppose there is. But at the moment I'm not sure which is the bigger thing to celebrate: the awesome deals I brokered this weekend or the fact that after a four-month dry spell I finally got laid.

Terry25: "I think I was looking for the way out."

She laughs, and it sounds husky and sweet at the same time.

BluesGirl88: "We all are, darling. Go on, have another drink. I'm a scotch girl myself."

She tips her glass to her mouth, holding my gaze as she takes a slow sip of the amber liquid. Her red lips glisten as she licks them with a dart of her pink tongue, and she looks at the glass appreciatively.

BluesGirl88: "Mmm. I needed that. It's been a long day."

Indeed, it has, I agree. I look at our liquor cabinet on the wall, remembering how good scotch tastes. Several bottles of various brands of single malt stand neatly in a line. I haven't had a drink of scotch since New Year's Eve and right now I can't think why. It's my favorite drink.

And I do deserve to celebrate this weekend's victories. Talissa might not have actually congratulated me for the awesome commission I brought in, but the sex was still great, even if brief.

I have a tumbler in the top drawer of my desk, which I pull out and fill to just under halfway with the thirty-year-old fluid. I was going to leave this chat, but one drink won't hurt. This bar isn't sleazy like Roger's pad. The music is great and BluesGirl is definitely easy on the eyes. I type a message to her.

Terry25: "You evil woman, you got me drinking at eleven p.m. on a work night."

BluesGirl88: "You only live once, Terry. And life is full of so many wonderful things to experience in the short time we get. Don't you think?"

Is she flirting with me? We chat for a few minutes about things like music, and how much of today's sound is pumped out by machines rather than true artists who feel real emotions. There's talk of family life and of where we both came from. My Australian roots and her third-generation Californian heritage. Of my childhood home in Salinas farm country, and her living out of a suitcase, traveling with her father from town to town as he played all the pubs and clubs. It's relaxed and easy to chat like this. Not sleazy at all. I get up to pour myself another half glass of scotch, enjoying the smooth burn it creates as it settles inside me.

BluesGirl88: "Come see my place. It's a beautiful little mansion I paid good money for."

Her voice calls to me from the speakers as I focus on not spilling my drink while I return to my seat at the computer.

I take a sip and study her. Her avatar is quite pretty. More real-looking than the others I've seen. Her hair looks so soft I could touch it. She could be a live person I'm drinking with rather than a virtual woman. And I'm intrigued to find out more about who she might really be. What was she saying about a house? Oh, yeah...

Terry25: "You paid money for a virtual mansion?"

BluesGirl88: "What's wrong with paying money for something that makes me happy? Some people spend hundreds on cigarettes or other hobbies. I love this world. We can be whoever we want to be, and spending money to enhance the experience makes perfect sense to me."

She has a point. There's no difference between that and me buying extra putters at the golf simulator I practice at.

An invitation appears to visit her mansion, and I study the floating envelope for a moment before returning my gaze to her. Her blue eyes are full of excitement.

BluesGirl88: "Come see. I have all kinds of upgrades you can't find in most places. But I got it all for an excellent price. It's a replica of a place some Hollywood starlet once owned in Bel Air. My realtor got an exclusive deal."

Terry25: "People need estate agents in the virtual world?"

BluesGirl88: "Why not? The paperwork is the same.

And people like to see what they're getting before buying, don't they? A man with your skills could make a killing here, Terry25."

She touches the envelope and disappears. I've sold a few mansions in real estate, but what would it be called here? Fake-estate? I laugh at my joke and take a swig of scotch. My head spins a bit as the booze settles in my stomach, but it's a good feeling. Warm and relaxing. What would a virtual mansion be like in this game world?

I take a deep breath and follow.

The scene must be heavily detailed as it takes a good few minutes for it to load. I take a few more nips of my drink while I'm waiting, and I'm more than a bit lightheaded now. The room is swaying when I turn my head. Scotch doesn't normally hit me this fast, but I've been tired lately as well. I'd better slow down a bit or else I'll be waking up a little under the weather.

The room loads in full, and I see her dressed in a black bikini sitting by a pool. From what I see of her virtual mansion, there are three levels in all, and an outside area containing the pool and a small deck area littered with various deck chairs.

BluesGirl88: "Do you like?"

She is now typing, and I wonder if she's asking for my opinion on her attire or the house she built in this virtual world.

Terry25: "Of course."

I lift my glass to my lips to take a sip, only to find it empty of scotch. I frown, trying to make out how that happened. I only just poured this one, didn't I?

BluesGirl88: "I even paid for some of these parts of my body."

I turn back to the screen. We're now in her bedroom instead of by the pool. And her avatar is doing a full three-hundred-and-sixty-degree turn. It's impossible not to notice her bikini hasn't made the journey with her to this room.

BluesGirl88: "Do you like what you see?"

Terry25: "Um... yes."

I admit it freely. Why not? Real or not, she's beautiful. Curvy and lush, just how I like a woman. Red lips. Long blonde hair spilling down her back. The detail is very lifelike, and I question whether it's healthy to be getting an erection from a virtual fantasy. But I am.

She touches one of her pink nipples and rolls it between her fingers. A husky giggle escapes her lips.

BluesGirl88: "These boobs and pussy cost a bit of money, but I couldn't be without them now that I have them. So much fun to play with."

What should I say to that? I opt for staying silent and appreciating the view.

BluesGirl88: "This is my own private place. You can be whoever you want here, Terry25. It's all just for fun, so don't be shy. I like that you like how I look."

I feel nervous and I'm not sure why. Yes, it's just a chat program, and none of it is real, but with the scotch and wine affecting my head more than I like to admit, the lure of her nudity is strong. I love the appeal of a beautiful woman. And I stand there staring at her while she steps closer.

BluesGirl88: "Do you want me to help you out?"

Terry25: "Yes."

With what, I'm not sure. To leave? To stay? To get rid of this hard-on that's tenting my boxers. I'd be lying if I wasn't thinking about her red lips wrapped around my cock. Or how perky and full her breasts must feel to hold. But this is uncharted territory I never intended to be in. I'm feeling more than a bit lost and definitely drunk. But she seems to know how to play this game, so I'll take whatever help she's offering.

She touches the waistband of my boardshorts, and, with a click, helps my avatar to remove his clothes.

Although now that he's naked, I realize he has

nothing but a bare patch of skin where his penis should be.

She takes a step back from me.

BluesGirl88: "Maybe tomorrow you should spend some money to get yourself a big hard cock, then come back and see me. Goodnight, Terry25."

With that, I find my avatar booted from her mansion scene and back to my own lobby.

Wait. *What the fuck?*

Did I just get shot down? How the fuck would I know my avatar didn't have a cock? And why the fuck would it matter anyway? It's just a stupid game. None of it is even real. But I can't help feeling a bit stung and stupid just the same. Still unable to find the exit button, I turn the whole damn computer off.

I check the time. Twelve-twenty-two a.m.

I groan, knowing how little time for sleep I have now before the alarm goes off for work. I feel tipsy and horny, but with Isaac being in bed with Talissa, I'll have to take care of my needs myself. Not that she'd likely put out anyway at this crazy time of night.

I stagger to the bedroom, strip off, and put on some fresh boxer shorts before climbing into bed. Isaac is in the middle but being a king size bed there is plenty of room for all three of us to fit. Talissa stirs, but I don't think she's woken up, and I lie on my back for a few minutes with my eyes open, and the room spinning, thinking about the blonde woman in the virtual world. I need to switch off and forget her, never return there again.

But the last thing I remember before I crash into sleep is the soft sound of her husky laugh while she played with her nipple.

CHAPTER 3

DAY 2

A SIX-AND-a-half-hour sleep doesn't work well for me, not when I wake with my head feeling like it's wrapped in lead. I hit the snooze button twice before dragging myself out of bed. The shower takes longer than normal, but by the time I've finished, the hot water has helped me feel semi-human and given me time to think too. At the breakfast table, Talissa looks at me as I enter the room. She already has a big mug of steaming hot coffee waiting for me and a plate of eggs and bacon.

I place a kiss on her cheek. "Baby, have I told you how awesome you are?"

There's a touch of guilt sitting in the pit of my stomach over my late-night activities with a stranger on a chat program. But in the light of day, I realize how much it's only a fantasy. A way of escape. And no different than the porn I watch on occasion. My avatar is not me. Enjoying the image of someone like BluesGirl88 is just like getting a hard-on when looking at porn. And Talissa has never minded that

I like porn. In fact, she's often told me she thinks having an outlet for fantasies is healthy. I'm pretty sure she enjoys her own.

She smiles at me. "Not for a while, but I kind of had an idea anyway. You haven't forgotten what the day after tomorrow is, have you?"

"I was thinking it must be golf day." I grin and wink at her. "I'll book a table somewhere. I'll surprise you."

She comes up behind me and wraps her arms around me and kisses my cheek. "And maybe you can have me for dessert." Her breath is soft as she whispers by my ear, and the tone of her voice and her suggestive words awaken me below.

Now this...this kind of interaction. This is the real deal. And I've missed her being so playful.

She disengages herself from me and walks over to the fridge. She hasn't showered yet so is still in her silk nightgown, and as she bends down to pull a carton of milk from the bottom shelf of the door, I can almost see her ass cheeks. I look at the kids, who are too busy with their bowls of cereal to notice me checking out their mother.

* * * * *

As soon as I get to work and hit the staffroom, Roger comes running in. "So, what do you think? You were still in the chat for at least two hours after you left my chat room. I saw your status as green in my buddy list."

Oh, shit! "Well, I found a much more subdued

place to chat, a blues bar. Good music and intelligent conversation. No offense, but it's more than I can say about your orgy party."

He laughs at my friendly jab. "So, you were listening to music until after midnight and talking politics? I find that hard to believe."

I glance around the room, although there's little point as no one else is in yet. "Okay, there was this blonde woman. She spoke about her love of the blues and—"

Roger cuts me off. "A blonde? Terry, the brunette-and-raven-haired-lover spends hours talking to a *blonde*?"

"Hey, I have been with a couple of blondes back in the day. Redheads too. If a woman has a pretty face, a great body, and a stellar personality, how does hair color change anything?"

Roger points at me. "Ha, ha. There's the old Terry I remember. So, did you fuck her virtual brains out?"

"No, and even if I wanted to, I don't have the necessary equipment on my avatar to do it. It's only been one night, but I'm done with the chat. I have a real-life wife with a real vagina, not these pixel chicks with animated tits and pussies."

Roger's grin stalls. "You just have to keep rubbing it in, don't you?"

I feel bad for him, even if he is a pervert. "Sorry, Rog."

We might be around the same age but we're at completely different points in our life. Before I can say anything else, Kate and George walk in.

"Looking a little tired today there, Terry. Should I even ask?" George's smile is more like a sneer this morning.

I don't give him an answer. What he probably thinks happened would be better than the truth. Kate says hi to Roger and me and then heads straight for the coffee machine. Even she's looking better than I am today.

"Well, these properties won't go out and sell themselves," I say and walk out of the room with a steaming mug of black coffee. I never drink it black, but this is a day where I don't need the cream to get between me and the caffeine my body desires.

Phelps is standing in my office as I enter it, his expression unfriendly as ever. "I sure hope you present yourself better to Mrs. Pellmont when you see her this week."

"You'll never be happy with my work, will you?"

"It's not your work. It's that smart-ass attitude you and your buddy Rog use around here. You two think you're the ones running the place? Well, I guess we'll have to see how some new blood in this office will pull you guys into gear."

"I'll sell the Pellmont mansion like I sell everything else that comes my way—like a damn boss."

"Make sure you do."

He grabs the door handle as he turns to leave my office, but before he leaves, he throws a parting shot my way. "You know it wasn't my choice to hire you and Rog, so I don't get why you're so shocked by the fact I don't particularly like the pair of you. But word to the wise, one day, you might be in my shoes and find yourself in a three-way deal, leaving you filling your branch with assholes."

The stupid prick is out my door before I can respond, which probably benefits me more than him given the circumstances. I can't imagine my tired retort would help my position in the company at all.

I close the door behind him and immerse myself on my computer in looking over the list of sellers with properties still on the market. It's a rare thing when someone has their property still up for sale after a month, but as soon as the month ticks over, my work computer will highlight it on my desktop screen.

Thankfully, today isn't one of those days. I have enough shit to deal with and I can't believe I feel as tired as I do. I should be able to skate through the day as long as I get six hours of sleep, but maybe being close to forty has slowed me down somewhat. And to make matters worse, today is such a quiet one. Why the hell isn't it acceptable to drink at work on days like this? A glass of scotch would at least make it bearable. I waste time until the end of my workday doing mundane tasks such as preparing leaflets for a letterbox run to try to drum up some more business for the ungrateful prick I work for.

* * * * *

As soon as I arrive home from work, I see Talissa and my mood plummets further as I realize I haven't booked anything for our anniversary dinner tomorrow. *Shit.* Since it's a ten-year milestone, I should have been prepared and put in a much better effort. Maybe take her away for the coming weekend. It's not too late. I could find something and spring it on her as a surprise.

"Oh. Hello, stranger. You're home on time today?" She blows me a quick kiss as she continues through the room with the basket of laundry she's carrying. She has the energy of a teenager it seems. I just wish I had the energy to keep up with her. I swear in the last ten years, she's kept as fit and athletic as she was when we first met. But then again, she does go to the gym several afternoons a week when she's off work and the kids are in school. She's got her own life going on while I'm busy working. And I'm fine with that. I'm glad she's independent as long as she's happy.

Apparently, Isaac is still not well and had to come home from school early, so she plans on an early night with him. They say boys always gravitate toward their mothers, and he is no exception. I know he loves me, too. We do a lot of boy things together like playing with cars and kicking soccer balls and playing in the backyard. But when it comes to bonding, he's all Mommy's boy.

While we eat dinner, things are quieter than normal. Talissa looks over at me from time to time, and the look she gives me shows me she knows I'm not my usual self. Isaac hardly eats a thing while Matilda is all eyes on Daddy tonight because, for some reason, I'm her hero.

* * * * *

IT'S ONLY EIGHT p.m., but already, I'm the only person in the house still up and not in bed.

I wanted to talk with Talissa a bit about our ten-year-anniversary plans, but she stayed with Isaac after she got him to sleep. I guess her energy does have its limits. She works hard at keeping the family organized as well as her own job. But we don't talk like we used to, and I'm wondering when the last time was that we had one of those chats where we would stay up until the sunrise just talking and feeling close.

Did we ever have one of those chats?

I'm sure we did at the beginning when we were dating. But how much have my wife's likes and dislikes changed in the years since then? Other than the obvious everyday things, I'm not sure I know.

Is that because she's not interested in sharing or because I haven't asked?

On an average night when the kids are in bed, we mostly just talk about them or our jobs or whatever news is happening in the world. But us? That topic gets shut down as soon as I even think about it because she usually says she's tired and heads to bed. 'Us' isn't a topic Talissa wants to discuss, I suppose. And she's okay with that.

But am I? I guess, I have to be.

But it makes me wonder sometimes if she has any real interest in me.

I flick through the channels using the TV remote, but there's nothing good on tonight. So, I

CHRIS HEINICKE

head to my office. I'm restless in a way I'm not usually, and the irritation from yesterday has settled in once again. My brain isn't in the mood for working on my business plan. I check out what's happening on social media instead.

The newsfeed is full of friends posting photos of their dinner, opinions on which celebrities are hot, which ones are losers, as well as multiple cat memes. Most nights I wonder why I even log on, but I have siblings, cousins, as well as old school friends who I like to keep in contact with.

Tonight, I can't even think of a witty status update to post.

Roger's posted a photo of himself sitting on his couch with his laptop, obviously not aware of the fact the screen of his laptop is in the picture. He's on the chat program already and with a lady.

For the first time since I got home from work, I think about the blonde from last night.

I've thought of her during the day though. And about how the whole 3DDreamChat game works. And maybe Roger isn't wrong in thinking a bit of fantasy is a fun way to blow off some steam. Not that I would want to engage in his sleazy perve orgy or anything. But that blue's bar had been okay. And if I got hard staring at BluesGirl88's magnificent tits, so what? There's nothing wrong with enjoying porn. Is this really any different?

Last night I hadn't known what to expect and the realism of the game world had caught me off guard. But the experience did teach me a couple of important things: fantasy is just fantasy, and always remember to bring your penis.

I snort, recalling that lesson. Fucking embarrassing to have dropped my pants with nothing to show. No wonder BluesGirl88 kicked my ass out of her mansion.

I'd vowed this morning that I'd never go back to the chat room.

Well, I'll keep that promise and never go back *unprepared.*

I grin. Since I can't focus on anything else right now, I open the chat program. Maybe a good wank fantasy will help me get rid of this restless mood I'm in.

I mark myself as offline to Roger. I don't need him in my face at work tomorrow, questioning me about appearing online and not stopping in to say hi.

At the virtual shop, I click on the body modification section. There's a selection of penises to choose from, and, predictably, they're all large in size and erect. The more lifelike they appear, the more expensive they are, but five dollars seems reasonable for a top of the range one.

I chuckle at the silliness of it, but it's just a bit of fun. I also purchase a black suit and then send my avatar to the blues bar. Several males and females are there, and a big group chat is happening. People are talking about the music playing in the background, and while it's not as good as the music played the night before, it's still quite decent. I don't see BluesGirl88 in the club, so I sit back in my chair and watch the small talk happening in the room. Not surprisingly, every avatar is good-looking, and most of the females are dressed in cleavage-and-leg-exposing attire. This whole thing is so removed from the real world I can understand the attraction to it.

I'm in reasonable shape, but then I do eat and drink sensibly and make sure I'm active on the weekends, unless my work drags me away. Which is often. But saying that, I'm not even close to the perfectly crafted piece of male flesh on my screen representing the real me.

The smooth blues playing over my speakers from the virtual bar reminds me of the scotch I had last night. I'm not a heavy drinker, and I've not had any wine this evening, so a half-glass of the amber malt won't be remiss. I've been craving the warm taste all day. Although, after the headache I woke with from yesterday's indulgence, I think I'll stop at the single drink.

The bottle of scotch is still on my desk from last night. Wait? Wasn't it in the liquor display with the other bottles? I don't remember moving it to my desk. But maybe I did in my drunken stupor and I just don't remember.

My unwashed tumbler is sitting next to it. I take it to the kitchen to rinse it out and grab a packet of potato chips before returning to the home office. Placing the tumbler on the desk, I half fill it with some of the silky-smooth alcohol. A chat request from someone named DancerGirl pops up on my monitor.

Taking a sip, I close my eyes and sigh. The scotch goes down as smooth as expected, and I can already feel the warmth soothing my nerves.

I study DancerGirl's request for a moment. The exit button is hovering near the side of the screen where I somehow missed it yesterday. BluesGirl88 seems to be absent tonight, but I'm not ready to leave the chat game yet.

I accept DancerGirl's invitation and almost immediately my avatar is standing by the ocean, looking rather silly in a full three-piece suit. A leggy brunette is lying on her back on a towel, catching virtual rays in a red string bikini.

Terry25: "Hi, do I know you?"

DancerGirl: "Not yet, but take a look at me—I think you'd like to."

I laugh and take a swig of scotch. The buzz that's coming on fast is feeling pretty good. I guess one of the advantages of getting older is how booze seems to hit me quicker.

During my wild single years, I could drink the night away with any woman I'd picked up to spend it with. But they were never as forward as these chat girls. The virtual world moves fast. But it's like what I've always said; the internet allows us the freedom to be who we want to be and the courage to say what we want.

Terry25: "Right."

I click on my suit and change to a pair of board shorts.

DancerGirl: "Now, that's better, Terry. How about coming over here and rubbing some oil onto my back?"

I'm not sure how this is supposed to work exactly. I hadn't interacted with anyone yesterday except to chat. The game must be programmed for characters to touch each other, but how could it possibly mimic any kind of real sexual stimulation?

I shrug and click on her back. My avatar moves to where DancerGirl is on the beach. He kneels, supporting his weight with his legs, one on each side of the brunette lying face down on the towel.

The pre-programmed animation makes my avatar's hands move up and down along her back in a crude-looking massage action. She responds with some kind of arching action while her avatar repeatedly groans in satisfaction. I know the sound is coming from the chat program and not a microphone; it has a cheesy pre-recorded tone to it. Other than her being practically naked, I'm not sure how this is supposed to turn anyone on.

Terry25: "Wow, I'm only rubbing lotion on your back, and you're getting all excited. I knew I was good, but not THAT good."

DancerGirl: "Don't flatter yourself, mister. It'll take more than this to get me off."

I nearly spit the drink from my mouth with her

comment. It takes me a minute to prepare my comeback.

Terry25: "Well, you best keep being nice to me if you want it to happen. I save my best work for the bitches who earn it."

I take a swig of scotch and wait. This will either bring the chat to an abrupt end or shoot things ahead at light speed. I'm not feeling the least bit turned on by her avatar, so I'm good if she ducks out. I'm here for the laughs anyway.

DancerGirl moves from the towel and is now knee-deep in the water, facing me. Her bikini top disappears, and her avatar has no tan lines. Trust me to pick up on those little details, but then my sharp eye has been a great asset to me in my occupation. When you appraise a house for a potential client, you need to take notice of every little thing that can add value or reduce it.

DancerGirl: "What are you waiting for, you big talker? Click on my tits... Stud!"

Her breasts aren't anywhere near the quality that BluesGirl88 showed me yesterday. But I can't help wondering how it would feel to cup and play with them. Or if I will feel anything. The simulation is just that, a simulation.

I do as she says, and my avatar re-emerges standing right behind her. His hands work their way from her back to her breasts, cupping, and rubbing them as the animation repeats itself over and over.

DancerGirl: "Oh, yeah, that's it. I'm getting so wet now."

I can't imagine how, because this pre-programmed animation isn't doing anything for me, but each to their own, I guess. Maybe more scotch will help.

A new chat bubble appears in the scene.

BluesGirl88: "What the fuck's going on here?"

As the avatar loads, I recognize the blonde from last night dressed in a short black skirt with a short-sleeved white blouse. Her hair is in a ponytail and not flowing free like yesterday, but the name doesn't lie—BluesGirl88 is back. And kinda pissed.

My avatar takes a step back from DancerGirl.

Terry25: "I was just chatting with my friend who was showing me some of the things this chat scene does."

BluesGirl88: "Uh-huh. Do you rub the boobs of all your female friends?"

Terry25: "Not as many as I'd like."

Cheeky, I'll admit. But she did ask.

Her avatar moves quickly to the edge of the surf

and glares at me.

BluesGirl88: "Get over here, now."

DancerGirl: "Gee, you found yourself a bossy one there, Terry."

BluesGirl88: "Who the hell asked you...slut?"

DancerGirl: "Go fuck yourself, psycho."

Terry25: "Hey, girls, can't we all just get along?"

BluesGirl88: "Listen here, Terry. It's either her or me. I didn't come here for a ménage á trois with two guys."

DancerGirl: "What the fuck?"

BluesGirl88: "You were rubbing a man's tits, Terry. So, if you want to stay here and pursue some homo fantasy of yours, that's fine. As they say, people can be and do anyone they want on an internet chat site."

I turn to DancerGirl, stunned over the fact she might be a guy.

Terry25: "Is this true?"

I'm not quite sure how I feel about the deception. But it's not like I was enjoying the simulation anyway.

The brunette glances between me and BluesGirl88, seeming reluctant to reply.

BluesGirl88: "Tell the truth or I'll find you and hurt you."

DancerGirl's avatar starts laughing hysterically.

DancerGirl: "You're not real and you can't hurt me, so don't throw stupid threats around."

BluesGirl88 transforms into a ninja in full white attire, including the head covering. She has a samurai sword in her left hand and swings it around in a high arc from behind and over her head. It connects with the neck of her target.

The lack of gore animation enabled for the game results in the sword going straight through DancerGirl's neck without decapitating her.

The brunette stares at her attacker for a moment.

DancerGirl: "That was cool but pointless. Yes, I'm a guy, but it's better than being a fucking psycho like you."

She exits the chat, leaving me alone on the beach with the blonde ninja.

BluesGirl88: "Fucking coward. Were you enjoying

his fun?"

Terry25: "Not really. No."

BluesGirl88: "Good. Because I'm not into sharing, Terry. If you're with me, you're with me and no one else. Let's go."

BluesGirl88 invites me to a private chat, and I soon find myself materializing in her virtual mansion. This time it's the entertainment room on the second level of the giant house.

She appears in a matching white lace crop top with G-string panties.

BluesGirl88: "Much better, don't you think?"

She picks a spot on the carpet in front of me and starts dancing to the subdued blues music that's playing in the room.

BluesGirl88: "Please be seated for the show. And make sure you're wearing something... comfortable."

She twists and turns, moving her body like the highest-paid exotic dancer at an exclusive gentleman's club. I pause, thinking about the word 'gentleman' and amused by the irony of the term. When I was a boy, my mother told me how gentlemen behaved, and I find it hard to believe ogling a naked woman while swilling booze qualifies

CHRIS HEINICKE

someone as a gentleman.

I click on the couch and my avatar sits down. Then I give him an instant costume change, and he's wearing nothing but a pair of black cotton boxer shorts.

Terry25: "Better?"

BluesGirl88: "For now. What do you think of a real woman's body?"

I grin and type my honest opinion of how she looks dancing erotically.

Terry25: "Fucking hot."

She laughs and twerks her tight ass at me, and I think I can maybe understand what the attraction is to this virtual game. It's like porn, but interactive. And while not all porn appeals to all people, when you find the right thing for you, it can become addictive.

She grins and runs her hands down her body, caressing her breasts and brushing her fingers over her thighs.

It could be the upgrades she's had done to her avatar, but the way her boobs move underneath her skimpy top definitely seems very real. But I wouldn't have known DancerGirl was a guy right away either.

Terry25: "How could you tell she was really a man?"

BluesGirl88: "You can't always tell. It comes with experience and time on this site. But a lot of the guys who pose as women here act a certain way. They don't care that in real life they're chatting with another man. It's what they like."

She touches her G-string panties, pulling them tight against her body while she sways her hips. I can see the outline of her pussy beneath the scant fabric. And I'm realizing that 'upgrade' doesn't just mean the quality of body parts, but in the animation too.

She grins at me and slides her hands up beneath her lace top to cup her breasts and tug her nipples.

Bluesgirl88: "Men are visual creatures and what they see is two people engaging in sexual acts, which they then use to assist them as they fist pump the trouser snake."

I take a long pull of my drink. I'm aroused by her dancing, I'll admit. The show she's putting on is great. Just the kind of fantasy I need today.

Terry25: "You have a way with words. Is there anything you can't do?"

BluesGirl88: "Lots of things, but I'm not about to advertise my shortcomings."

There's a shiny pole in the middle of the room

we're in, and her avatar materializes, instantly swinging on it in tune to a slow rock song. I look at my scotch bottle and see I've almost drained it.

It certainly explains why I'm feeling so lightheaded and carefree. Right now, I couldn't care less about anything happening in the real world. Inside this fantasy game, there are no stupid office politics or a jerk-off boss. No sick kids or hour-long commutes in the morning and late afternoon. Or a wife who is too tired most days to notice my needs. The packet of potato chips is almost empty, and I'm not feeling good in the stomach for it.

BluesGirl88: "You've gone quiet. Is something wrong?"

Terry25: "I've been drinking and put down the whole packet of chips. I'm too old for this shit."

BluesGirl88: "So you're not twenty-five years old then like your name says?"

Terry25: "I was once."

BluesGirl88: "You lied about your age? It doesn't surprise me. You don't seem like a twenty-five-year-old. But age doesn't matter here, does it? As long as we're both consenting adults and we are the opposite sex to each other, I'm okay with it. But please tell me you're not seventy."

I type 'LOL' in a speech bubble and my avatar bursts out laughing.

Terry25: "I'm thirty-nine, actually."

BluesGirl88: "Well, you better not lie to me about anything else."

Her character loses her top. I stare, transfixed by the sight of her bare breasts.

Terry25: "Wow, I love the way your boobs swing as you do that."

BluesGirl88: "Like I said, I paid some good money for these. Have you been spending some money on yourself?"

I make my character's cotton boxer shorts disappear, and his penis is visible in its default erect state.

BluesGirl88: "Wow, that's impressive. We should go to the top floor and test it out."

I have no idea how this sex simulation is supposed to get me off, but my real-life erection tenting my pants is willing to find out.

She stops dancing and walks toward me, a drink appearing in her hand. She raises it to her lips and glances at my avatar's erect cock then at my eyes.

Her blue ones are very lifelike, mesmerizing.

BluesGirl88: "This place is like drinking scotch. This glass might not be real, but when I take a sip, I know how it tastes. And it feels pretty good to have that burn."

I raise the virtual glass that's appeared in my avatar's hand to his lips and simultaneously take a sip from my own glass of scotch, and, for a moment, reality and fantasy blurs. The sensation is stimulating. Like I'm really drinking with BluesGirl88 in that virtual room. Smooth, easy, and exciting. And a fucking turn-on. I want to know how it feels to enjoy this fantasy to the fullest. My very own personalized porn.

Terry25: "Lead the way, baby girl."

I could facepalm myself for the cheesy comment, but it's too late once I hit enter and it's on the screen.

Her character appears in the bedroom. I zoom in and see she's now fully nude. I send mine up there too and move to the bed. The mattress has different points to click on and each location my avatar goes to, he engages in a different sexual position.

BluesGirl88: "You starting without me?"

She sends herself to the middle of the bed where she lies on her back with her knees spread wide, as is her very realistic-looking pussy. I click on her and my avatar moves on top of her in what looks like missionary position sex.

I watch the animations from my chair, taking the last drink from my bottle. Every few minutes, BluesGirl88 goes to a different spot, and I follow her. We engage in virtual sex in different positions. The last is her on top of me, her boobs bouncing above my face while she rides me. I'm lost in the motion, mesmerized. God, she's got great tits. There's not much typing going on, and if she's doing what I'm doing while watching this from my chair, I know why.

When I finally look at the time, I see it's three a.m. Shit. That late? I tell BluesGirl88 I have to get up for work in a few hours, and I really should leave and go to bed.

BluesGirl88: "I'll see you tomorrow, and when I do, I want you to take me to a place you've bought. I can tell you're a man who earns a lot, so I don't want to hear any whining about having to spend money."

Her character is standing by the bed with her hands on her hips.

Terry25: "I'll see what I can find. Thanks for the fun tonight, BluesGirl."

I leave the chat and exit the program. Where did the time go tonight—and what does it mean when one pixel-built entity has sex with another one?

It wasn't my physical body. It was a fantasy. But

a fantasy I enjoyed because it seemed real. My mind was connected with another's mind, involved in intimate activities. I may not have been there in the physical form, but emotionally, I was with another woman.

I'm dizzy from the scotch and the rush I've experienced as I stagger to my bedroom. It felt good to play with BluesGirl, piqued my curiosity and need for release, but should it?

I sneak into bed and Talissa doesn't even move, nor does my son who's sleeping in the middle of us for the second consecutive night. Here I am, looking at the woman who loves me and the little boy who looks up to me as if I'm some sort of hero.

I'm no hero, and after my actions tonight, I'm thinking I might be an awful husband.

CHAPTER 4

DAY 3

"TERRY, WAKE UP. Terry."

I open my eyes and see my wife peering down at me, rocking me with her hands.

I dart a glance at the clock. *Damn.* It's nearly eight a.m. and I don't remember my alarm going off at all.

"I'm awake," I mumble and shut my eyes again for a second. My head hurts like a crew with jackhammers have taken up shop in it.

"What time did you come to bed? I woke up once, at two, and you still weren't in yet."

"Yeah, I know, sorry. I'm still brainstorming a business plan of mine, and I was coming up with all sorts of strategies." Damn it, I'm lying through my teeth to cover my sick, self-serving activities from last night.

"I worry about you when you don't sleep well. Get in the shower, and I'll have an extra-strong coffee and hot breakfast ready for you." As she gives me a big kiss on the lips, a frown creases her brow.

"You were drinking last night?"

"I had a couple of scotches. It helps with the creative streak."

She rubs a hand through my hair. "Be careful, Terry."

Her serious tone makes me pause, but before I can ask what she means, I receive another kiss on the lips, and she smiles at me. "I love you," she adds and then quickly leaves to see to the children.

I could cry. She's the most beautiful woman inside and out, and I'm doing sneaky shit behind her back while she's comforting the boy we brought into this world a little over seven years ago.

I shower, drink my coffee, and eat some bacon and eggs at the table with Talissa and the kids, but my mind is still fuzzy and my body dragging. I barely say anything. Why am I carrying so much guilt about this virtual blonde girl?

It was just a fantasy. Nothing more than personalized porn.

I kiss my kids goodbye, and then after I give my wife a big kiss, I say, "I love you so much. Please don't ever forget it."

Today, I take a large flask of hot coffee with me to work. I'm going to need all the liquid energy I can get. I have about forty-five minutes to do a drive, which usually takes me just under an hour.

* * * * *

"Geez, Terry, you look like shit," Roger says as I get into the office at about five minutes past nine. The rest of the staff are already there, even Phelps.

"Did you forget to shave or just couldn't be bothered?" Phelps asks.

I put my hand on my jaw, and I come to the realization that I clean forgot. I never forget to shave for the office. "Oh shit, sorry Phelps."

He turns away from me and addresses the room. "As I said on Monday, we have a temp working with us for a while to help us catch up with the increasing workloads. If we do well enough, she may stay on longer."

"She? Wow, I won't be the only girl here anymore." Kate smiles as the door opens and the new temporary agent walks in and...the pounding in my head increases. I blink, trying not to stare as my mind does a double-take.

"Everyone, this is Emily," Phelps says. "Not only is she pretty, but she has a brain that'll make any of you look like a single-celled organism in comparison."

Kate is the first to shake hands with her. Then George and the cheeky smile-wearing Roger are next. I feel faint. I take a deep breath and shake her hand. She looks me in the eye with her bright blue ones as she says, "Pleased to meet you, Terry," and flashes a smile.

My head's spinning. Her long blonde hair is pulled into a ponytail. She's wearing a short black business skirt and a white short-sleeved blouse that is very tight fitting against her high and mighty breasts. I try not to stare, but it's damn near impossible when she reminds me of the woman I had virtual sex with only a few hours earlier.

"Are you okay?" she asks me in a husky tone.

"I'm not feeling well today. I...excuse me." I run out of the office to the men's room and almost dive for the bowl in the solitary cubicle. My throat burns as my breakfast makes an exit and splashes into the water, a couple of drops hitting me in the face.

How the hell am I supposed to work with the woman I've been chatting to on 3DDreamChat? I mean, it's impossible that it's her. But she looks damn like her. She's wearing the same clothes and has the husky voice of BluesGirl88. And her face, while not exactly the same...her blue eyes and the shape. Damn. The avatar has an uncanny resemblance to the woman.

Get a grip, Terry, I silently admonish.

I take a deep breath and shake my head to clear it. No. It's not possible. I'm losing my mind. Too much scotch or something. I've overindulged and now it's messing with me. I haven't felt well since yesterday. It can't be her. How can it be?

"Terry, you okay, dude?" Roger's familiar voice cuts through the fog in my head.

"I'll be fine," I say. I flush and walk to the sink to clean my face and hands.

Roger grabs my shoulder and turns me to face him. "Hey, I've known you for a long time, even longer than Talissa has. What the fuck is going on?"

The room is spinning dangerously. I clutch the edge of the counter for balance. "You won't believe me if I tell you."

I splash water on my face and rinse my mouth.

The cool liquid is refreshing, steadying. I repeat the action.

"Try me," Roger says.

I pat my face dry with a towel and look at him.

"Okay. She's her."

"Who's her?"

"Emily. She's the girl from the stupid 3DDreamChat. I texted with her again last night and she was wearing the same clothes as Emily is right now. Her face, her tits, even the voice—I'm telling you, she's her."

Roger blinks at me.

"I told you you wouldn't believe me." Why would he? I don't even believe myself. I toss the paper towel into the trash.

"Do you have any idea how ridiculous you sound? Yeah, Emily is hot and definitely worthy of a night of hot steamy sex with yours truly, but she's like a hundred other blondes with a nice body."

"Yeah, I know. But I'm telling you, she's the same girl."

"You mean, she *looks* like the same girl. She can't be the same girl." He shakes his head. "Buddy, you need to get it together and get back in there."

"But what if she is? What does that even fucking mean?"

He sighs. "It means the world is one big fucked-up coincidence. But it's not her. You're just on edge from lack of sleep. Now, come on, let's sell some properties."

* * * * *

I GET BACK to the morning brief. Phelps glances at me and carries on talking as if he doesn't care whether I'm there or not. I tune in and out and steal an occasional glance at this Emily. At one stage, she catches me and gives me a small smirk.

Is she messing with my head on purpose? Or is this some kind of weird karmic coincidence meant to guilt me? All I can think about is whether she looks the same naked as that avatar I fucked last night.

Dammit, I'm a pervert. Roger's right. It has to be the lack of sleep causing this paranoia, making me think this chat girl has invaded my real life. There are millions of people living in the San Francisco Bay area, and what's to say BluesGirl88 even lives here? She could be from another state or living in another country. But then again, I didn't detect an accent.

The brief goes for another ten minutes before Phelps decides someone else should talk. He invites Emily to speak about herself.

She stands with one hand on her hip and uses the other to enunciate her words. She looks at each of us as she talks, describing her education in real estate sales and small business management, her employment overseas, and lastly, her goal to anchor herself and settle down. Listening to her speak is like sexual chocolate, and she exudes enough confidence to put even Roger in his place.

"So, you're single?" George asks.

Roger looks at him and raises his eyebrows as if to ask, "What the fuck?"

"Recently single, yes, but I don't think I'm your

type," Emily says with a wink.

George laughs. "Well, I thought we could go out for drinks sometime and you can see what's on the market in this city. At least, if they're not your type, they might be mine."

"Hey, George, we're not here to play Mr. Matchmaker," Phelps says. "Now, Emily, you can work with me today, and tomorrow you can go out there and do your magic."

We all go our separate ways, and I trail behind, watching as the newcomer follows the boss down the hallway. As she turns to the left to go into The Dragon's Den, otherwise known as Phelps' office, she catches me staring at her. A smirk tips her lips before she disappears from view.

Great. She probably thinks I was checking out her ass. Which I was, but...dammit!

I walk to my own office and close the door and the blinds. The glare from the sunlight diminishes along with my headache. I boot up my work computer and wait for it to load. Why the company doesn't update their hardware is beyond me. I have enough time to go make a mug of coffee in the staff room and bring it back before the system is finally ready.

Accessing the web browser, I type in the internet address for 3DDreamChat and begin the software download. While waiting for the program to finish the process, I call up Mrs. Pellmont. A younger-sounding woman answers, explaining she's her assistant, and confirms our appointment for Friday. Then I do a few follow-up calls for clients who have expressed interest in buying property in certain areas. While discussing two or three properties with each prospect that might meet their needs, I do a kick-ass job of disguising my tiredness. I need to ensure they are confident in my abilities to help them find their dream property.

Checking on the progress of my download, I see the chat program has completed, so I install it. I know this goes against the company terms and conditions for using their computers, but I need to check to see if this BluesGirl88 is online so I can eliminate my suspicions. It takes a few minutes for the PC to install the software and then restart, so I refill my coffee mug again while waiting.

I've lost count of how much coffee I've ingested today, but what does it matter anyway? Three cups or ten, I still feel like hell warmed over. The computer is ready, so I run the 3DDreamChat software. After entering my username and password, a quick search reveals no sign of the blonde I've spent hours chatting to online.

But what does that prove?

BluesGirl88 could just not be online right now. How would I know what she's up to in real life?

Damn, I've loaded contraband software to the company computer and haven't achieved anything to dispel my suspicion about the chat girl and Emily being the same person. I exit the program and make sure there isn't an icon for it in my start menu, desktop screen, or quick launch buttons. Someone would have to search to find it if they wanted to see if I have anything on my system that shouldn't be there.

I look at my appointment book. There's a young couple booked in to take a look at a property in their price range an hour from now. It's a great opportunity to get out and try to clear my head, and if I leave now, I'll have time to grab a latte-to-go from the cafe a couple of blocks from the property I need to be at.

I shut down the computer, grab my briefcase, and head toward the back entrance to make for the parking lot at the rear of the building. I manage to avoid human contact until I exit the rear door of the building. Shielding my eyes from the sun's glare, I see Emily out back, smoking a cigarette. *Shit.* I breathe in long and hard, then let it out at the same pace. I was trying to avoid seeing her, but while she's still out here smoking, it might be a good chance to confront her. Or ... I could just make a quick escape. I head for my car.

"Terry. Are you feeling better?" she asks.

Sensing her gaze tracking me, I glance back at her. She's staring at me, cigarette hanging between her fingers. She brings it to her lips and gives it a drag with the same casual sexiness as a sip of scotch from a tumbler.

Fuck it.

I change course and head her way. "What the hell are you doing here?"

I stop in front of her with just a foot between us. Taking a long drag on the cigarette, she stares at me while exhaling smoke in my face. "I work here."

"That's not what I'm talking about. I mean, why

are you following me from 3DDreamChat to my real life?"

Damn. The words sound stupid even to me, but she has to be BluesGirl88. The similarities are just too much. Either that or I should quit my life now because I've gone insane.

She laughs. "3DDreamChat? Hey, whatever you're smoking is obviously a lot more fun than this menthol. What are you talking about?"

I point at her shirt. "You were wearing the same blouse and skirt last night when you arrived on the beach. You dressed like this on purpose to mess with my head. Even your ponytail." I gesture at her appearance. "It's all the same."

"You're funny but clearly nuts. How would you know what I was wearing last night?"

"Like I said, 3DDreamChat. You had me at your mansion, and you had a white shirt and black skirt on. We talked for ages and then we...did...other things."

She blinks at me. But I can't tell if it's a cool and calculated expression or what she's thinking.

"Oh, Terry, I'm sorry, but you must have me mixed up with someone else." Her gaze settles on my ring finger. "And what's a married man doing chatting to a woman like me on the internet?"

I could throw up again right now. I've made myself look really stupid. I guess this is what happens when one stays up half the night drinking a bottle of scotch and playing foolish games.

"Never mind. I'm so sorry. My mistake. I didn't sleep well, and it's messed with my head."

P a g e | **66**

She throws down her cigarette butt and grinds it out with her heel. I turn to leave, but she grabs my hand with hers, stopping me.

"It's okay, Terry. You've obviously had a rough night." She releases my hand and feels around her handbag, pulls out a small coin purse, and opens it. "Take one of these. It will help you get through the day." She places a small white pill on my left palm.

I stare at it. "What the hell is it?"

"You're tired. This will make you not tired." She grins. "Don't worry, it's just an upper. It doesn't have any hallucinogens in it, but when it wears off, you'll crash pretty hard."

Being out in the midday sun is making my head hurt even worse than the pounding hangover I woke with. I'm more than tired; I'm a walking disaster, and I still have clients to meet and impress. "How long does it work for?"

"Eight to ten hours, give or take. Depends on the person, but for me, it's normally ten hours. They work great though. I had one this morning."

Her hand is warm and soft as she closes my fingers around the pill. Her touch lingers a few seconds longer than is comfortable.

"I have to go," I say, and back away from her hypnotizing blue eyes. As I walk toward my car, the feeling of her hand covering mine stays with me.

Fuck it. I unclench my fingers and throw the pill down my throat. Maybe it will work or maybe it will kill me, but anything is better than this relentless pounding in my body and mind. I avoid looking at Emily until I'm in my car.

She waves as I drive away, her smile wide and satisfied.

* * * * *

WHEN I'M TIRED, I like to tell myself that coffee will fix it, but today it was a little round white pill that fixed it. I'm driving home, and despite the intense hours I've put in, I haven't felt this good in days. Emily was right about the pill.

The afternoon was a success. I may have secured another property sale before it even hits the market. The clients, Yvette and Robert, made such a nice young couple. One of those couples who always hold hands and finish each other's sentences. They had a bright-eyed reaction to every part of the house I showed them.

They reminded me of how Talissa and I were during our first few years together. Even in my late twenties and early thirties she made me feel like a boy happily suffering an intense form of puppy love. Yes, we still love each other, but the intensity isn't the same, and I miss those days when we could just do what we wanted, go out for dinner whenever we felt like it, and fuck each other's brains out at a moment's notice. Of course, I love my children and could never be without them, but sometimes I wish I could go back to being the solitary center of her universe. I know it's selfish to think like this, but at times, I feel like growing older and responsible sucks.

"Enough," I yell out loud. The road ahead is full

of traffic traveling at a snail's pace. I soon see why. A little white hatchback has been t-boned by a red SUV, and the traffic has been restricted from four lanes to two. A man is talking to a blonde woman, his body language seeming apologetic. As the woman turns her head, I do a double take. Emily, my new work colleague, looking like there aren't enough cigarettes in the world to fix today. Her mouth opens as she sees me, and at that point, I know she's recognized me.

Shit! I can't just drive past her now. It takes a few minutes before I find a safe spot to pull over past the collision site where tow trucks are hooking up the damaged cars to clear the scene.

As Emily runs over to me, I push the button for the window to come down so she can speak through it.

"Terry! You wouldn't believe what happened. This idiot went through a red light and slammed right into me. I think he's been drinking."

Shit. "Are you okay?"

"Yes. Just shaken up a bit."

"Do you need help? A ride somewhere?" I can't leave her stranded like this.

Her face breaks into a relieved smile. "Really? You would do that for me? I need to grab my gym bag from my car though. I'm supposed to be at a class in twenty minutes."

I was expecting maybe a lift to her place or an Urgent Care clinic to be checked out for injuries. But to a gym? "You've just had a car accident. Does the gym class matter?"

Her smile falters. "Yes, people depend on me. I'm not hurt, and I've already spoken to the police, paramedics, and tow truck driver, so I'm all cleared to leave. I was going to call for a taxi, but since you've offered..."

She runs off before I can say anything, and in my side mirror, I see a police officer walking toward me. It's a female cop wearing a SFPD uniform with a bulletproof vest. They say a female's uniform is loose fitting so as not to feminize them, but this one seems to have the opposite effect. Rapidly approaching my side of the vehicle, she has her police badge produced as she arrives at my door. "Excuse me, sir, do you know this lady?"

"Yes, ma'am. We work together. Thought she could do with a ride."

"That's awfully generous of you." She looks at my hands on the wheel, and I can almost feel the intensity of her gaze as she does a quick check of the interior of my car as well as me. Her eyes settle on mine. "I trust she will get home safely?"

I hold her gaze and flash my million- dollar-property smile. "You have my word, ma'am."

I can't help noticing her good looks and blonde hair that's been pulled up in a bun under her hat. And her eyes. Damn, they're a clear blue. Seeing her reminds me that I still need to get Talissa a naughty police officer costume for our 'private time.' Just another sexual fantasy to tick off on my bucket list.

"Name and registration."

I give her my name and show her my license and registration as asked. She jots down my information, her expression unreadable.

As she hands my registration back to me, she says, "Thank you. This young lady should be heading to the hospital to be checked for a concussion. But she's declined to go with the Paramedics." She glances at Emily and I catch a glimpse of disapproval cross her expression as she turns her attention back to me. "If your friend doesn't make it home in the next couple of hours, you'll be getting a visit from me."

Okay. I could think of worse things. But I understand her point, I guess. The streets aren't what they used to be and not everyone who appears as a Good Samaritan is necessarily just that. I know, when my daughter gets older, I'll be the most paranoid father on the planet.

"Yes, ma'am, I understand, and I'll remind her to call you as soon as she's home."

Emily gets to the passenger door, gym bag slung over her shoulder. She pulls the door open, says 'bye' to the officer, and gets in.

We get waved off and I turn to Emily. "Please remember to call her when you get home."

"I told her you're my friend. She put the hard word on you to leave me alone?"

"Not quite, but it felt kind of like a father watching his only daughter go on a first date. I'll be getting chased with a shotgun if you aren't home by curfew. So how far away is this gym?"

"About fifteen minutes up this road." She glances at her watch. "Shit. It's gonna come down to the wire."

"I'll do my best. Are you going to have time to get changed?"

"Yes. Just try and watch the road though." She starts unbuttoning her blouse.

It takes all my strength not to break and crash the car. *Jesus.* I didn't mean to get changed *now*.

"Uh...that's...creative," I stammer, trying to look straight ahead and failing.

She grins. "Time saver. I didn't think you'd mind."

Through my peripheral vision, I see her slip the blouse off her shoulders. I sneak a quick look while pretending to check for traffic as we sail through a green light at a major intersection.

Her white lacy bra is in full view and her boobs are as magnificent as I thought they were. As magnificent as the 3DDreamChat avatar's. This is too much.

She opens her gym bag and pulls out a black crop top and slides it over her head and bra. It sits a few inches above her navel and shows off her toned abs. Jutting her hands up the back of her top, she unhooks the bra, slips it off, and places it in her bag.

"I've done this a few times. You can probably tell."

"I'm trying not to look, but I'll admit, you've got skills." And I think I'm on a slow boat to hell that just got swept into a fast current.

She giggles and pulls a pair of red Spandex shorts from her bag. Lifting her ass off the seat, she slides her hands up her tight skirt and then tugs a pair of white lacy panties down to her feet.

Holy fuck. I think the boat just hit the rapids.

Clinging to sanity by a tattered rope, I keep my eyes on the road. After a couple of minutes of hearing fabric rustling and the sound of a zipper, she tells me it's okay to look. Her skirt is gone but the red shorts are on, and I wish I could be in her class—whatever class she's in.

She puts on a pair of ankle socks and white sneakers, and her transformation from businesswoman to gym junkie is complete.

"I really appreciate this, Terry."

I shake my head. "I don't know how you do it, work in the office all day, and then, even after being in an accident, head to the gym. That's some serious dedication." I work out when I can, but I'm not as committed to it as to not miss a session if life gets in the way.

"Well, I kinda need to be there. They're counting on me. I instruct what we call Weights and Beats. We lift light dumbbell weights in time to music. We get people of all ages coming in to do it. Maybe you should try it once."

"Wait. Let me get this straight—you smoke but also *instruct* classes at the gym?"

"I'm trying to give up smoking, but it's damn hard. I've cut down to ten smokes a day, which is great considering I used to smoke a pack a day from the age of sixteen. I'm doing the best I can, Terry."

"Sorry. I didn't mean...you look very...great."

We drive a little further, and she points at the sign of the Heavenly Bodies fitness company where she needs me to stop, and I recognize it as the same chain that Talissa goes to in Half Moon Bay where we live. There's a parking lot in front of the large, glass-walled building. I pull up to the door and bring the car to a complete stop.

"Are you sure you're okay to do this? That cop said you might have a concussion."

She studies me for a second, her expression a mix of humor and surprise. "You really care, don't you? That's so sweet." She leans over and gives me a quick kiss. Am I startled that it's on my lips rather than my cheek? Maybe a bit, but after today's events I'm not sure I'm surprised by much of anything anymore.

She grins at me. "I'll be fine. And I owe you big time for this."

"No, you don't. Now get going, so I can get home before the wife sends a search party for me."

"Thanks, Terry." She blows me another quick kiss and exits the car.

I stare at her ass as she runs to the front door of the gym; one could bounce coins on those tight round cheeks.

Fuuuuck.

I bang my head repeatedly against the headrest on my seat until I'm able to push thoughts of Emily's hotness away and concentrate on getting home to Talissa and my children.

As much as I like to sneak in a look at a hot body, being attracted to a work colleague can only lead to trouble, especially when said colleague looks so much like the avatar I had cyber-sex with last night.

That can't be a coincidence, can it?

Either way, I have the feeling that the slow boat to hell has made it through the rapids only to be in danger of approaching a waterfall.

* * * * *

As soon as I walk through the door at home, the mouth-watering scent of fresh baked lasagna hits me, and I know that dinner is ready to be served. Talissa smiles as she asks how my day was, and I tell her about Phelps hiring a temp to help with the workload, but I don't mention the fact the temp is female and a hottie. Not that my sweet wife would get jealous—she never does—but sometimes less information is better. And I'm pretty sure this is one of those times. I doubt I can handle any questions right now without sounding like the completely perverted lunatic I think I've become.

I pick Isaac up and twirl him about the room.

He squeals, laughing. "Daddy, you seem really awake tonight."

"I had a good day at work, son, so I'm really happy." I smile at him. "It makes all the difference."

"Good thing that one's feeling better too, or you'd be cleaning vomit from your shirt." Talissa nods at Isaac as she grins at me.

I grin back and put Isaac down, just to be safe.

He looks up at me. "Mommy says you work too hard and that's why you're so tired lately."

"Mommy's right. I promise to try and work less on weekends though. We have a new worker who might be able to do some more of Daddy's work."

"Yay!" he says. Matilda echoes his cheer and wants a twirl-hug too, which I'm happy to oblige. Then we're all sharing a smile at the dinner table.

I look at the time and realize it's been seven hours since I took the pill. I'm feeling more than good right now, but I don't even want to contemplate what will happen when it wears off. Surely, it couldn't be something as drastic as falling asleep at the table.

There's a knock at the door, and before I can even think about getting up from my chair, Talissa is up and greeting the person interrupting our meal. I hear a familiar woman's voice introducing herself as Officer Hannah Hall.

"Terry," Talissa calls out, and when I turn the corner from the dining room to the hallway, I see the blonde cop from the car accident scene.

"Good evening, officer. Is...everything okay?" I ask.

"I haven't received a call from, Emily Philips, who you gave a lift to earlier this evening. Can you account for her whereabouts?"

"Terry?" Talissa furrows her eyebrows.

"I dropped her off at Heavenly Bodies in Mission Bay and then drove home, ma'am."

"Sounds like a strip joint," the officer says as she pulls out her notepad and jots down the information. "Sure you didn't stop in for a while?"

"It's a fitness center, ma'am. She teaches classes there." I give the officer the address in San Francisco and approximate time I dropped Emily off.

"Do you know if she had any arrangements to

get home?

"None that she mentioned. I assumed she'd call for a taxi, ma'am."

"Have you tried calling her, Officer Hall?" Talissa asks. "You must have her details from the accident report, ma'am."

Hall turns her attention to my wife. "As a matter of fact, I have tried several times, but her phone keeps ringing out. Is your husband in the habit of giving women rides?"

"Well, he rides me at least twice a week, ma'am," Talissa winks at me. "So, I guess that would be 'yes'?"

"You think this is a joke?"

"Yes, I do. Terry did a favor for a work colleague and because she hasn't called you, you drop around here, disturb our dinner, and try to accuse him of something. Either make a charge or leave us to our kids."

The cop stares at her for a long second. As Hall opens her mouth to speak, the ring of her mobile phone cuts her off. She glances at the phone, then at me as she answers it, "Officer Hall."

She nods with every 'uh-huh' she says, and, a minute later, she ends the call. "That was Emily. Her phone ran out of charge and she only just got home. Sorry for the inconvenience." She steps back from the door as she puts her notepad away. "Have a good evening."

"You should be sorry for the thinly veiled accusation. Good night, ma'am." Talissa closes the door. As I'm about to walk back to the dining room, she grabs my arm. "You didn't tell me about your taxi service this afternoon."

"I didn't think it mattered. Emily had a car crash and I saw her and couldn't just drive past. She just needed to be dropped off at the gym. That's all."

"Is she pretty?"

"Talissa, this isn't like you to be jealous. Yes, she is pretty, but she's blonde."

She smiles. "And here I was getting all concerned about your late nights. Then when I heard about you driving a female workmate around, my mind went to a dark place and I jumped to a scary conclusion."

I wrap my arms around my wife and look into her beautiful cat-like eyes. "It's okay, baby." I still haven't booked a place for dinner for our anniversary. "We should go away this weekend, just you and me. Drop the kids off at my folks' place and go to the lake. We can do what we want, a bit of late-night skinny-dipping, a few drinks, just like we used to."

Her smile is wide. "You know I'd love to, but it's getting a bit last minute to dump them at your parents' place like this."

"I'll call them after we put the kids to bed. You know they'd love to have them stay at the farm again."

"I love you, Terry." She gives me a big kiss. "I'll think about it."

* * * * *

THE KIDS ARE in bed and Talissa and I are in the

living room, cuddled up on the couch. I run my hand through her long hair, and she turns to face me, meeting my hungry mouth with her own. The lust in our kiss builds, quickly heading toward a bursting point. Her hands slip beneath my shirt. She's wearing a long dress made of very light fabric, and I run a hand up to the zipper at the back of it. As I begin its downward journey...Matilda walks in and vomits all over the carpet at the entrance of the room.

"Oh, great," I say as our romantic plans are quashed for the night and a chunky pile of vomit is sitting on the carpet. Talissa comforts our little girl while I grab the carpet shampoo and paper towels and hold my breath. It takes a good fifteen minutes to clean the stain and the smell.

I find Talissa in our daughter's bedroom. Both of my princesses are fast asleep huddled up together in the single bed normally only used by our five-year-old girl.

I sigh as I close the door softly, and head to the office. Might as well get some work done instead. As I boot up the computer, I question whether I should be logging onto the chat program, but I know I'm going to anyway. I need to find something out. The 3D game loads, and I realize my avatar is naked with a big hard-on due to the activities he was engaged in the night before. I dress him in a black leather jacket, white t-shirt, and jeans.

A chat request pops up immediately from none other than BluesGirl88. I accept, and belatedly remember she had asked me to buy a scene to take her to.

Terry25: "I'm sorry. I haven't had time to buy anything yet. It's been a crazy day, and I've only just switched on the computer."

Her avatar loads, and she's in a police uniform of a naughty type with a super short skirt and a tank top for a police shirt.

BluesGirl88: "About time you showed up. Do you like this?"

Terry25: "This is getting all weird. The new girl at work is a blonde who looks just like you did last night. Then I get harassed by a blonde cop tonight...and here you are dressed up like Lady Horny Slut Officer."

Her avatar laughs hysterically.

BluesGirl88: "Are you serious? Was I nice to you in real life?"

Terry25: "So your name isn't really Emily Philips?"

BluesGirl88: "You don't need to know my real name. You just need to know I'm in charge of this thing we have, and you'll do as I say or else there'll be trouble. Now go buy me a new scene."

Terry25: "I'm tired and my daughter is sick. Can't

P a g e | **80**

we just play at your mansion?"

Her avatar punches mine in the nose, but without gore animation turned on, her hit goes through my avatar as if he were a ghost.

Terry25: "What the hell?"

BluesGirl88: "Daughter? Are you telling me you're married?"

Terry25: "Does it matter? What we have is fun, but it's not real and never can be."

Her avatar kicks mine in the nuts. Then she grabs his hair and punches him in the nose with her other hand. She exits the chat and my character is suddenly sitting alone in the lobby.

I should just go to bed and get a good night's sleep for a change. But I could do with a nip of scotch first. I've been craving one all day. As I go to turn around, I see a chat request from BluesGirl88 again.

My head tells me to ignore it, but another part of my anatomy tells me to accept it. I shouldn't, but this animated blonde keeps drawing me in, and I keep wondering what she will do next.

The scene is loading slowly as if it's operated by a team of turtles. Parts of it begin to appear. Flickering torches. An iron gate. My avatar is chained to a wall by manacles? She is still in the slutty police uniform but has a baton in one hand and a whip in the other. The scene is dark, and each wall has a rough-cut stone appearance, like a medieval dungeon.

Terry25: "What the hell is this?"

BluesGirl88: "I asked you to do something and you didn't do it. Now you will be punished."

She cracks the whip and hits me on the back with it. This time it doesn't go through me but makes a stinging sound as it connects with my virtual flesh. I turn the speakers down.

Terry25: "I told you what happened today and why I haven't bought anything for us to play with tonight."

Her avatar hits mine in the knee with the baton. It doesn't hurt me, but she's clearly getting something out of it.

Terry25: "What's the point of all this?"

BluesGirl88: "You lied to me about being married as well as not buying a scene. I should just kill you."

Now I think she's truly deranged. I should go to bed. I get up from my chair intending to do so, but instead of heading to my bedroom, I walk to the booze shelf and grab a glass of scotch. As I return to the computer, I take a long sip of my drink.

Damn. It burns extra hot and fast tonight. I put the tumbler on the computer desk with a heavy 'clunk' of glass on wood. My head is spinning and my vision blurry. My pulse is sluggish, like thick molasses. What the hell is going on?

"Where are you, Terry?" A female voice calls from the hallway.

Talissa! Shit.

I turn the computer off and stumble from the chair. Just one sip of scotch and I've lost my balance and coordination. What the hell is wrong with me?

One foot in front of the other is all I need to do. I crash into the wall, steady myself, and hit the opposite wall. My legs feel like they're made of concrete.

I see a blur of dark blue and black. It's making a noise and coming straight for me. My upper body battles through the fog...the fog my mind keeps trying to insist isn't there. And then I feel her touch. Talissa. No matter what state my body is in, her touch is my haven. She helps me walk and lets me collapse on the bed.

My world turns black.

CHAPTER 5

DAY 4

"GOOD MORNING, HANDSOME."

Talissa's smiling face is the first thing I see when I open my eyes.

I smile back. Although my recollection of last night's events is blurry, I know she was the beacon of salvation who steered me to bed. And today is a special day. At least, I think it is.

"Today's the 14th?" I haven't slept through it have I? I shake my head to clear it. I feel like a human pinata that's been hanging on a rope at a kids' party.

She chuckles. "Last time I checked."

I grin. "Happy anniversary, beautiful."

"You remembered," she squeals and rolls over to lie on top of me. She's warm and soft, her nightgown silky as I wrap my arms lazily around her.

She brushes my cheek with the tip of her index finger, a sly smile pulling at her lips. "I went and got a special present for you yesterday."

"You shouldn't have. I haven't got you anything

yet." *Oh, shit.* Did I even place that order for roses? The realization I also didn't call my parents last night to arrange for the kids to stay with them smacks me in the forehead. With the weekend fast approaching, I'll have to get on it as soon as I get to work.

She quirks an eyebrow. "You'll have to search for my prezzie though." Her breath is warm against my cheek. "Maybe you might have to check under my nightgown." The brightness of her smile is on par with the morning sun.

She squirms against me, and I realize I'm fully naked. Talissa must have stripped me down after I blacked out last night. I slide my hand up her leg, all the way to her thigh. As usual, she's wearing nothing underneath her blue nightie. I touch the heavenly place between her legs...and something is very different. "Oh, my God." My heart skips a beat.

"I got it all waxed for you. Feels so smooth, doesn't it?"

I can't deny it—she's delivered something I've always fantasized about and seems all the rage with the young women these days—if all the beauty salons advertising the waxing service are to be believed.

"I love it." I can't stop touching her, enjoying the feel of her smooth pussy. She's getting wet already. And I can't stop enjoying that either.

"I never thought I'd go from carpet to polished floorboards—if you know what I mean." Her smile seems almost shy now. But the look in her eyes is all sexy she-devil. She nips my bottom lip. "We have time before the kids get up. Let's celebrate our ten years."

She grabs my penis and slowly caresses it with her soft hands. Her touch is always sublime, but as much as she treats my man downstairs with her massaging greatness, he doesn't rise to the occasion.

I stare at my uncooperative cock and try to will it to behave. But it's not listening to me any more than it's listening to Talissa.

Fuuuuuck. This has never happened before.

She's everything I could ever desire. Curvy, lush, and her beautifully presented gift to me should be able to double my excitement. I could just disappear forever right now. All this built-up tension, and now that I have the chance to release it...I don't see it happening.

"Terry?" Her brow furrows as she looks at me. "Maybe you've just been working too hard."

I suppress a tear but nod. Lying might come easy when you get used to it, but it's never easy to forgive yourself when you do it to those you love.

She lifts the nightgown over her head and throws it to the floor, revealing her naked body to my captivated gaze. Her pear-shaped breasts sway as she straddles my groin and rubs herself against my uncooperative member.

I groan and cup her breasts. God, it feels good. Everything she's doing feels so damn good. But my cock refuses to behave.

Fuck it! Why the hell in fuck's name am I looking at the most angelic sight and nothing's working?

"I'm sorry, honey. You know this never happens."

She stops what she's doing and lies next to me, cuddling me close. Her finger traces my lips. "Maybe we can finish this tonight?" She gives me a soft kiss.

I cup her face in my hands and look into her eyes. "I promise we will after I take you out for dinner." I kiss her long and deep. When I let her go, she's smiling. I glance the length of her fit body. "I don't think I need to say you'll need to wear something really nice. You're doing just that now."

"I love you, Terry." She gives me another kiss, gets out of bed, and heads for the shower.

I sit on the edge of the bed for a moment to steady my spinning head. Goddamn. What the hell is wrong with me? My head feels heavy like I've been hit by a truck. What happened last night? This is more than working too much.

I put on a pair of boxers and head for my office. The monitor is off, but my computer is still running. *Shit*. Didn't I turn it off before bed? Has the chat game been running all night?

I sigh in relief when I see the game is logged off. At least I didn't leave it playing. I can't imagine it would go over well if Talissa had seen it.

My email notification says I've got several new messages. Checking through them, there are five with the sender name of BluesGirl88. How the hell did she get my email address? Is it listed in my game profile?

I start with the oldest email.

Where the fuck are you? I don't appreciate a man who takes off as soon as things start to get serious. Get

back to the chat now.

The second oldest email gets worse.

There are consequences for those who think they can just do what they want to me and abandon me when they think they need to take some responsibility. Come back. NOW!

The third email isn't as bad.

I'm so sorry, Terry. I need you. I want you, and I could never hurt you. It's very late now, so you're probably in bed with your wife. Maybe you're using all your sexual tension on her, and I wish it were me. PLEASE come back!

She's crazy, she has to be. Damn me for listening to Roger in the first place. I open the fourth email.

I tried to be nice, I tried to be fair, but you've really done it now, Terry. You think you're safe? Think again. It might be you, or it might be someone you love.

What the hell? Should I be worried? I think I am a little worried. What if these threats carry any real substance? But unless this chat girl truly is Emily, how the hell can she do anything? She can't possibly know where I live.

The last email makes my blood become ice.

Someone once said, "If you're not real, you can't hurt me." Do you ever wonder how they're doing now?

Oh, shit.

I check back on the chat program and find there's no sign of BluesGirl88. I do a search for a DancerGirl and go through the results, picking the one I'm certain is the user I chatted to a couple of nights ago. She, or should I say he, accepts the request.

DancerGirl: "Are you sure you're allowed to chat with me?"

Terry25: "Listen. I think you might be in danger. Like, real-life danger. The woman who threatened you the other night has somehow found my email address and has sent me a disturbing series of emails, one of them mentioning you."

DancerGirl: "Calm down, Terry. Anyone with a little bit of IT knowledge could find out your information, if they knew where to look. I recommend you don't reply, no matter how threatening she gets. She may have just had a wild guess at your email address and is fishing for you to reply. If she can confirm it's you, she's a step closer to finding you in real life."

Terry25: "I just wanted you to know she might be looking for you."

DancerGirl: "Thanks. But I'm fine. I keep who I really am private."

Terry25: "Is that why you masquerade as a woman?"

DancerGirl: "Partly. I like the anonymity. And when a male and female avatar gets down and dirty, it's all the same, isn't it? I even see a lot of girl on girl action. Ironic to think in real life they both could be guys. Anyway, I got to go to work, stay safe, and maybe get out there and find some real action. It's not that hard."

Terry25: "Now that would get me in trouble with the wife."

He exits the chat.

I look at the time. I've wasted half an hour on the computer, and I still haven't had a shower yet. At this rate, Talissa will leave the house before I do. At least I can go to work knowing the man behind DancerGirl is safe. But what do I do if Emily really is BluesGirl88?

* * * * *

I GET TO work feeling like hell warmed over and ten minutes late, a fact quickly noticed by Phelps. He calls me into his office and asks why the hell am I slipping up this week.

"I'm sorry, but how often am I late, Phelps? Do you have some kind of bug up your ass about me?"

His eyes are dark and glittering with anger as he stares at me. Definitely an ass-bug. "If Emily proves her worth this month, she may well get something full time here, and as you know, things will get quiet very soon leading up to the holiday season. So, you best make sure you don't fuck anything up, or else this bug up my ass will come out and bite your stupid head off. Now get out of here and sell something."

He flicks through some papers and signs them, not even looking up as I leave the room. I pull the door closed a little harder than I should, and as I enter the hallway, I notice Roger standing outside his office.

I point at him and head straight in his direction. "I need to talk to you."

"Of course, buddy." He smiles and stands aside to allow me to enter his office before him. Closing the door behind us, he asks, "Is something wrong?"

"Yes. Everything. The new girl, Emily—she's messing with me. I guess you heard about her accident on the way home yesterday?"

"Yes, she mentioned she had a collision." Roger frowns. "Did Phelps tell you about it?"

"No. I gave her a lift from the location of the crash to the fitness center where she instructs classes. But the thing is, she changed from her workwear to her gym gear in my car. She was careful not to let me see anything good, but she took everything off in the process, and I mean *everything*."

"Wow, you lucky man. Your 3DDream girl stripped down beside you and you managed not to crash your own car? Was she as good in real life as the game?" He smirks as he teases me, like a cat who ate all the goldfish and didn't get caught.

I don't address his comment. I know he doesn't believe what I'm saying. I gesture at him to keep quiet. "Just listen. She had these gym shorts with obviously nothing on underneath—seems a bit weird for fitness gear, all the sweating and stuff."

Roger smiles. "There's an entire line of gym shorts with a reinforced crotch to go with the tops with the built-in bra. They're a big hit with gym junkies. More comfortable or something."

"Why does it not surprise me you know about this type of thing?" Was there anything Roger didn't perv after? "But there's something else, too. There was this blonde lady cop at the accident, making sure Emily got home safe. When she didn't report in for a couple of hours, the cop made a visit to my house, asking questions like maybe I would know why."

"Well, Emily's here today so I'm assuming you didn't rape and kill her." Roger laughs and I smile with him. "You know how cops need to investigate everything. She would probably be the same if I was giving a woman a lift home from an accident scene."

"Roger, if she saw you giving Emily, or, in fact, any woman a lift home, she'd be calling in the Special Forces."

He leers at me. "So, was she hot?"

"The cop? Or Emily?"

"The fact you actually have to choose who I

mean is impressive, you horndog." We share another laugh. "What did Talissa think of the cop showing up?" he asks, which makes my bleary head begin to ache.

"She wasn't particularly impressed." Remembering I need to sort some things out for the anniversary, I disengage from the conversation and leave Roger's office. On my way down the hallway, I notice Emily walking toward her temporary office. The sight of her reminds me of another matter I need to take care of.

I call out to her and she smiles, gesturing for me to go into her office after her. As soon as I'm in the room, she closes the door and the blinds before she sits on the side of her desk. Taking a deep breath, she says, "Sorry about the whole thing last night. I didn't expect that cop to be all 'mother hen' like when I didn't report in straight away."

"It's okay, Em, but something else is wrong."

She studies me. "Are you okay?

"Not really, no."

"You look tired if you don't mind me saying. You crashed down hard last night, didn't you?"

"Yes. Too many late nights." I study her expression to see if there's any reaction to that comment. If she's BluesGirl88, she'd have been up late too. But she looks fresh as a daisy as usual. And the only thing I see in her blue eyes is concern.

"The pills will do that when you first start taking them. But after a bit, it gets better. They really get me going every day, you know?" She winks at me and starts rummaging in her purse. "You should have another one. It will help you out."

"Well, that's what I wanted to ask you about. Do the pills have any weird side effects—as in really bad man problems?"

She laughs. "I'm not following."

How can I delicately put this without completely embarrassing myself? "The general was ready to go into the field this morning, but the soldier refused to march."

She laughs harder, and I don't know what I fear most. Is it because she's laughing at my misfortune or laughing because I don't make sense to her?

I can tell I'm just going to have to spell it out. "Oh, dammit, Em. I couldn't get an erection this morning."

Her expression freezes, and I hope to hell no one heard my raised voice. *Please, Earth, swallow me up now.*

"Okay...um, I guess being a female I wasn't aware of such a side effect from coming down off the pill. I mean, it's not, ah, something that happens to me." She gestures loosely at her groin area as if I'm not acutely aware of the fact she's very much female down there. Is she wearing pretty lace panties again beneath that tight skirt? Or is she even wearing anything?

I realize I'm staring and wrench my gaze back to her face. "Well, it's my anniversary tonight, and I want to be able to... perform."

She purses her lips and nods. "I'm not a pharmacist, you know, but I think what you need is just a higher dose, so you avoid the crash until later on." She pulls out her handbag again and sifts through, locating her secret stash of pills inside the coin purse. "Just take the whole thing. I can get more. And I'll ask for some answers from my supplier."

"Considering what happened to me last night and this morning, I'm not sure that's a good idea."

"Well, why did you come to see me then? You want a solution? Keep taking these pills. I suggest you take one now and another at four or five o'clock, so you stay alert and erect. If she wakes up and wants some more action in the morning, find a way to pop another pill."

"If I keep taking them, will I ever be able to perform without them again?"

"You said it yourself, Terry. Tonight's a special night for you. Just take it a day at a time. Were there any other side effects?"

"No."

"Well, take the fucking pills then and worry about it again tomorrow if popping pills upsets you that much."

I look in her eyes and think it over for a few seconds. As much as this idea worries me, I need to be able to rise to the occasion tonight. And the pill really did help me get through the day yesterday. I felt better than I'd felt in ages. Which is far better than the emasculated zombie I feel like right now.

I accept the offer and stare at the small round purse in my hand. I open it and pop one of the pills in my mouth. A few pills remain inside, so I put the coin purse in my pocket.

"Mmm. There you go. You'll be feeling better in seconds. They always give me such a rush when I take them. Uppers. Perk you. Up." She grins, emphasizing each word about uppers with a little bounce that makes her breasts jiggle.

"Yes, they do," I admit. I can feel it working already. The rush of adrenalin pumping through my veins is clearing my head. It's even faster than yesterday, and it feels great. Better than coffee and scotch combined.

"It's exciting, isn't it?" her voice is soft and husky, smooth and warm like a shot of scotch.

"Yes." I can't stop staring at her breasts. The way her blouse fits them so nicely. They have a perfect curve and fullness to them, and I don't think it's the bra that's making that happen. They were just as perky beneath her sports top without one.

Her fingers trail along the top edge of her collar.

"Why don't I help you test it? So, you know you can perform tonight?"

"What?" I glance upward to catch her gaze, not quite sure I heard her correctly.

Emily stands and slowly undoes her blouse, her fingers making easy work of the small buttons. She's wearing an identical blouse to yesterday, but with a dark grey skirt only covering her upper thighs.

"Ah, hang on..." What the hell is she doing? My pulse is racing. I should get the hell out of her office while I still can. I try to take a step backward, but can't seem to make my feet cooperate. I'm frozen in place, mesmerized by the movement of her breasts as she slides the shirt over her shoulders and takes a step my way.

"Hey, you saw me in a bra yesterday. Why so shy now?" She takes another step toward me.

I have no response. I can barely think straight. Her bra is lacy and white, revealing a hint of her dusky pink nipples beneath. I want to see more. I want to leave too, but my cock is screaming at me to enjoy what she's freely offering, and I'm beyond any ability to not listen to it.

A soft smile touches her lips as she reaches behind her back and unclips her bra, then lets it fall to the ground. I can't look away. Her breasts are magnificent. Not as big as my dear wife's, but still a decent handful, and Emily is less than a foot away from me. No one can see into the office when the blinds are drawn, thankfully.

I swallow hard. "Is this a trap?"

"No, it's not, Terry. It's a confession." She cups her breasts with her hands and squeezes them gently. Her nipples are hard and pointing at me. She plays with the one on the left and bites her bottom lip as if it feels really good. And now I want to play with them too and make us both feel good. But I keep my hands at my sides and clench my fists, trying to contain the desire.

Her gaze drops to my groin, where I'm sure she can see my erection bulging my pants, and God help me, she licks her lips.

"I don't know about you, but after my ride in your car yesterday, I was so turned on knowing you were watching me change my clothes that when I went home from the gym, I jumped in the shower and pretended you were with me." She's in front of me now. The heat from her bare skin is scented with a faint perfume. Her breasts fit perfectly in my palms; her nipples tighten as I tweak them gently.

"Shit. You're so damn hot," I whisper.

She's rubbing my cock through my pants, exploring the length of it, making it harder.

"Mmmm," she moans. "I want to see."

So, do I. My lust for her is making me shake. I've not been this aroused in ages. I want to see all of her. Experience all of her. I lift her skirt and...oh, fuck. She's bare there. No panties. And she's waxed. I place my hand between her legs.

She closes her eyes and moans as I touch her, moving her pussy against my hand.

Dammit. Goddamn. Fucking fuck.

I'm at the point of no return now. I was at the point of no return as soon as she took off her top. Maybe even yesterday as soon as I saw her.

I unclasp my belt, and my pants are quickly down around my ankles. She puts a hand down the front of my boxers and grips the part of me that's standing firm like the handle of a baseball bat.

"That pill's great, isn't it?" She smiles and pulls herself close to me. "Makes me fucking horny as all hell too. So, you better put it to good use."

* * * * *

AFTER WE FINISH, the guilt smacks me in the head like a brick.

Yes, it was an epic release, screwing Emily on the

edge of her desk, and I feel better for it physically. But I've now crossed a line I never in my life intended to cross and become something I never wanted to be. I'm now officially a cheater. Cyber-sex is one thing, but this...this is...I can't believe I just did this. I hadn't intended on this happening when I walked in her office feeling like a half-man, half-zombie. And yet, I just banged the fuck out of my very hot co-worker as if I was twenty years younger and not married. And this morning I couldn't even get it up for my wife.

What the fuck is wrong with me?

She's already put her clothes back on, including a pair of panties dug out from her handbag.

"Thanks, Terry, I needed this." She smiles at me as she pulls her hair back into a tidy ponytail. "When I go without sex for too long, I start to get all crazy." She gives a light giggle.

What the hell do I say? Here she is, a hot thirty-year-old, throwing herself at a man nearly ten years her senior when she could have any gym junkie her age.

"I need to get back to work," I say.

"Yeah, I know. Have you ever been told you're an awesome fuck?"

Well, have I? The thought whispers through my brain, resonating in parts of my ego I'd thought long dead and buried. I shake my head to clear it. "We shouldn't have done this. I'm a married man, and this is our workplace."

"You haven't done anything bad, Terry. You satisfied an itch for me that you started yesterday.

Men like you make women crazy. You're good looking, confident, and you know what you want and throw yourself at it. If you weren't married, you'd be getting more action than most men half your age. And when it comes to the married thing, to most men, it doesn't matter. So, don't feel bad. If this was the first time besides your wife, you're one of the good guys."

"Thanks. I think." I don't feel like a good guy. I feel like a piece of shit. I look away from her and eye the door to her office.

"It's okay to have secrets. Terry, I have no reason to tell your wife what we did. I wanted to feel you inside me. I don't want to take you from your wife and kids, so what harm has been done?"

"I'll always know what I did."

And why did I do it?

Why?

I rush out her office and head to my own. Is she right? Am I really the kind of man women desire? Wrinkles and grey hair and all? I was a much younger man when I was trying to nail anyone with a pussy and a pulse.

It had been exciting back then, but now?

Now, I'm not sure who I am anymore. Or like who I've become. Maybe I should get checked out by a doctor. See if there's something really wrong with me. I've not felt myself for the last few days. Maybe it's more than just being tired and run down. Is this what a mid-life crisis feels like? *Shit.*

I'm not sure what is happening to me.

But I am sure of one thing; I still love my wife.

P a g e | **101**

I need to book somewhere for dinner. I have to carry on with my day as if nothing has happened and try to give Talissa an anniversary to remember. There are a number of places we've been before, but I need somewhere special tonight, a place where they will cook the kind of food so good that I don't need to focus on making conversation or deal with my guilt.

I call Roger on the internal network. "Rog, I need to take Talissa somewhere really nice for our anniversary tonight."

"I can recommend The Grand Resistance. They do a wonderful selection of French food, and by the time you get to dessert, Talissa will be ready to lose her panties."

I close my eyes and lightly smack the receiver against my forehead. "Rog, all I needed was the name of a restaurant, not you thinking of *my* wife and her underwear, or lack of. But thanks all the same."

"Uh-huh. Terry, what happened in Emily's office just now? She had the blinds closed while you were in there. And...when you left, I couldn't help noticing your shirt was untucked."

Oh, fuckballs of fucking hell. For all his faults, Roger is the most observant bastard on the planet. It's made him a good real estate agent, but right now, I'm wishing his attention to detail was a little less sharp. Despite being my best friend, there's no way in hell I can tell him what happened.

"Terry? You there?"

"She had some files she didn't want anyone

walking past to see. So, I...hid them." *Dammit.*

"Secret files? What is this, the CIA?" He pauses and I can hear him sigh. "I'm your best buddy, right? No judgment zone, no matter what you did."

"I didn't do anything I shouldn't have so get your mind out of the damn gutter."

"I was just joking, Terry. Come on, lighten up. This isn't like you, man."

"Yeah, I know. I'm just under some pressure, you know. Phelps wants me gone so he can keep Emily on after the busy period."

"Fucking tight ass prick. It's only our commissions putting food on our table. Not the stupid grey-haired wanker who sits at his desk all day and tells us to sell. We should take our network of contacts with us and start our own business. Are you up for it?"

Shit, I have plans, but not ones that include bringing him on board. "I don't know, Rog. I have a mortgage and private school tuitions to pay and a private babysitter we're hiring as of tonight for the kids. She'll be watching Matilda while Talissa's at work."

"What happened to the daycare you had her in?"

"Company's gone under, so we're going from forty dollars a day to a hundred for the babysitter. Talissa has done all the background checks, and she says it's just for a few months before she starts school. I wish I could take the plunge into our own business, but it's just not the right time for me."

"Hey, no worries, buddy. Anyway, I better get back to work."

CHRIS HEINICKE

We end the call, and I waste no time in finding the name and phone number for the restaurant Roger recommended. There's no trouble getting a table for two, and it overlooks the infamous lake where Talissa and I used to visit when we first dated. The next call I make is to arrange a big bouquet of her favorite flowers to be sent to her, and I make it in time for her to get them at work.

* * * * *

I MANAGE TO avoid Emily for the rest of the day, and the pompous prick Phelps, as well. I'm feeling pretty good physically. Clear-headed. At home now, and ready for my date night to begin. The pill did help. Emily had been right about that, at least.

I made an epic mistake today. One I can't undo.

Maybe I needed to experience it, so I could know that I'm just as flawed and prone to temptation as any other guy. In all honesty, it was awesome to be seduced by a hot, horny babe. Ultimate fantasy, right? The only thing that would have made it better for me would be if she'd been dressed as a slutty cop. I quickly push that thought aside. I'm not going to do this ever again. Morally, it had been wrong on all kinds of levels. Satisfying my sexual fantasies isn't worth the risk. Now I just need to move on and let time pass by—pushing it slowly to forgotten history.

I'm dressed in a dark suit for our evening, feeling sharp and classy. And when Talissa walks out of the bathroom in that same low-cut, sleeveless, red silk dress she wore when we first met, I'm reminded the pill is definitely still working. As she stands to the side, I get an eyeful of side-boob. And a full dose of her stellar cleavage when she strikes a sexy pose front-on. She's going to turn heads at the restaurant. The dress ends a couple of inches above her knees, and I'm already thinking of what I want to do to her after dessert.

She's the hottest woman I've ever seen in my entire life.

"Oh, babe.... You look...wow." I can't find the words I need to fully emphasize how much the sight of her wearing this dress again thrills me.

She smiles and does a little twirl. "Still fits." She steps close to me and plants a big kiss on my mouth. Then whispers by my ear, "No touching until I say so." A devilish grin spreads across her face. It makes me want to do things with her that would make a prostitute blush. *Fuuuuuck.*

"I'll keep my hands to myself, milady." I grab her hand and brush a kiss across her knuckles.

The doorbell rings.

"That'll be the sitter," she says. Talissa leaves the room to answer the door while I wipe her dark red lipstick from my mouth and cheek. No need to arrive at dinner looking like I've been seduced by my wife, though later on tonight, I'm not going to mind.

As she greets the newcomer, I hear Talissa ask, "Do you always dress like this for work?"

"The kids never mind what I wear," I hear a young-sounding female voice answer.

I walk toward the entryway and peek around the wall. A tall blonde who I'd guess to be in her late teens is standing near the door with Talissa. Her white tank top shows off her pierced navel and slim abs. Her light denim shorts are the style with pockets hanging below the shorts themselves. Her legs have a light natural tan about them and go on forever. Oh, God. This is the new babysitter? I shouldn't be looking and finding her hot. I'm old enough to be her father.

"Terry, Brittany's here," Talissa calls out, meaning we can get our date underway soon.

I round up our two children and lead them to the cute blonde. Isaac runs up to her and tells her she's pretty.

"Hi, there." She offers a hand to me, which I shake lightly. She stands about an inch taller than I do, which makes her over six feet, and she's wearing sneakers, not heels. Shit.

She turns to my son. "And you're a very handsome little man, Isaac. And who's this pretty little princess?"

Matilda smiles at her. "I'm Matilda, and I'm five."

"Wow, so grown up already. Do you go to school next year, young lady?"

"Yes, I do, and as soon as I turn six, Mommy says I can go."

"O-M-G, that's so awesome!" Brittany's eyes light up as she speaks to the kids, and they return the smile and giggle with her.

I move next to Talissa and whisper in her ear, "I think she'll be fine."

"Okay, Isaac and Matilda, if you're good for Miss

Brittany here, she'll be back again. Now come give us a kiss before we go."

Children's emotions are the most genuine of anyone's, and they both squeeze us tightly, telling us they love us before we get to say it first. It's been a long time since Talissa and I have had a date night, and I intend to make it count.

* * * * *

I COULDN'T HAVE picked a more romantic setting if I'd tried. We're seated at a candlelit table by a window overlooking the lake. The moon reflects its light to the surface of the water, reminding us of times gone by when we wore the clothes of our much younger selves. And the times we didn't wear them.

I need to get my mind elsewhere. These last few days, I can barely get sex out of my brain, and my work is suffering for it. Not to mention what it could do to my marriage.

During the lavish three-course meal, we talk about work, and I mention Roger's idea of going into a partnership.

"He'll just be riding on your coattails, Terry. You could do it on your own. You could do anything, if you put your mind to it. You are the most amazing man I have ever met."

Oh, damn. A tear comes to my eye. "I love you, Talissa." I lean over the table to kiss her, my tie nearly hitting the flame of the candle.

She laughs, and as the dessert is served up, she reaches under the table and grabs my hand. She slides forward in her seat and says, "I forgot something before we left." She moves my hand up her bare thigh and puts it between her legs.

No wonder she walked very carefully in her dress tonight. One long stride and anyone around would be seeing what's normally reserved for my eyes only.

"Everything's working tonight," I tell her.

And by the smile on her face, I'm certain she knows what I mean.

* * * * *

I SETTLE THE bill and we walk toward the car. There are only a few cars left in the rear parking lot of the restaurant, and looking over at the lake, we see the area is deserted of people. I catch her eye and ask, "Are you thinking what I'm thinking?"

Talissa giggles, and I let her take the lead as she turns away from me and takes off her high heels. Carrying them in one hand, she runs from the parking lot past the front of the restaurant and then to the downhill grassy mound that leads to the lake. Following behind her, I get a good view of the pale perfection of her ass as it's exposed when her dress rides up. I stay on track as she takes a turn to the right and heads for an area out of view of anyone still at the restaurant.

As she comes to a halt near the edge of the lake, I stop running. My dress shoes are covered in fresh grass cuttings. I kick them off and remove my socks, which are also grubby from the run.

"You better not be stopping there," Talissa tells me with her hands on her hips.

I wink at her, then remove my tie, followed by my shirt and pants. Standing out in the open in only my underwear, I say to her, "Your turn."

She pulls her dress up and over her head, throwing it to the ground. No bra. No panties. She stares at me, as I admire the beauty of her lush, porcelain figure in the moonlight. She giggles and runs to the edge of the water and splashes in. I have no choice but to follow her—which I do after removing my last item of clothing.

The lake is like black glass, reflecting the lights from the hotel and beyond, broken into ripples by the movement of Talissa's presence. It bites at me with its icy temperature, but I swim to where my wife is treading water a few feet away. She puts her arms around me, and I return the gesture, our legs kicking at the water to keep our buoyancy. We release each other and paddle around, splashing each other for a few more minutes until she leads me on a race to the shore.

The moonlight illuminates her nice, large ass. A lot of men aren't into big bums, but Talissa knows I'm not one of those, and she knows I'm watching it wiggle as she runs in front of me. She stops and lies on the grass, stomach first, presenting her gorgeous ass for my admiring eyes. I kneel behind her and slap her healthy rump before planking on top of her. Moving her long hair aside, I kiss her neck, reveling in the softness of her skin. She arches against the ground and we shift position, lifting upward until we're on all fours with my body cradling hers. I cup my hands around her plump breasts, enjoying the feel of them. I'm so excited I can barely control myself. There's something about the water and being out in the open like this that has always appealed to some inner instinct to ravage my she-devil wife. Tonight, that instinct is beyond strong, growling inside me to be let out.

Guiding my cock along her smooth, waxed pussy, I enter her from behind. She lets out a satisfied groan that mixes with mine. And we fuck like a pair of wild wolves.

* * * * *

"WOW, BABY, YOU'RE back to your super stud form tonight," Talissa says as we cuddle into each other's warmness after we've climaxed for the third time. She sounds as happy and satisfied as I am as she trails her finger through my chest hair, making a lazy figure eight.

"Mmmm." I kiss her. "Happy anniversary, baby." At least I managed to make up for this morning's disgrace.

I look at my watch. We've been fooling around for two hours. It's now past eleven p.m. We don't care about the extra money we owe the babysitter; this date has been well worth it. My head's beginning to feel heavy though. I know what is happening. The inevitable crash is coming on fast, and I need to stop it before I lose consciousness right here and now on the grass by the lake. Our clothes are in a heap just a few feet away with the pills in my pants pocket.

"We should dress and go," I say.

Talissa groans and stretches. "I could just stay here forever. Tonight has made me feel young again, and I know it's because of how you make me feel inside."

I sit up and study her. "Why don't we just take off? You, me...and the kids, of course. Just sell everything and go travel for a while. Nothing to hold us down and nothing to keep us stuck in this shithole city."

"We can't, Terry."

"But why can't we? Why can't we live the life we want and go out and enjoy all there is in this world? We don't have to be like everyone else."

"You know I would love to, but we have a responsibility to our children to provide stability, security, and consistency. I hate to be the stick in the mud here, but that's how life is."

My vision begins to blur, so I dive for my pants and fiddle around for the small bag that holds the key to me being able to hold it together.

"Are you okay, Terry? Is this like what happened last night?"

"I'm fine. I just need to take one of these..." I locate the pills and quickly pop one in my mouth. I close my eyes and take a deep breath. The change is almost instantaneous as my head clears within a few seconds, and fresh energy rushes through me with almost euphoric relief.

Talissa takes the bag from my grasp. "Why do you have a pink coin purse?"

I sigh. No point in lying about everything. "Emily from work was worried about me being so tired, so she got me onto these pills."

"Emily did."

"Yes."

"Do you know what they are?"

"Not really. Uppers, I think."

"You think?" She sucks in a breath. "You took pills from someone you hardly know, and you don't know what they are? Geez, I can't see anything going wrong with that."

I grab my shirt and slide it over my arms. "Talissa, let's not ruin the great night we've had. Let's go home and get a good night's sleep."

It seems a shame to leave. She's in her glory here, naked and bathed in moonlight, but the night must end sometime. Our date tonight has almost erased my memory of everything that happened earlier today. But the guilt lurks like a shadow, and I know tomorrow I must face it all again.

But that's tomorrow's problem.

We dress in silence, Talissa glancing at me from time to time. But whatever she's thinking she keeps to herself as we stroll hand in hand back to the car. She leans her head against me so it rests on my chest as we walk together. I'm lucky to have this woman in my life, and I have to make sure I don't fuck it up.

When we reach the car, I open the passenger side door for her as if I'm a proper gentleman.

She gives a husky chuckle. "Thanks, kind sir, but I've hardly been a lady tonight."

"Nor have I been a gentleman." I wink and close

her door. Once I'm in the driver's seat, we share a long, deep, passionate kiss, both of us grateful for this evening but sad it's at its end. I start the car and in seconds we're on our way home to reality.

As we drive through the parking lot, the lights of a white Honda hatchback switch on, and I catch a glimpse of a mass of blonde hair through the driver's side window of the car.

Emily?

No, it can't be. Otherwise, it would be a hell of a coincidence, wouldn't it? But my mind seems hell bent on taking any opportunity it can to think of my blonde workmate.

Who I banged.

On her desk.

Today.

And thanks to the pill I just took, despite having had sex with my wife three times this evening, my cock is stirring again.

"Terry? You okay?"

I can feel Talissa's gaze on me as I exit the parking lot, and I've never been more grateful for the cover of darkness.

"Yeah, babe. All good."

I turn toward home, but a few minutes down the road, I can't help noticing the same white Honda is following me at a distance.

* * * * *

I PARK THE car in the garage and close the electronic

door immediately. I don't know if we were followed all the way home or not, but I don't mention it to my wife. I don't want her to be wondering why I'm obsessing about my new co-worker. It was probably just a coincidence anyway and not Emily following me. Sure, it looked like the same white Honda that she drives. Sure, I think the driver was blonde. But it's dark and late and my mind is apt to be playing tricks on me at this hour. Lord knows it's been a hell of a day.

We hustle our way inside and find the babysitter curled up asleep with a blanket and pillow on the couch. A quick look in the children's bedrooms assures us that they're both well, and truly deep in slumber.

"Oh, sorry." Brittany stretches and yawns as we return to the living room. "It got late, and I couldn't stay awake any longer."

"Well, it is nearly midnight so it's understandable. You're more than welcome to crash on the couch for the night," Talissa says.

"Thanks. If you don't mind?" she looks over at me. "I promise I'll be gone before eight. I don't like driving at night when I'm tired."

"No trouble at all. Oh, yeah, here's some extra money for you. Thanks again for staying longer." I pull out two fifty-dollar bills and hand them to her. "We're going to bed, goodnight."

"Night," she says stifling a yawn and flashes me a cute smile just before I look away.

Talissa gathers Brittney some extra bedding for the night and towels for the morning, and I go to my room and get changed and shower.

Half an hour later we're lying in bed and Talissa is lightly snoring, but that damned pill I took has me tossing and turning, unable to shut my mind off—the white car, the blonde hair, and those headlights that followed us.

What if it *was* Emily? The damage from the accident wasn't serious, so she could have her car back already, but how would she know we were at that restaurant?

If she's one of those jealous, possessive types after just one fuck, then I have a world of other problems about to crash down on me. BluesGirl88 has definitely shown she's a psycho. Maybe this could be the definitive link I need to connect her with Emily. I'm still not convinced that she and Emily aren't the same person, despite them both denying it.

I'm not one to believe in fate and things happening for a reason. I prefer to think the universe is governed by chaos theory. It was a stroke of good luck I happened to be in the club the night I met Talissa, just as I believe it was bad luck that I met this BluesGirl88 online—especially if she really is Emily. Because that would mean Emily is a secret psycho stalker.

Was Emily already lined up to be the temp before I met this chat girl? The most logical answer would be yes. But if not, and Emily is the girl in the chat room, then she would have had to find a way to get my personal information, including where I work, in order to take advantage of the opportunity.

Seems a bit far-fetched. I did talk about myself a lot to BluesGirl88 the first night we met in the online bar, but not any specifics about my life. Except that I'm in real estate.

Would that be enough for her to find me?

I can't get her husky voice out of my head and the likeness of the avatar to Emily. I need to press both a lot more individually in a not-too-obvious manner. They say to be a good liar you need to have an excellent memory, so I need to find the crack in one or the other's stories.

Talissa is truly asleep. I could probably sneak out and check to see if BluesGirl88 is online. Lying in bed and not sleeping and overthinking all that's happened these last few days won't do me any good anyway, and if I wake Talissa with my restlessness, I'll be in deep shit.

Rolling carefully toward the edge of the bed, I extract myself from the covers and slip my feet over the edge as quietly as I can. My wife rolls from her side onto her back and starts snoring. Excellent. Maybe I should have been a navy seal or a marine. *Yeah, right!* I've been shooting at the range with my wife a couple of times, and I don't think I could hit an elephant in a hallway. My wife, on the other hand, is a crack shot. At least, my attempts at hitting a target were good for giving her a laugh.

As I'm about to exit the bedroom, I remember Brittany. I can't be walking around the house in just a pair of boxer shorts when we have the babysitter staying in the house. The poor girl would be horrified. Tiptoeing around the room, I find a shirt

P a g e | **116**

and a pair of sweatpants and take them to the bathroom to put on. Talissa continues to snore, not loudly, but with enough volume to reassure me she's still fast asleep.

Each step I take down the hallway, I live in fear of causing a fateful creak in the floorboards, which my mind stupidly thinks will wake the entire house. As I pass the living room, I pause. The room is dark, but I hear soft, steady snoring that reassures me Brittany is deep asleep too.

Once in the study, I fire up the computer and load the chat program. I barely see my avatar render in his own lobby when a chat request pops up from none other than BluesGirl88.

Here we go.

I accept and find my avatar in a boxing ring. BluesGirl's wearing a black sports bra with matching sports panties like those favored by athletes. Or maybe Emily when she's teaching at the gym?

BluesGirl88: "You fucking prick. Where have you been?"

Her character punches mine in the face. She follows with a kick to the groin and a punch to the stomach. Being a fighting simulation, my avatar reels with each blow he takes.

Terry25: "Why are you doing this? We may as well be playing an online martial arts game."

BluesGirl88: "You will stand there and take it until

I'm done."

She strikes my avatar with a roundhouse kick to the chin. I don't bother to fight back. It's a stupid simulation.

Terry25: "I'm not in the mood for this shit, woman."

BluesGirl88: "I don't give a shit, Terry. You left me hanging the other night, wondering what happened."

Terry25: "I passed out. I came down after taking an upper and couldn't stop my plunge into sleep."

BluesGirl88: "Seriously? You obviously exited out of the chat before that happened. What? Did your wife find you on the computer with your pants around your ankles while I was chatting with you?"

Terry25: "Don't be ridiculous. You've never turned me on that much before."

BluesGirl88: "Bullshit, you fucking liar! What about the other night when you went all quiet while our avatars were banging each other like a pair of horny goats?"

Terry25: "I was having a drink and a cigar."

BluesGirl88: "You don't even smoke."

I pause. Of course, she's right, but how does she know I don't smoke? Emily does, though. And she knows it's not my guilty pleasure. I decide to try and push her buttons.

Terry25: "You're right. It's a filthy habit that disgusting people partake in, not people like me."

BluesGirl88: "Listen to you, Mr. Self-righteous. Would you call screwing someone else behind your wife's back as being NOT filthy?"

She thinks she has me, but I've got her.

Terry25: "I call it the biggest mistake I've ever made, and I wish I could undo it."

BluesGirl88: "You think you can have sex with me and show me no respect afterwards? You're really a piece of shit, after all. You wait, Terry. I'm gonna get you and tear you to pieces and destroy you. You messed with the wrong girl."

Terry25: "You're just a blonde slut on a chat program, who probably has the looks of a bucket of horse vomit in real life. You won't do shit to me, you psycho bitch, because you can't do shit. You can kick me and punch me and insult me all you like here because this isn't real and you're not real. And if you're not real,

you can't hurt me."

I exit the chat and then the program itself. I shut down the computer and grab a glass of scotch from the full bottle that has replaced the empty one I left on my desk. Talissa must be keeping me stocked so I can work without interruption. I stare at the amber liquid in my glass and smile. I'm glad I decided to go online tonight. BluesGirl88/Emily has exposed herself, and I'll be ready for her when she decides to come after me.

"Cheers," I say aloud while holding my glass up and clinking it to an imaginary drinking partner's.

The scotch goes down smooth and easy as always, hitting me hard like it does these days. I enjoy it though, the quick buzz and the way it makes me relax and feel at peace. I drain the tumbler in one long pass.

Now I know I'll be able to get to sleep.

CHAPTER 6

DAY 5

I WAKE UP feeling the best I've felt in days. Groggy and sore from yesterday's activities, but with a sense of peace I've been missing for longer than I care to consider.

Talissa gives me a kiss.

Then another one that's harder and more insistent. She looks in my eyes while she grabs my cock and starts rubbing it, demanding a follow up on last night's performance.

Unlike the previous morning, my cock is more than ready to cooperate and stands to attention quicker than the rest of me. My mind is struggling to process the quick turn of events. This isn't the normal way I wake up.

"Babe?"

"Shhh." She places a finger across my lips.

Talissa must have pulled down my boxers while I was sleeping because I'm naked as I lie here, completely at her mercy.

She straddles me and keeps pumping my cock,

smiling at how quickly I've become hard and ready. I grip the sheets with my hands and struggle to keep breathing. My pulse is racing from going from zero to sixty in the space of a minute.

I can't hear the children making any noise yet, but it is only six a.m. Quite often, we have to wake up early if we want any morning glory, and it would appear Talissa is ravenous for some.

"Babe?" I ask again as her pace quickens. If she's trying to jerk me awake today, she's doing a good job.

"No talking." She wags a warning finger in my face and grins.

I nod. Clearly, she has a plan in mind this morning and though her grip's a little too rough and hard, I'm pretty sure I like where this is going. Beats the hell out of the months where she's ignored me and didn't even want to be kissed in the morning.

Releasing my cock with an almost painful flick of her hand, she bites her bottom lip and watches my expression as she flings her silk nightgown up and over her head. Before I've had the chance to enjoy how magnificent she looks naked, she rises and takes my cock inside her.

Damn. Oooh, daaamn.

I close my eyes and arch back against the mattress, enjoying the sensation of her hot pussy.

But she grabs my face with her hand, urging me to look at her. Her gaze holds mine, the look in her eyes intense. Wild. I'm not used to her being so aggressive, but I'm not going to complain an inch. Whatever's gotten into her, I approve.

Talissa's bouncing with more vigor than usual, and I don't know how much longer I can last at this pace. I was close to the edge with the jerk she was giving me before this fast ride started.

Just as I think I'm about to explode, she stops. Still fully hard and aching, my dick slides out of her pussy as she moves off me.

"We'll finish this later," she says as she bends forward and kisses me.

Woah. What?

"But, babe, I was so close. I'm gonna burst here." My balls are already aching in protest of this breach in the normal flow of events.

She wags her finger at me. "No finishing the job in the shower either. I want you to think about this all day. I want you to miss me and crave me. I'll know I'll possess your desire all day."

Well, damn. She really is a she-devil.

"Wow, this is something new. I think I like it."

"Promise me," she insists. "Or I won't be able to reward you later." She touches the tip of her finger to the tip of my still-erect cock, making it flinch reactively. "No touching yourself or getting off until I say."

"Okay," I choke out. "But it's gonna kill me. How will I be able to go to work and function?"

"You will be fine, my big stud. Think of how good it will feel when you get what you want later." She gives me another kiss and heads for the shower.

I cover my head with a pillow and let out a long groan. What a way to start the morning. Blue balls and a cock that isn't sure it likes this new game. All I want to do is scratch this itch she's left me. But Talissa made me give her a promise, and as much as it pains me, I'll make sure to keep it.

I decide to squeeze in some more sleep while I wait for my turn to shower.

* * * * *

AT THE BREAKFAST table, I hear music from the living room. I ask Talissa if Brittany is still here, and she explains that the sitter will stay on to look after Matilda until my wife returns home from work. I finish my eggs and bacon and wander into the room where I hear the music coming from. The babysitter is doing aerobics to a morning fitness show on TV. Her shoulder-length hair flicks around as her long, trim body moves to the beat.

I can't be watching this. She can't be more than eighteen years old, and even though that would legally make her an adult, I'm sure there's a special place in hell for dirty perverts who have sex with females half their age. She bends down to grab her toes, and her upside-down face smiles at me as she notices me by the doorway.

"Hi, Terry." She waves while maintaining her position. She presses her body against her legs and tucks her shoulders behind her ankles, and I think of the pain it would cause me if I tried the same thing.

"Terry, I think one of my earrings fell out in your car last night. I'll be back in a minute," Talissa calls out.

"Okay, honey," I call back.

Brittany smiles as she stands back up and turns to look at me, giving me a good view of what she's wearing—a black aerobics top not much larger than a regular bra and a pair of black sporting panties.

"She's so nice, your wife, and pretty, too. And your kids are so cute and well-behaved...and you, you're a handsome man for your age."

I take it as a backhanded compliment, but I have to say something.

"Um, thanks." While trying to think of something wittier to say, I hear the front door slam shut.

"Terry, bedroom now. Brittany, take the kids out back for a minute, please." Talissa's tone matches the scowl in her features.

Well, what the hell is going on now?

I do as I'm asked, and Talissa comes storming into the bedroom after me, pulling the door shut behind her with a bang.

"So, did you find—"

A slap in the face cuts me off. "Yes. I found *these!*" She holds up a pair of white lace panties, ones that look like the pair Emily slipped off two days ago.

I stare at the panties, then at Talissa's angry expression.

"I can explain."

"I sure hope so, Terry, because I know my big ass wouldn't fit in them. It was that blonde skank from work, wasn't it?"

"Ah..." I gape like a fish out of water. This is tough. Yes, the panties probably do belong to the skank she's referring to. But they were left in my car before I fucked her. So technically, this is an innocent misunderstanding. "Where did you find them?"

"Under the passenger seat."

"When she was in the car, she changed into her gym gear and slid them off from under her skirt to put her shorts on. She had a gym bag and I assumed she put them in there."

She stares at me, her angry expression unwavering. "You expect me to believe that, Terry? Seriously? Why didn't you tell me any of this stuff—if this is actually what happened? If you had nothing to hide you should have said straight out, but now I have to wonder what else you're hiding from me."

"I'm sorry, honey, but I thought you wouldn't believe such a story." I take a step closer to her.

She puts her hand up, blocking me from moving any further in her direction.

"Just go to work and let me digest this. I'd like to believe what you're telling me, but you were so secretive about even giving her a ride the other day. Maybe because you gave her a ride, and then she let you ride her as a thank you gift."

"Please don't do this. I love you. There's no one else for me but you—and you're all the woman I need."

She points to the door, no longer even looking at me.

I can see she's hurt and needs time to cool down. Anything I say right now isn't going to help.

Fuck.

I leave the room and head to the car, the peaceful feeling I woke up with now shattered.

Emily. Did she do it on purpose? I slam the car door as soon as I get in.

I know who I'll be seeing first when I get to the office today.

* * * * *

I ARRIVE AT work with an hour of built-up anger brewing inside of me, and I don't wait in the staff room as I normally do each morning. I go straight into my office where I can keep watch for the blonde bitch's arrival.

It's rare I'm here even before Phelps, but as the nature of our job as agents means we all need access to the branch at any time, we each have a key. It's only 8:25 a.m. and the place is still deserted, which gives me an idea.

I'm sure I have a few minutes before everyone else gets here, time in which to make a stealth mission inside Em's temporary office. If I can find something there that I can use against her, it might help even the score for setting me up with those panties she left in my car two days ago.

After thinking about it during the drive here, I'm certain it was a setup. If she'd been missing the panties and left them by mistake, she would have asked about them.

Her office is in pristine condition. No papers sitting on the desk and the drawers are all neatly organized. There is no notepad to be seen, which is unusual as we all need to jot down notes in this job. I riffle through as carefully as I can, then at the sound of someone unlocking and entering the front door, I freeze.

Listening for the sound of footsteps, I'm certain I hear the distinctive 'click' of high heels on linoleum.

Damn.

I close the drawer I was searching through as quickly and quietly as I can, careful not to make a crash when it shuts. After darting a glance to check that nothing is out of place, I tiptoe on the balls of my feet and exit the blonde bitch's office. Pulling the door shut behind me, I walk in my normal fashion down the hall toward my own office.

"Hi, Terry. You're early today." Kate smiles at me as she approaches.

"I have the Pellmont House today. I want to be extra prepared for this one." I flash my used car salesman smile.

"I'm sure you'll do well." She giggles like a teenage girl in the learning stages of flirting. It's pathetic. She's in her mid-thirties and probably hasn't had her first fuck yet. I could be wrong, but Roger and I are pretty sure this would be the case.

I shake my head once she's passed me. If I gave a shit right now, I might try to line her up with one of Talissa's male friends. Instead, I'm preoccupied with needing to check something quickly on my work computer.

I boot it up, load the chat program, and see no sign of BluesGirl88. Okay, fine, no surprise there.

But another of my contacts shows up as being online—DancerGirl. Sending a chat request, I don't expect my invitation to be accepted with any promptness, and after a few minutes I'm not surprised there is still no answer. This is achieving nothing, so I exit the program and shut down the computer.

I'm best to head for the staff room and go through the usual ritual of coffee, chat with Roger, and then saying hi to everyone else as they arrive. Phelps is already in there, which is strange because I didn't hear him make his normal song and dance about arriving to work. But then, I think about the fact he's usually the first in the door.

I don't want to be alone with him in the staff room, so I slide on over to the coffee machine as if I have an invisibility power.

"Morning, Terry."

Obviously, I don't have the ability. "Morning," I grunt back to the prick and focus on getting my coffee so I can leave.

"Don't mess up the Pellmont property today. If you do, your life here will be a living hell. Make me happy, okay Terry?" He pats me on the shoulder, which makes me wonder if hell has frozen over. In the entire time I've worked here, he's never done that—in fact, he only ever shook my hand the first time we met when he agreed to take me on board.

Roger saves the day. "Morning, Terry, Mr. Phelps."

I return the greeting with a look that he knows well, the unspoken, *'We need to talk'* brow quirk that's been used by us for years.

George is next to arrive, and lastly, Emily, looking like she ran a five-mile race to get here. "Sorry, I'm late," she addresses Phelps and avoids making eye contact with me.

"No problem, Emily. We try not to make it a habit here though on any day, let alone a Friday when we have our end of week briefing."

We all take a seat at the table, and Phelps waffles on for what seems like half a day, but in reality only half an hour has passed. Once he's finally done, we all get to go about our business, and I follow Roger to his office.

"What's up, buddy?" He pulls out a chair for me and takes his spot behind his desk.

"I've made a terrible mistake." I go on and tell him about what happened with Emily in the office yesterday, and then about Talissa finding the underwear in the car this morning.

"Oh, shit, Terry. I kind of feel responsible for this, for introducing you to this chat program and encouraging you to chat with other women. But I didn't say to go fuck the new girl on her desk at work."

"You didn't force me to do anything. I chose to do it. I don't know how it happened, though. I've had so many chances over the years to cheat on my wife and haven't been tempted. And then yesterday it all fell apart. What the hell was I thinking? I think there might be something wrong with me."

Roger smiles. "It's okay, Terry. It's your one little indiscretion in twelve years."

"It's not okay, Rog. Talissa found Emily's panties, and while I was innocent at that point when she left them in the car, I did cheat later."

"You'll work this out. Maybe you could ask Emily to give Talissa a call and smooth things over."

"Geez, I can see holes in that idea bigger than the Grand Canyon. She won't do it. I think she left the panties in my car on purpose. And besides that, she's pissed that we screwed, and I've treated her with contempt since. I confronted her last night on 3DDreamChat."

"You still think Emily and this girl from the online chat are the same person?"

"After everything that's happened? Yes, I do. I know it sounds far-fetched, but there's just too many coincidences." I don't tell him about my suspicions that Emily followed me in her car on my anniversary date with Talissa. I know he'll just come up with the same argument I've already had with myself that it's a coincidence. Which sounds logical...except my gut is saying different.

He shakes his head. "Okay, well. Listen, buddy. Maybe I can chat with Talissa, tell her you came to me all upset and scared that she's going to leave you over the panties incident. She'll listen to me rather than Emily anyway, and if she realizes how torn up you are, there's a chance she might buy your story. Come on. Let me give it a shot."

I rub my chin and take a few seconds to respond. "I'll let you know, Rog. Thanks very much for the offer. If I can't smooth this over, I might just have to take you up on it."

I should give Roger more credit than I do. He might be a sleaze and a joker, but he'd dive on a grenade for me, and yet, I'm not sure I could do the same for him. I'm starting to think I'm not the good person I thought I was. And it may have just cost me my marriage today.

"Well, get back to me as soon as you figure this out. My offer's good all day."

I thank him again and leave. Taking a few deep breaths, I build up the courage to approach Emily. She's a formidable foe, and if this goes pear-shaped, I'm in for a whole world of trouble.

"Hi, Terry." She pops out of her office and stops a few feet from me. Then she says in a voice louder than necessary, "I have to go do something, but I'd love to chat later."

I step toward her and grab her wrist. "Why did you do it?"

She laughs at me. "Whatever do you mean, Terry?" she looks around to see if she's attracted the attention of anybody else in the office.

I speak in a low voice. "You left something in my car the other day. You did it on purpose, didn't you?"

"Terry, let me go." Her voice is louder again.

George appears down the other end of the hall. "Hey, Terry. What's going on?"

"Get back to your office, George. This doesn't concern you." My voice is firm, but not large in volume.

He takes a few steps toward me, and I know Emily's won this round so I release my grip. Now, it's my turn to speak in a loud voice. "Sorry, Em. Just a misunderstanding is all."

She smiles at George. He glances between us, and then retreats to his own office. I stare down the blonde who has caused me so much trouble.

Her blue eyes are wide as she smirks back at me, making my blood boil and providing the catalyst for me to rush back to my own office. I slam the door shut behind me and close the blinds, making myself invisible to anyone curious as to what's going on.

Pressing my fingers to my temples, I squeeze my eyes shut. *Get it together, Terry.*

Emily's a conniving bitch, trying to derail my life. Best revenge is to not let her win. I need to focus on doing my job before I fuck that up too. The Pellmont account. If I can charm the poor widow into picking me as her agent, the Pellmont property will be the key to a big pay cheque that no one can take from me. I've done it before. I can do it in my sleep.

Real estate is easy.

The hardest sell of my life is going to be convincing my wife to take me back.

* * * * *

I DECIDE TO leave a little earlier for my midday appointment to try to get a feel for the area where the Pellmont estate is. As I drive through the up-market suburb's streets, I can't help hoping I can one day afford one of the oversized houses.

Not so much for me, but my sweet wife and children. Talissa deserves the best of everything and

I'd like to give my kids the chance to grow up in a life of luxury, not just getting by week to week like my family did on the farm. For each generation, it gets tougher to find one's financial feet, and I want my kids to walk on marble instead of dragging their feet through mud. A home like this would be a legacy for my family.

If I still have a family to pass a legacy on to, I remind myself. Talissa still isn't returning my calls or texts. She's shut me out with a wall of silence.

She could need time. Or she could be done.

My heart aches at the thought of what I might have lost. Damn. I need to stop thinking about it so I can do my job. I need a clear head if I want to win this contract. I can't lose everything in one day, can I?

I drool over a few more luxury estates until the time is right to approach Mrs. Pellmont's place. I can't believe my eyes as I pull up and park on the side of the road in front of her house. There are three levels to it, and the stonework is white and appears to have been recently cleaned. The front gardens are well kept, and the hedges trimmed. The immaculately groomed lawn circles a fountain as tall as me. It's the color of a green tree frog.

It's a view not unlike the cover of a gardening magazine, and I take a moment to admire it. This place could probably fetch over five and a half million on the current market. If I can build a reputation in this area, I can tell Phelps to go shove this job where the sun don't shine.

I take my time walking to the front door,

enjoying the view and the warmth of the sun. Even the air feels so much cleaner and crisper here. As I near the door, it swings open, and I'm greeted by an attractive woman wearing a long white summer dress. Her blonde hair is styled in a bob and her bright green eyes are like beacons, drawing my gaze. Mrs. Pellmont must have sent her daughter to meet with me, and now I find myself in a different scenario than what I originally expected.

"Good morning, Mr. Cooper. Please, come on through." She smiles as I head toward her.

I extend a hand for her to shake. "Please, call me, Terry."

"Nice to meet you, Terry. I'm Lauren, Lauren Pellmont."

This is Mrs. Pellmont?

I recover quickly. "You look so young. I thought you must have been the daughter. Sorry for your loss, Lauren."

Her smile is thin. "Donald wasn't a well man for some time, but he made sure I would be taken care of after he passed away." She leads me into the vast entryway, her expression seeming touched with sadness. "The truth is, I no longer want to stay here. Too many memories. I need to get away for a while and see the world again."

I nod. The file said that Donald was seventy-two when he died. I'd expected Mrs. Pellmont to be an older woman, but perhaps he'd married a second time. Was Lauren a trophy wife for him? She can't be more than thirty.

Part of me is disgusted, and the other part of me

has nothing but admiration for the old guy landing such a young hottie for a wife.

I gesture to encompass her vast home and flash my most charming smile. "It's such a nicely presented house from the road. If the inside is anything like the outside, I think we could get five and a half for this place. That will get you a lot of traveling."

Her brow quirks ever-so-slightly. "I promise not to disappoint you, Terry."

She leads me through to the open kitchen, dining, and living area that screams open-living entertaining. I wander to the middle of it and let the beauty wash over me. It's expensively decorated, but not ostentatious and the placement of the windows and lighting is to die for. I could really see myself in this place, or something very similar to it. There's a study, and a library and laundry fill out the rest of this level. We take the staircase to the second.

There are three large bedrooms, which I know my kids would lose themselves in, and another living area with a steel pole in the center going from floor to ceiling. A couple of couches and a large television screen have been arranged parallel to the wall adjacent to a guest room.

I stare at the pole, remembering one very similar. Do all mansions have this kind of accessory or is this another weird coincidence with that 3DDreamChat program? "Interesting pole you have there."

"I use it for practice and to keep in shape. I used to dance on one regularly in a club, if you catch my drift." Her smirk is full of deeper meaning and that left eyebrow does its quirk-thing again.

Why is she telling me this? Now I'm remembering BluesGirl88 doing her pole dance routine. And as much as I'd love to see Lauren demonstrate her skills, my mind needs to go back to the job.

I glance at the spiral stairway. "This level is immaculate. I would love to see the top one."

"And I'm dying to show it to you." She leads the way up the stairs, holding the hem of her long dress in one hand. The white fabric molds the firm round shape of her ass nicely as she moves, swishing from side to side with each step.

Don't look, don't look.

I keep repeating the words like a mantra, a lifeline for my already diminished sanity.

When we reach the top level, we enter a sitting room. Sunlight sparkles throughout the area courtesy of a large domed skylight window. The cream-colored furniture and decor contrast beautifully against the dark carpet. A doorway is directly ahead, which I assume is the entry for the master bedroom.

"We have just one more room to look at, which I'm sure you will love." She smiles and walks slowly to the door. Her feet pad lightly against the flooring, and I realize she's no longer wearing shoes. I look around me but don't see any left behind. I also don't recall her taking them off, though I'm pretty sure she had shoes on when I met her at the front door.

She gently pushes the double doors inwards. I

follow a few feet behind, not quite certain what to expect.

The room she leads me into is a bedroom like I have never laid eyes on before. The ceilings are twice the height of me from the floor, and an extra-wide bed sits in the middle of a space almost equal to a basketball court. To the left is the en suite bathroom, including a shower cubicle with twin shower heads and two hand basins, each large enough to bathe a baby in.

On the far side of the bed a large sliding door opens onto an outdoor deck. The room is lush and lavish, but again, not pretentious. If anything, it's perfection.

"This is incredible, Lauren." I walk onto the deck and see it includes a built-in four-person hot tub. Wicker lounge chairs lined with cushions sit on paving stones either side of the generously sized tub.

While I'm standing by the railing, wishing I could afford to live in this place, she comes up beside me. She has two drinks in her hands and passes one to me. I stare at the tumbler of amber liquid. It smells like a fine blend of scotch. How good would the drink of choice of the uber-rich be? But I shouldn't indulge while on the job.

"I really shouldn't—"

"I insist."

She takes a sip of her drink, watching me as I hesitate. "You don't want to offend my hospitality, do you?"

I shake my head. "No, of course not."

She raises her glass to mine. "Then cheers to a

successful business venture."

Okay. I guess if the commission's on the line, I don't have a choice. I take a sip of the scotch. And like I suspected it's the best I've ever tasted. I close my eyes and savor the smoothness and flavor as it goes down like warm fire.

Damn. It's like a drug in my veins the way it hits me so hard and in just the right places.

"You like?"

"Yes."

She smiles. "Good."

I take another long sip as she gestures at the balcony.

"My husband and I spent a lot of time out here. The nighttime view is amazing. Reminds me why I married a rich guy." She sighs and I turn from admiring the coastal view to look at her. "It's hard to let go of this place, Terry, but it's something I have to do if I want to move on and spread my wings."

"I can't imagine how hard it is to lose a spouse, but we each deal with it in different ways."

She smiles, flashing her exceptionally white teeth. "I did love my husband, but everyone knew what this marriage truly was. I earned a lot of money dancing at clubs, baring my all for the pleasure of men." Her free hand grips the railing. "But even with the good money I made, I knew I'd never be the sort of rich where I felt I was entitled. Mr. Pellmont didn't want to grow old with an old woman. I was his third wife in fifty years. So, we each got what we wanted from this marriage."

She touches my arm with the tips of her fingers.

"Do you like the house, Terry?"

There's a look in her eyes that makes me feel like prey. I can't say she's not attractive, and her voice has a slightly husky tone that would sound great on the radio. But I want to keep this strictly professional.

"Lauren, I wish I could buy it myself. But I'd have to sell a number of houses in this price bracket first to be able to do so. I think you could ask five-point-eight mill for this place, maybe even six."

"A girl could do a lot with that money, don't you think? A girl could buy a little pink convertible and travel the country, stopping when she wanted and where she wanted. When she got sick of it, she could sell it and travel to every country around the globe."

"Yes, she could."

"But you know what? I need to have an afternoon in this place first, one that's so mind-blowing it'll wash away the taint. I want to start my new life off right. I don't want to remember the one I had."

Holding my gaze, she pushes the straps of her dress off her shoulders, allowing it to fall on the deck.

Oh, fuck. Oh, fucking fuck.

What the hell is with my life lately?

She's got great tits, I'll give her that, voluptuous and sitting high and firm, supported by a red lacy bra that barely covers her nipples.

I shake my head and move a step back. "Lauren, you are a very beautiful woman, but this isn't appropriate for many reasons."

She places her drink on a table. "Who cares about appropriate?" She moves closer, her generous bust almost touching my chest. "I'm your client, and you owe me the services I require to sell this place. Which comes with a condition where you need to do what I say."

"I'm a married man."

"That hasn't stopped you before, has it?" She looks in my eyes with such intensity, I feel like she can read my mind...and it all suddenly clicks into place. I stare at the drink in my hand.

How stupid am I?

The scotch. This house. I've seen parts of it before, not in real life, but in that stupid 3DDreamChat game. These past few days, I was barking up the wrong tree, thinking BluesGirl88 was Emily. But she isn't, is she? No, no. She's the freaking so-called grieving widow, Lauren Pellmont.

"Your body is telling you to take me and make me yours for the afternoon. I can see that bulge in your pants."

I wish she was wrong. But my cock seems to have a mind of its own lately. And even though Lauren isn't what I want, my manhood doesn't care. After Talissa doing what she did to me before work, it wouldn't have taken much for me to lose control. But with the scotch buzzing through my veins, making me crave every pleasure available, control isn't even an option.

I feel dizzy as she stares at me with her mesmerizing green eyes. "Why me? You could take any man home and do wicked things to him for however long you wanted."

She quirks her brow and takes my empty tumbler from my hand, placing it on the table next to hers. I don't remember doing it, but I've drained the glass.

"You're a man bursting with sexual confidence. I picked your branch to sell this house because I wanted *you* to sell it...after you sell yourself to me in the bedroom, of course. I won't tell your wife about this, or your boss, or even your friend, Roger."

She pushes me back toward the bedroom. I stagger a bit as I cross the threshold but manage not to fall.

"Roger?" The name echoes in my mind. "How do you know Roger?"

"The idiot tried to pick me up in the bar a couple of weeks ago where you and he were having drinks after work. He might think he has a way with words, but he knows nothing about women."

"If you were at the same bar as me, I would surely remember you." Her green eyes alone would have burned themselves into my memory. But then again, I see a lot of faces in the bar we like to visit every Friday afternoon and I don't remember most of them.

"From where I was sitting, you wouldn't have. I observe people, and when I do, I make sure they can't see me. I watched how you carry yourself. The sound of your voice made me so hot that night. I wanted you then. But Roger was always by your side, and I couldn't have him see us talk." Her hands run to my top shirt button, and then the next, moving down my front, loosening each button from its respective hole. I'm so dizzy and my cock so hard, it's all I can do to keep standing.

"Once you left the bar, I sat near him and glanced in his direction from time to time. A few drinks later, he almost pounced on me. Men are so predictable when they drink; they need a few under their belt before they can chat to a beautiful woman."

She spreads my shirt wide and studies my chest. "Mmmm. I love a bit of hair on a man."

I gasp as she rakes her nails over my pecs and plays with my chest hair.

"Did you do this to him too?" I ask.

"Who?"

"Roger."

She shakes her head. "You're not paying attention. I spoke to him. I had him talking about what he did for a living and where he worked. I went home that night and couldn't believe my luck. I used him to make an appointment with you, the poor unknowing bastard."

This is the strangest story. Maybe I'm so dizzy from the booze, I'm just not understanding.

She shrugs and plays with my belt buckle, loosening it. "I have to sell this place anyway, so why not get some hot sex out of it? You get exclusive rights to sell this high-priced property in exchange. I believe in fair payment." She grabs my tie and tosses it on the floor.

I moan as she rubs her palm over the bulge in my pants. I can't cheat on Talissa again, but this woman has me so horny right now, even if she wanted me to fuck her while watching goat porn, I don't think I could say no.

"Terry." She presses her thumb and finger into my cheek, dragging my attention to her face. She sways before me, slightly bleary. And I wonder what proof that scotch is. "I don't want to take you away from your wife and kids. I just want to feel your cock inside me."

I move my shoulders back as she tugs my shirt down my arms and allows the garment to slide to the floor. She runs her fingers over my chest again, massaging my skin with her palms.

Wanting to do the same to her, I unclasp her bra and pull the straps off her shoulders. Her breasts spring free, revealing the best pair of boobs I've ever seen in real life.

They are surprisingly perky for their size. Gravity-defying. I grab them with my hands, which are dwarfed in comparison to her magnificent tits. Are they real? I don't care. They are fucking hot to play with.

She leans forward and kisses me. I take one hand away from her breasts and slide my fingertips down the front of her, slowly passing her flat stomach, and then her navel, which is one underrated area of the female body that I find an extreme turn-on.

Her hand takes a similar course. She rips my belt through the loops of my pants and throws it to the floor. Then she starts working on the zipper and the button of my pants.

I stagger, trying to keep my footing as I grip each

side of her red, lacy panties.

She leans close to my ear, her soft breath tickling my skin and adding to the fire burning in me. "Go on," she whispers, "take them down."

My pants have already hit the floor. I realize that's what I must have tripped over. She's got her hand molding my erection through my cotton underwear. It feels so good, I'm about to pass out from the blood thundering through my veins.

I clutch her panties and practically rip them down, falling to my knees in the process. She releases my cock and stands with her legs apart, her pussy fully exposed an inch from my face. Beautiful slit. She smells good. I lean forward to see how she tastes and almost fall on my face as she moves back to sit on the bed. I can now see she mustn't be a natural blonde as she throws herself against the covers, her legs draped wide over the end. She touches her pussy as she looks at me, exposing her hot pink center.

"Stand up and bang me like a whore," she yells.

And powerless to do anything else, I do as she commands.

* * * * *

I WAKE UP to see darkness through the sliding doors. How many hours have I been sleeping? I turn the other way and reach for the woman who I spent the afternoon with, only to discover I'm alone in her bed. The house is silent, and I have no idea what the time is until I press the light button on my watch. It's now seven-twenty-four p.m.

As I jerk the covers back, I wince and abort the idea of springing out of bed. My head is splitting. I get up more slowly, pressing my fingers to my temples.

What the hell happened? I couldn't have been so tired that I needed that much sleep in the afternoon. Picking up my phone, I see there are a few missed calls—two from Roger, one from Phelps, and three from my wife. Well, at least she's talking to me again. But I didn't hear a single call come through.

I pick the one I least care about. Phelps's voice has an erratic tone, asking what the outcome of the meeting with Mrs. Pellmont was. The first call from Roger inquired why I wasn't at our usual Friday meeting spot for drinks after work, and the second call saying he had a call from Talissa asking where I was just fifteen minutes ago.

The first call from Talissa sounds very formal as she requests I bring home some bread and milk. The second sounds concerned, asking why I'm not home yet, and the last one, just five minutes ago, sounds ticked off and worried, as she says she's on her way to the place where my boss, Phelps, said I was meeting with a client.

Oh, shit. She's coming here? And I'm lying naked in a messed-up bed in someone's house reeking of booze and sex?

From my calculations, the longest she will take is twenty minutes from our house in Half Moon Bay to this place, which doesn't take into account if she's already on her way. There's no time for a shower, but

I do the best I can with a quick wipe of soap and water. My clothes are scattered around the room. I pick them up, trying to dress as quickly as I can. My shirt and pants are wrinkled. *Shit.* Nothing that I can do there. I run back to the bathroom and grab a hairbrush to try to fix my bedhead hair.

I gather my briefcase and jog through the house and down two flights of stairs, stumbling in my haste to the front door. I'm slightly breathless and dizzy as I exit the house. Making my way to my car, I grab my phone and try Talissa's number.

The glow of headlights heading up the driveway makes me pause before getting into my car. Is it Talissa? Or Lauren returning? Whoever it is, they've already seen me. Putting up a hand to filter the brightness, all I can make out is the car is dark. But it doesn't take long to discover what I first feared.

My wife's car pulls up and parks beside mine. I put on a smile I don't feel inside.

How the hell do I explain this, being at a client's house hours after the appointment? I don't have a filing cabinet inside my head full of readymade lies I can utilize at a moment's notice. But as Talissa throws off her seatbelt and opens her door, I find something.

"Baby, I'm sorry. We got caught up in some tough negotiations," I say as I walk to her.

Our children are seated in the back of the car, looking pale and quiet as they stare at me through the window. A lot of stuff is packed there with them. Things for a trip away. Backpacks. Toys. Matilda is clutching her favorite bear she can't sleep without.

*Oh, no. No, no, no...*this doesn't look good at all. "Talissa?" I turn to see her standing beside me.

Hands planted firmly on her hips, she looks me over from top to bottom. In the bright beams from her car's headlights, I catch the flash of anger in her eyes. "Tough negotiations that wrinkle your clothes?"

"It's not like that at all."

"Then why the hell didn't you call me and give me an update?"

"I called you earlier, but you weren't answering—"

"Well, you should have tried again, shouldn't you? I'm sure a client could understand if their agent wanted to let their wife know they would be late coming home from work." She shakes her head. "You're up to something, Terry."

"You're acting silly, there's nothing—"

A slap across my face stops me in my falseness. She counts off my sins on her fingers. "Women's panties in your car, no phone call to say you'll be late, and I see you in wrinkled clothes, and those late nights on the computer as well? And you've..." She leans in closer and sniffs near my face. Her eyes narrow. "You've you been drinking on the job, too?" Her expression wrinkles in disgust. "Jesus, Terry. You're obviously sleeping with someone else."

I put my hand up, trying to stop her thoughts from continuing down that path. "Please, Talissa—"

"The kids and I are going to my mother's for the weekend, so just do whatever the hell you want. We'll talk about this on Monday. Maybe my mother will calm me down, but I can't be in the same house as you this weekend. I don't want to have to tell the kids I murdered their father. Goodbye, Terry."

I stand there, mute with shock as she gets back in the car.

What's left to say when your life's just imploded? What can be said? All I have is lies. The truth is that she's right.

Darkness surrounds me as she drives away, black shadows that creep between the accent lights of the front garden.

Long after the taillights from Talissa's car disappear around the end of the driveway, I finally move. A shiver takes me as I get into my car.

My wife and kids are gone.

And I don't know if they are ever coming back.

* * * * *

I GRAB SOME take out burgers on the way home and a bottle of rum. I'm staying off scotch for the rest of my life. The taste of it now will only make me vomit. Did Lauren Pellmont drug my drink?

It's possible. I never saw her pour it, I don't think. It would explain why I couldn't control myself and the missing time from the afternoon.

Yes, Lauren had been attractive, but I'd had no intention of sleeping with her. And yet... I did.

And now I'm alone in my own house and my life is a piece of shit.

I unscrew the cap from the rum bottle and bring it to my lips. Maybe if I drink enough, I can drown away the mess I've created. How the hell did I walk into this trap?

I turn the computer on and take a big bite from the mess of a thing resembling a cheeseburger. Logging into 3DDreamChat, I soon find BluesGirl88 and summon her to a private chat.

Terry25: "You, fucking bitch! Where the hell did you go today?"

I alternate between taking a bite from the burger and taking a swig of rum.

BluesGirl88: "I don't understand what you mean."

Her avatar is dressed in a long white dress almost covering her feet.

Terry25: "Do we really need to keep shoveling the bullshit? You were wearing that dress today, in a house just like the one you first took me to in this God-damned chat program. Stop lying and admit that you're stalking me in real life."

BluesGirl88: "You wish, you damned pervert. I bet you already have your pants down and your two-inch dick in your hand."

Terry25: "You know it's bigger than two inches. I had it inside you today in your bed, you lying slut."

Her avatar slaps mine.

BluesGirl88: "I don't appreciate being called a slut, nor the accusation that I would actually have sex with you in real life, you dirty old creep."

Terry25: "Stop messing with me."

I throw the rest of my burger onto the wrapper and take a longer gulp of my rum. Not normally being a rum drinker, it doesn't go down nearly as smooth as the scotch. But I can feel it fogging my head and messing with my coordination.

BluesGirl88: "Why can't we just have fun like we used to do, Terry? Why can't you get it out of your head that you know the real-life me and just accept this for what it is—a fantasy?"

Terry25: "Are you insane? Thanks to you, my wife's gone to her bitch mother's house for the weekend and taken MY children with her so they can have their minds poisoned with her demented view of the world."

"You're angry. I can see that. But I can fix it and help you relax. Forget everything and everyone else. This is just you and me. Our little fuck fantasy."

Terry25: "Why the hell would I ever want that now?"

As I take another sip from the bottle, she changes the scene to a beach setting. There are several avatars here, each one fully naked. Some are in pairs, some in multiples, but all engaged in animated sexual activities. And all are female. The audio is filled with moans and groans.

Her naked avatar is lying face down on a beach towel.

BluesGirl88: "Terry, come here."

I stay where I am on the beach.

Terry25: "I thought you liked it private? You told me you didn't like sharing."

BluesGirl88: "I know you like to see girls fucking. It's the ultimate male fantasy. You can fuck me while you watch them."

She raises her ass in the air and twerks it for me.

I should be aroused by this. The sounds of the orgy. All the naked women fucking each other.

I'm not sure if it's the consumption of rum or just the amount of sex I've had in the last couple of days, but the sight of BluesGirl88's pussy is making me feel sick right now.

Fucking psycho bitch. She's ruined my goddamn life.

Terry25: "I have to go."

BluesGirl88: "Who the hell do you think you are? If you disappear on me again, I'll fuck you up so bad, you'll wish you'd drunk yourself to death."

Terry25: "Maybe I will, and you can have this on your conscience."

BluesGirl88: "Asshole. You'll regret this, Terry."

And with those words, I find myself booted from the chat. I raise the bottle in the air. "So long, cunt."

I drink for a few seconds flat, the dry liquid feeling like sandpaper going down my throat. It does nothing to settle my stomach.

As I put the bottle down on my desk, I see a piece of paper folded in half near the keyboard.

Opening it, I read: *I would like to talk soon. Look me up. Love, Babygirlblonde.*

The writing is done in those cute fonts teenage girls like to use, including a little heart for the dot on the "i". I stare at the message for a long moment.

What. The. Hell?

Brittany?

It must have been left by her.

Babygirlblonde. Brittany the teenage babysitter is on 3DDreamChat? Jesus. Is that even legal?

And she wants me to fucking chat?

I groan and shut my eyes as the room spins for a minute.

It's too late at night to look her up even if I

wanted to, which in my current state of mind, is probably not a good thing to do. I shouldn't be online chatting with the babysitter, least of all rum drunk.

Shutting off the computer, I stagger to the bathroom, barely making it to the toilet before I vomit.

CHAPTER 7

DAY 6

I WAKE UP at nine-thirty-seven a.m., and once again, I'm reminded why I don't drink rum. It's done me in even worse than the scotch.

My head is thumping, and my tongue feels like I've been licking beach sand. All I can think is that at least it's Saturday, and I don't need to race to the office today.

I check my phone. No one has called or messaged me. I need to get myself together so I can call Talissa and fix this. Do I be honest and tell her I've slept with two different women in two days, as well as her, or keep telling lies?

I have no explanation for my behavior other than maybe I was drugged for at least one of the times. But maybe I'm just a piece of shit guy, going through some kind of mid-life crisis.

Either way, I've managed to seriously fuck up my life and hurt the person closest to me. We've drifted apart during the last ten years, but I've never wanted to hurt Talissa like this or cheat with other women.

So, why now?

Things were good until I tried out that stupid 3DDreamChat.

Donning a pair of silk boxers, I head for the kitchen in search of a mug of strong coffee. Some eggs and bacon would help, so I open the fridge and start grabbing what I need. This is a hard day to tackle, and I wish my head didn't feel like a useless lump of stone. The house seems empty without the kids running around and Talissa being her usual busy self.

I need to fix this.

The coffee is lava hot, but I drink it anyway and savor the goodness as it goes down. I turn on the stove and grab a pan, ready for a big fry up, when I hear the doorbell.

I'm not expecting anyone, and I know it can't be Talissa. She would just walk in rather than ring her own doorbell. We might be separated for the moment, but this is her home.

The buzzer rings again.

"Coming," I yell and quicken my pace. Whoever it is, is an impatient prick, and that buzzer is misery for my head.

As I reach the door and open it, I bark out, "What?" not caring to conceal my irritation.

The blonde police officer from the day Emily had her car accident stares back at me. "Mr. Terry Cooper, I need to ask you a few questions."

She pushes inside before I can even agree to it.

I rub my jaw while I stare at her, my heart

thumping a mile a minute. I've not shaved. I'm only wearing boxers. My head throbs like an Irish dancer doing a jig. And now this? I shrug mentally as my mind gives up trying to make sense of why my life is in a state of perpetual chaos lately.

"Officer Hall, I'm starting to think you can't get enough of me." I spread my arms wide and gesture toward the room on the left. "Can we go to the kitchen? I need another coffee." I head that way without waiting on her answer.

"You better make me one too, then," she calls out behind me. She follows me to the coffee machine.

"How do you like it?" I ask.

Looking me up and down, she says, "White and strong."

Right. Ignoring that innuendo, which I might be misinterpreting anyway, I ask, "So what is this about, ma'am?"

I put her hot drink on the kitchen counter.

"Homicide division had a report about a murder committed yesterday. A man in his forties found decapitated in his home. He had his computer switched on, running a program called 3DDreamChat. The team searched through his recent chats and found a few names. Yours is amongst them."

I freeze mid-sip. "Are you serious? Who was this person?" My mind races to DancerGirl. Could he be who the cops found dead?

"You tell me, Terry. What were you doing talking to a man on a chat program designed for casual hook-ups?"

"Does it matter? I'm sure I'm not the only person ever to use it."

"This will be easier if you answer truthfully. I'd rather not have to take you down to the station for questioning."

Holy shit. She looks serious. "I don't understand. You said you found a man murdered who'd been using the program? If my name was listed in his contacts, I can't be the only one. I've only been on the game for..." I do a quick mental count of when Roger first talked about the stupid program, "...five days." Less than a week, but it feels like a lifetime has happened. "Why am I being questioned? Am I a suspect?" If so, I need to go call my lawyer right now.

"Not yet. Depends on how cooperative you are. What do you know about the chat program and how it works?"

"I know it's got different levels of interest. And that some men get on there disguised as women, and vice versa. It's some sort of kink people have for cartoon characters and virtual sex."

"Is that something you like to do? Do you get on there and play with your tiny little dick while pretending to have sex?"

I almost drop my coffee. "*Excuse me*?" Maybe I didn't hear her correctly.

She stares at me, pen poised over her note pad as if waiting for me to answer.

I cross my arms and lean against the counter. "I thought you were here to ask a few questions about my connection to a guy who was murdered—which incidentally, I can't actually do unless you tell me who you're talking about—not question the size of my genitals, and masturbation habits."

I must have some rum left in my system to rail on a police officer like this. But really, what kind of cop is she to make such an unprofessional judgment as that?

She sets her barely touched coffee on the counter. "Hit a nerve, did I?"

"Listen. If you want to find his killer, maybe you should try a user by the name of BluesGirl88. She sliced the head off a person I was chatting to the other night, with a samurai sword I might add, and basically, threatened his life."

She jots down some notes. Then turns back to me, her expression blank. "We have reason to believe he was murdered by a married man pretending to be a sixteen-year-old girl. The suspect is also thought to have a tiny penis. Can you verify this as fact?"

"This is hardly professional, officer. What is your badge number? I'd like to call your superior."

"If you drop your shorts right now, you can eliminate yourself from the list of suspects very quickly. Unless you have something to hide?"

Maybe I should just call her out on her bullshit and do what she says? But after the past few days I've had, there's no way I'm dropping my drawers for a cop, no matter how cute she is. She can bloody well arrest me.

I keep my arms folded across my chest and stare

at her in silence.

She sighs and speaks into her walkie-talkie. "Back up requested. Suspect is to be taken into custody for questioning."

"What are you charging me with? I haven't done anything wrong."

"Obstructing justice." She pulls out her baton and raps the knuckles of my left hand with it.

"Arrrgghhh!" I scream as the metal stings my skin. "What are you doing?"

"I told you to cooperate," she says, as a dark-haired officer who appears to be a few years younger than her runs into the house with his pistol drawn. He must have been ready to jump out of the car at any given second.

I raise my hands in the air as I look him in the eye. "She asked me to prove I wasn't the murderer by showing her my penis."

"And did you?"

I stare at the gun in his hand. "No. Of course not."

"He's being difficult. I had to use my baton on him, Ed," Hall says.

Really? I turn to her, my hands still raised. "Lady? If you really want to see my dick that badly, why don't you drop my shorts and suck it?" I cringe as soon as the words leave my mouth. But really, this is all too much.

"You, sick fuck," the officer named Ed says. "Soliciting sexual favors from a police officer is a serious offense. Cuff him, Hannah."

"Hey, what? What is going on here?" I yell as

Officer Hall grabs my hands and twists them behind my back where she forcefully restrains them with the metal cuffs.

"I want to call my lawyer!"

"You can call your lawyer at the station." Ed holsters his weapon and starts pushing me out of the kitchen and toward the front door.

This can't be legal. Are these two even cops? None of this is making any sense. Aren't they supposed to read me my rights or something? I don't like how this feels but there's nothing I can do as I'm led down my front garden path in my underwear to the waiting police cruiser.

The neighbors must have heard something going on, as they all seem to be out in their front yards, watching my moment of shame unfold. I can't think of anything more embarrassing right now. I'm completely naked except for my boxers.

No one asks anything. They just look completely shocked, and I'm sure this won't be the end of the embarrassment as I'm shoved into the back of the police car.

The journey in the car is quiet, and after twenty minutes, it becomes apparent we aren't heading in the direction of the local police station. The sinking feeling I've had that something's up with these two cops settles into the pit of my stomach like lead.

Suburbia behind us, we're now on the open road. And I'm wondering if I'll ever see my family again.

* * * * *

HALF AN HOUR later, we stop near a deserted barn. The officers pull me from the car and lead me with an arm each toward the wooden structure that appears to be over a hundred years old.

"Well, this looks fun," I say. "The SFPD has a secret shoot-me-now-and-they'll-never-find-my-body cozy, rural hideaway, does it?"

"Just keep walking." Hall gives me a shove to get moving faster.

"I don't deserve to be treated like this. I've done nothing wrong."

Hall's brows flick as if she's amused by my claim of innocence. "How about I just shoot your junk off if you don't shut up?"

"Hannah, I thought we had an agreement," Ed says, looking me up and down with a grin.

"Oh, yes, I forgot. You get to do what you want with him first."

Ed laughs, but he doesn't sound like he's joking. And I'm really thinking I should have just stayed in bed this morning. So far, it's been a disaster of epic proportions.

My bare feet seem to find every rock and dry piece of dead vegetation with each step. I try not to stumble as I walk, but the behavior of these two cops increases my anxiety with every second.

I've heard about corruption in the force. And I'm certain these two might be the textbook definition of bad cops. But why the hell would they want anything with me? And what the hell is going to happen as soon as we're in the barn?

I'm not allowed the opportunity to slow my pace, no matter how sore my feet get. But I dare not complain in case Ed decides to take offense and shoot me.

"Nearly there, Terry. I hope you like a bit of rural life. We have some fun lined up in there for you," Hall says.

"I thought you were trying to solve a murder, and now you have me out here handcuffed and nearly naked with threats of shooting me. If you're gonna kill me, just fucking do it."

"Hmm. Tempting," Ed says. "But that would defeat the purpose of going through all this trouble."

What? I don't know what he means, but I'm afraid to ask. The big barn doors sit crooked on rusted hinges, and as Ed takes the lead and opens the left door outward a couple of feet, they emit a loud squeak. From where I stand next to Hannah, all I can see of what's inside the old farm building is darkness.

"You next," Hannah says and pushes me forward. She follows close to my bare heels, and as I poke my head inside the old barn, I hear the clicking as the vice-like grip of the handcuffs is released from my wrists.

Lighting flickers on. I stare for a moment as a second set of doors opens and I try to make sense of what I'm seeing. Instead of the hay bales and abandoned farming equipment that I'd expected to find inside a barn, a long wooden desk sits in the middle of what appears to be an office room, with several chairs, laptop computers, and piles of manila folders. A pinboard has been hung on one of the walls, covered in pictures, printouts, and a map.

Though the room appears as though it houses a team of several people, it is unoccupied apart from the three of us.

"What the hell is this?" I ask.

Hannah grins. "Welcome to Operation Chat Kill."

Ed powers up two laptops and points to a locker labeled "Nelson". "There's some clothes in there. Put them on so I'm no longer tempted by your manly goods." He barks out a laugh.

I pause, not quite sure what's happening. One moment I think I'm about to get killed, the next I'm standing in what looks like a secret police hangout.

"So...I'm not under arrest?"

"No," Hannah says.

"And you're not going to kill me?"

Ed rolls his eyes. "No, we're not going to kill you. Hannah won't let me." He turns to her. "Geeze, you picked a bright one."

Inside the locker I find a t-shirt and sweatpants that are probably Ed's but will likely fit me. I turn my back to the others as I pull on the pants and fasten the ties. I don't know what the hell is going on, but I have the feeling someone's been dicking with me. Pulling the t-shirt over my shoulders, I catch Hannah's eye.

Has she been watching me get dressed? I don't care, but this whole thing is more than just a bit weird.

"This would be the part where you tell me what

the hell is going on," I prompt her. "What exactly is Operation Chat Kill or whatever you called it?"

"Ed and I are undercover detectives in the Cyber Crimes Division, and this is our remote base of operations." She gestures at the barn-that-isn't-a-barn. "We've been monitoring some unusual online activity for the past several months. There's been a spree of murders of chatters who have engaged in activities of a sexual kind—six that we know of in the last two months."

"An online serial killer?"

"Could be. The man I mentioned earlier is the latest victim."

"Okay, but what does this have to do with me?"

"We think you're being targeted by this killer, and we'd like your help to catch them."

The revelation of the undercover mission raises even more questions from my already overactive mind. I frown at Hannah's words. "Why not just tell me this before? Why the embarrassing arrest, threats of violence, and the threat of letting your partner here sodomize me?"

"I never said I was going to fuck you, Terry." Ed looks me up and down with a sneer. "Was just having fun with you. Maybe it's something I need to work on during my anger management meetings." He barks out a laugh. Hannah frowns and shakes her head.

"We had to make it look convincing, for anyone who might be watching your house. It's important to not tip off the cyber-stalker that we're onto him or her. If you'd known what was going on, your reaction to being taken in for questioning wouldn't have looked real."

Okay. That made sense. Maybe. "You could have explained once we were in the car." I cross my arms in front of my chest and lean against the locker wall. Ed barks out a laugh. "Yes. But what would have been the fun in that?"

The guy is clearly a bag of dicks. I focus my attention on Hannah. "Am I allowed to leave if I want to?"

"Yes, but you'll be safer here with us for the moment."

"It's that serious?" Well, shit. "What about my wife and kids?" If a psycho is stalking me, that means Talissa and the kids might be in danger too. My heart pounds with renewed urgency at the realization.

"They've gone to your mother-in-law's for the weekend, correct? We have a team watching them under remote surveillance. They are safe."

Maybe Talissa taking a break from me wasn't a bad thing after all. I close my eyes and try to find humor in the irony, but I can't. All I feel is a sour lump in the pit of my stomach. "I should never have joined that stupid 3DDreamChat program." Everything had gone crazy since that day.

"Well, that's another reason we brought you here. We have a plan to flush out the suspect before they strike again. And we'd like to use your association with BluesGirl88 to do so."

"Investigate Lauren Pellmont then. Or maybe Emily Philips. I'm pretty sure BluesGirl88 is one or the other of them."

"We need to catch whoever it is in the act to make a prosecutable arrest. And that's where you can help us."

"Um...okay, what do you need me to do?"

She gestures at the laptop and an empty seat beside her. "I want you to log in and find this chat girl. Engage her in your usual conversation and behavior. I want to observe exactly how she acts, to see if she follows any similar patterns we've observed. She may operate under different online identities. If so, we may well have a definitive suspect and can move forward with our investigation."

The idea of chatting with a psychopath makes my skin crawl. "What if she comes after me?"

"We're hoping she will. If anyone tracks you here, Terry, they'll be in for a big surprise." She grins. "This place might look like an abandoned barn on GPS, but it has surveillance and sentry equipment around the perimeter. And only someone tracking you through the breadcrumbs we're going to leave in the game when you log in now would come here." She nods at her partner. "Ed, could you please hide the car?"

She removes her police cap and undoes the hairband, allowing her blonde hair to fall past her shoulders. It's shiny and is a few inches shorter than Emily's but still long enough for my liking.

Ed walks out of the barn and out of sight. Hannah guides me to the chair she wants me to sit in and then grabs the one on the left. She shuffles herself and her chair close to me, our thighs almost touching.

"I'll be going online as Erika19. You and I will be in a pool party scene flirting and doing whatever we need to draw attention. If you see this BluesGirl88 online, invite her in."

I log into the chat, the laptop taking a while to load my character and his clothes. I change him into a pair of board shorts and see Erika19's invite. I accept and appear near a giant in-ground swimming pool with a few deck chairs scattered around it.

Her avatar is a smoking hot blonde with enormous boobs, a dark tan, and ridiculously long legs. She's wearing a skimpy white bikini, which only just keeps her avatar's most intimate parts hidden from sight.

Hannah grins. "I designed her to be as tacky as a man wants in a chick online."

I let out a quick laugh. "Well, I think you nailed that."

"Roleplay, undercover detective style. I'm the slutty dumb blonde, and you're the refined gentleman who picks up women like a modern-day Casanova."

"Right." A Casanova is definitely something I'm not. But I'm grinning as I start typing to her in the chat. She's lying on a deck chair on her back while I'm swimming in the pool.

Terry25: "The water's nice, babe. Why don't you come on in?"

Erika19: "I'm gettin sum sun here get sum1 else 2 swim wit u."

"Are you going to keep typing like that? It will do my head in," I say out loud to her.

"Just playing a part, Terry." She looks me in the eyes, and for the first time since I've seen her face, I think I catch a genuine teasing smile from her. She sure has a pretty face, but when her hair is hanging down naturally and framing it, she goes up in levels to downright beautiful.

This has been a pretty messed up day so far, and I still don't know how I'm supposed to feel about the events that have unfolded. I do a search for BluesGirl88 and see she's online, a fact I point out to Officer—or rather Detective—Hall.

"Call me Hannah, please. Okay, ask her in."

I invite BluesGirl88 to the chat I share with Erika19, and it takes just a few seconds for her to accept.

BluesGirl88: "Nice place. Am I supposed to get naked and jump in the pool with you and forget about last night?"

Erika19: "I woodn't have a prob with tat."

BluesGirl88: "Who are you, girl? You type like a ten-year-old?"

Terry25: "She's a friend of mine."

BluesGirl88: "From where? Daycare?"

Erika19: "Ur not nice."

BluesGirl88: "Well, fuck off then and leave me and Terry alone."

Terry25: "This is her scene. If she goes, we can't chat here."

BluesGirl88: "I'm surprised you even came back for me, Terry. All those things we said to each other. One minute you want to have sex with me, and then the next, you go on threatening me."

Hannah raises her eyebrows and looks at me. "Threatening her?"

"She goes all crazy after a while. She has like this split personality thing going," I say back. "She's threatened me more than once."

It's time to lie to the psychotic bitch.

Terry25: "There's a part of me that needs you for some reason."

BluesGirl88: "What? Your dick?"

Hannah bursts out laughing, and then types:

Erika19: "I wanna c his dick."
BluesGirl88: "Fucking whore!"

BluesGirl88 runs over to Erika19 and punches her in the face.

Terry25: "Hey! Will you stop it with the hitting? We're at her place, be nice."

BluesGirl88: "Fuck you, Terry. This little bitch needs to learn her place. Get naked, you dumb slut, and sit by the edge of the pool."

"Somebody's a femme domme," Hannah says in a sing-song voice and purses her lips as if faking surprise.

I shake my head. "I don't understand what that is."

"Power and control. Some people get off on it. Just like some people enjoy submitting. Was she always calling the shots with you?"

I think about that for a moment. "Yes."

Hannah nods. "Fits her profile. She could be a guy, you know, acting out a femme domme fantasy. Or a girl who likes to be in charge."

"Lauren Pellmont likes to be in charge. So does Emily." So does Talissa, now I'm thinking about it. Sex was almost always initiated by her and on her terms. What does that say about me?

BluesGirl88: "What the fuck is going on? Does the baby need a spanking?"

"Uh-oh. Bossy bitch is getting antsy. Better give

her what she wants." Hannah smirks. Her eyes have a sparkle to them, and I can see she enjoys her work as an undercover cop.

Erika19 suddenly appears onscreen naked and picks a spot on the edge of the pool. She opens her legs wide.

"Wow," I say out loud. The details are amazing. I cough to cover up the awkward realization I feel a stirring in my pants.

BluesGirl88: "Looks good enough to eat."

Within a second her avatar is in the pool with her face buried between Erika19's thighs.

Hannah turns down the volume on her laptop speakers as the room is suddenly filled with the sounds of female moaning. She looks at me.

"I guess she swings both ways," I say. I'm trying not to be affected by what I'm seeing and hearing, but I can feel my skin heating anyway.

An invite for a private chat box with BluesGirl88 pops up on my screen.

BluesGirl88: "Do you like what you see?"

Terry25: "I thought you didn't do more than one person at a time?"

BluesGirl88: "That girl's not real. Can't you tell by the obviously oversized tits and eagerness to get naked?"

Terry25: "You seem to know all about this sort of thing."

"Well, this is interesting," Hannah says looking over my shoulder.

"Told you she was unstable," I say. "Doctor Jekyll and Mister Hyde."

BluesGirl88: "I think you've been sucked in by another man pretending to be a girl. You're pathetic, Terry. Or are you a homo and not ready to come out yet?"

Terry25: "Hey, I'm a pussy fan only, but I don't have a problem with homosexuals."

"You should take a peek at our group chat, Terry," Hannah says.

I hear footsteps behind us. Ed has come back from being outside. He stands behind the two of us, and I can only assume he's watching both laptop screens. I click back to the group chat and see BluesGirl88 punching Erika19 in the face while her own face is still between her legs.

Terry25: "Stop hitting her."

BluesGirl88: "Then be a man and give me what I want."

"Fucking psycho," I mutter. I make my avatar strip his shorts off. With his ever-ready penis revealed, I click behind BluesGirl88 and my animated character starts pumping her from behind.

"Wow, a cartoon threesome. This is useful police work," Ed says.

"Shut your stupid mouth, rookie. We're trying to draw this user out to see if she or he is the real killer," Hannah says.

"Do you need me here then?" he asks.

"Not really, but you're welcome to stay or leave."

"Call me when you're done, but make sure you watch the pervert scum next to you. If you feel any way in danger, shoot his brains out."

I stare at him for a long moment. Maybe BluesGirl88 isn't the only psycho I need to worry about. I turn to Hannah. "This is highly irregular, isn't it, for police?"

Hannah swivels on her chair and faces me. "Sometimes you need to do what you need to do to get the job done. Including stuff that isn't officially sanctioned by the top brass. Ed and I have been working this case for a while." She comes in close and whispers in my ear, "He's only my partner, but he gets jealous of anyone he thinks has a chance with me. And the online sex turns him on."

"Um...okay," I say, and try and focus on the onscreen action. But with that bit of too-much-information screaming in my brain, all I can think about is whether or not Officer Hall just insinuated she likes me, and if I'll survive today without being dropped in the nearest lake wearing cement shoes.

"I think I'll stay close actually, make sure this guy keeps his hands to himself." Ed walks away to a far corner of the barn, grabbing a manila folder full of papers on his way from the desk Hannah and I are sharing.

BluesGirl88: "You've gone quiet, Terry. Are you playing with yourself?"

Terry25: "Well, this is a pretty hot threesome."

Hannah giggles.

BluesGirl88: "I wish you could see me right now, Terry. I'm at home with my legs spread, gently rubbing myself, and getting close to the edge. I want you, Terry, I want you inside me for real, your hot, sweating body pressed up against me while you bang me so hard it almost hurts."

Terry25: "Why don't we do it? Why can't we meet and do this properly? I want to feel your body with my real hands, my real mouth, and my hard cock. This animated porn is great, but I want to experience the physical beauty of real-life sex."

"That's impressive, Terry," Hannah says to me.

BluesGirl88: "From what I've heard, you've been getting plenty of real-life sex."

Terry25: "I'm talking about having sex with you again."

BluesGirl88: "What the hell do you mean? We haven't even met."

Terry25: "Are you sure about that, Emily? Or Lauren? I know you're one of them."

BluesGirl88: "You really have no idea, Terry, and that's what I like about you. It's time for me to leave this party."

Her avatar grabs Erika19 by the throat and holds her head underwater.

BluesGirl88: "But first I'll make your little girlfriend here pay for your stupidity."

Hannah exits the chat and shuts down the program.

BluesGirl88: "You think that little bitch can hide from me? I'm gonna find her and make her pay."

Terry25: "You think you can hurt her, as in really hurt her? I thought you said she wasn't real? I think you're just full of bullshit."

"Excellent. She's tracked this address," Hannah looks at an app in the corner of the laptop's screen.

"Once she gets here. We've got her. Well done, Terry." She flashes me a smile and then yells to her partner, "Ed, call for backup, I need to get the witness to safety."

BluesGirl88: "You were warned, Terry."

Her last words stare back at me, filling me with unease. Is it wise to poke a bear with a stick?

Hannah clicks the exit icon on the chat program and tells me to get going. Ed's voice carries across the room as he makes a call requesting more cops come to this barn, saying he has a strong lead on the internet murders.

Hannah stands and puts her cap back on. "Come with me, Terry. I'll take you somewhere safe."

* * * * *

AN HOUR LATER, we pull up out the front of a block of units in South Beach.

We're on a street full of apartments, condominiums, and townhouses. It's not a low-income section of suburbia, but an area more common to the habitation of middle-income property renters. The owners of the properties in this area generally reside in the richer parts of the city, investing here to boost their wealth portfolio.

"Which one is the safe house?" I ask, hoping it's the ground floor unit just in case.

"Number 2. The one with the red door."

She locks her car and walks to the front

CHRIS HEINICKE

entrance, which is painted a shade similar to blood, and I'm really hoping that's not an omen. I follow her, curious about what the inside of a safe house might look like.

She uses her key to unlock the door and turns to me before entering. "Please excuse the mess. I wasn't expecting a guest today."

"A guest?"

She smiles as I step through the doorway after her. "Welcome to my place, Terry. You'll be safe here."

Her place? "Ah...thank you." I glance at the nicely organized foyer, decorated with a painting of bold, blocky abstract colors. "Are you sure? I can probably go to a hotel or something."

"Yes, I'm sure. I want to make sure that you are safe, personally. Our officers are fine, don't get me wrong, but I'll still worry unless it's me protecting you."

Which means...what? Either I'm in a lot more trouble than I thought, or she's the most dedicated cop I've ever met. Or both.

I'm pointed to a living room containing little more than a couch and a TV sitting on a short wooden cabinet. There's a pleasant smell in the air, almost like the carpets have been shampooed recently. Her footsteps fade away, and I hear a door open and close.

"Right," I say. This day has certainly been an interesting one. In my wildest dreams, I couldn't have predicted the events that have happened. Or that I'd be spending time at a sexy female cop's house for my protection. To say I hate the idea of a woman knowing how to use a gun would be a lie. I've always thought a female cop in uniform was damn hot.

As I settle onto the couch, I call Talissa to check on her and the kids. She doesn't pick up. Not surprising considering how pissed she was when she left. I leave a quick message, hoping they are okay and telling the kids I love them.

Talissa and I will have to work things out later. A message isn't the right way to say all the things I have to say about how my day has rolled. Would she care anyway?

Maybe that's not fair to think but relationships are a two-way street, and I've been feeling for years like what I have to say or do doesn't really mean anything. I love her, absolutely. But maybe love isn't enough.

My eyes do a quick tour of this room, looking for mementos or photos or any artifacts to shine light on the woman in the uniform. Next to the TV is a picture of her with an old couple, who I assume are her parents, at what looks like her police academy graduation.

In the corner of the room is a sealed cardboard box with a trophy sitting upon it and a digital clock on a small table to the right of the two-seater couch. Maybe being in the police force occupies so much of her life she has little opportunity to personify her surroundings.

"Would you like a drink?" she yells from the end of the hallway. "I'm off duty here, sort of, and am hanging for a beer."

Off duty at one p.m.? She must have started work early today. I do feel for shift workers and the crappy hours they have to keep at times. "Beer sounds great," I call back.

The sound of bare feet connecting with creaky floorboards moves into a room closer to where I'm seated. A refrigerator door opens, and I hear glass rattling and a few seconds later, Hannah is standing in the doorway of the living room, a beer bottle in each hand.

But it's not the beers I notice. It's her, wearing a long T-shirt that comes halfway down her bare thighs. The top part has tank top like sleeves if you can even call them sleeves, and they hang halfway down the sides of her athletically toned torso. There's visible muscle definition in her biceps and triceps, and from the way her nipples poke through the material, I guess there's no bra underneath.

Her blonde hair is soaking wet, and if there is a sexier sight on a woman than shower hair, my mortal body will not be able to cope. She takes a long sip from one of the bottles, giving me a generous view of side boob.

Noticing my glance, she takes the bottle from her mouth. "If you don't like it, I can put something else on. I like to be comfortable at home.

"It's fine. It's your home. You can wear what you want."

"Good." She walks slowly to the couch and takes a seat next to me, passing me the other bottle.

"Thanks." I immediately take a big swallow, the

cool liquid wetting my parched throat. It tastes like just what I need right now, and I'm glad it's not scotch. Or rum.

"Don't worry, I'm stopping at one. I want to relax, not get drunk. Never know when I might need to shoot someone."

"Um, yeah. Like how you threatened to shoot my dick off earlier?"

"Yeah." She laughs. "I wouldn't really, you know."

"I'm so confused about today, how you set me up and treating me rough, right up to the point of showing me the place you have in that old barn. You do realize I was scared the whole time?"

"We needed to convince your neighbors you had been arrested. The other part enabled me to make Ed believe I don't like you. I am really sorry about it, Terry." She takes a swig of beer, her eyes never leaving mine, and filled with a look I find hard to interpret. She seems genuinely sorry but sad too.

Oh, shit. Is it about to happen again? I'm looking at her face from less than a meter away, wanting to comb her wet hair with my free hand. Out of the police uniform, Hannah seems to have lost her hard edge and the tough façade.

"Terry, do you love your wife?"

What? Way to kill my erection, but she brings up a good question. "Of course, I do."

"But you're like every other man. You have needs, desires, and an unquenchable thirst for all the good things in life. You're a normal male, driven by the instinct to spread his seed. It's not your fault. It's the way the male brain is wired."

An unexpected line of conversation. Is she trying to justify cheating? Or imply all men are incapable of commitment? I take a sip of beer. "But we aren't brainless animals. We have the ability to say no."

"Very true. But it's hard when you don't want to, right?"

"Yes."

"You've been through a lot the past few days. I know it's been confusing."

I stare at her, not sure what to say. How much does she know of what's happened?

"I've been watching you for a while."

"I see."

"Actually, I don't think you do." She takes another sip of beer. "It's far from me to get involved with other people's lives, but... Did your wife leave you because she thinks you're cheating or because of something else?"

"I..." I'm not sure why we're having this conversation or if its part and parcel with how crazy my life has gotten. But there's something comfortable about Hannah. The way she's casually discussing my mess as if it's important to her and cares how I'm feeling instead of judging me. "She was upset because I haven't been truthful, I think."

Her brows flick. "Truth is a many-layered thing. And not always what it seems."

I take a sip of my beer. "I guess so."

As she takes another long drink from her beer, she leans backward against the side of the couch. Her shirt rises as she moves, exposing her black panties. She's certainly not shy, I'll give her that. And I can't say I mind.

She purses her lips as she studies me. "It's like in that chat program, people tend to hide who they are. But you seem very real to me." Leaning sideways, she puts her beer on the table and gets to her feet. "I'd better let you rest. You've had a hell of a day."

"You don't have to leave," I say.

Her smile is fleeting as she bends forward and cups my cheeks with her hands. Her eyes are clear and steady as she stares into mine. "You're a good man, Terry Cooper. You don't deserve to be hurt, so be careful who you trust, okay?"

Does she mean her? Or someone else?

Her lips are soft as they brush my forehead. "I'll be in my room. If you need anything, just holler." She steps away from me but then turns back almost immediately. "Oh. I almost forgot. The A/C isn't working right, so if you get too hot, feel free to strip down. You don't need to hide anything from me." She looks me over, seeming to take me all in with a knowing grin.

Well, damn. As if my erection isn't already creating a visible bulge in my pants. How the hell do I keep finding myself with women making the moves on me?

To hell with it—if she can say whatever she wants, then so can I. "Maybe you should take yours off, too."

"Cheeky man, aren't you?" She lifts her shirt over her head and throws it at me. Her breasts are small, but with her muscular build, it's perfectly normal to expect that.

My expression must reveal my admiration because she lets out a sexy chortle. "I shouldn't be teasing you like this, but it's hard to resist when you are so open to it." She glances at my groin where my erection is a very obvious item of interest. "But that's just it, you are very open and vulnerable right now. And my role is to protect you. So, I'm not going to seduce you. Not today. Not now."

"What if I say I'd like to?"

She shakes her head. "Don't get me wrong. I'd love to take your pants off and suck your cock like you invited me to earlier at your house. You're a very attractive man in many ways. But this isn't the right time. Not now."

I feel crestfallen and elated at the same time and I'm not even sure why. But Hannah Hall might just be the most beautiful person I've ever met in my life.

"When your situation changes," she says, "look me up. Until then, help yourself to the food in the fridge and whatever else you need. My house is yours. I'm going to go check in with Ed and see if we've caught our psycho yet."

She leaves to go to her room, and it's not lost on me that she didn't bother to put her shirt back on.

It's also not lost on me that despite the sexual energy she's giving off, I'm more relaxed than I have been in days. There's something honest about Hannah Hall that I find refreshing.

I'm at peace. She puts me at peace. She also teases the fuck out of me with her hot body and lack of shyness. Which is something I wouldn't have expected from a cop. But this day has not gone according to normality since I opened my eyes this morning.

I finish my beer as I turn on the TV and flick through until I find a movie to take my mind off things. But before I've even lasted five minutes, I'm fast asleep.

* * * * *

IT'S THE SOUND of urgent speaking that drags me awake. Or maybe the crick in my neck from sleeping in an awkward position. I groan as I sit up and turn my head from side to side, trying to ease the stiffness from my body.

Hannah is pacing near the living room window, her body silhouetted by the late afternoon sun streaming into the darkened room. She's speaking on her phone in hushed tones, having what appears to be a heated conversation, but ends the call when she sees me watching her.

She taps her cell phone against her hand as she stares at me for a moment. Even without a clear view of her face, I can see something has upset her.

"Is something wrong?"

"Yes and no." She gives a nervous laugh as she comes to sit beside me on the couch. It's warm in the room, and she's got her hair up in a messy bun. Her breasts are hidden by the loose T-shirt again, and I'm struck by a sudden wave of disappointment. Something has changed.

Two glasses of ice water are on the table. She takes a sip from one, her thoughts seeming miles away.

My throat is dry. I pick up the other glass. "This is for me?"

"Oh, yes. Sorry." She nods apologetically, but her flash of a smile is quickly replaced by a frown again.

Taking a sip, I study her. "Things didn't go well with Ed at the barn?"

"Yes, they did, actually. Our suspect didn't show at the barn like we wanted, but the team was able to use a ping-back from the location tag to track the IP address. They have a suspect in custody for questioning while they investigate."

"Was it Lauren or Emily?"

"Neither. A man in his mid-forties, who's been living in his parents' basement after he lost his job about a year ago."

"Oh." I put my glass on the table. "BluesGirl88 is a guy?" That would mean I've been having virtual sex with another man all this time, which makes me feel like vomiting.

"Not necessarily. It looks like he's been stealing other user's logins and avatars to use while he stalks his victims."

"That would explain the split personality BluesGirl88 seemed to have."

"Yes."

"Catching him was a good thing, right? So, what's the problem?"

"I don't trust it. Seems a bit too...easy, you

know?"

"You think they caught the wrong guy?"

"I'm not sure. There might be more to it." She looks down at her glass. "But I've been instructed to take you home now the danger to you and your family is over. I'm being reassigned to another case."

"Oh." It shouldn't matter to me, but heaviness settles inside my chest. Her tone suggests she isn't happy about being reassigned. I hope I haven't gotten her into trouble. "Did I...did I...complicate things for you?"

She shakes her head. "No. I did. And Ed is—" she closes her eyes and sighs deeply, abandoning what she was going to say about her partner. She shakes her head again. "It doesn't matter." She pats my knee and forces a smile. "Come on. I better get you home."

She puts on jeans and a t-shirt, while I use the bathroom. Then I follow her to her car. We share the trip to my home in silence. I can't stop thinking about her naked and playful, teasing me with her perky tits and toned abs. She's hot, I'll give her that, but I really just want to see her smile again. This silence isn't comfortable. She's worried, but not saying the whole reason why.

She stops the car outside my house and turns to me.

"You're safe now, Terry. But...promise me you'll be careful, okay? Things may not be all they seem."

I nod. "Thanks for all you've done for me, Hannah." There's a tightness in my throat as I stare at her. Why do I feel like I'm saying goodbye to a best friend that I'll never see again?

"Fuck it," she whispers and leans toward me, placing her lips on mine. The touch is soft and warm, and I deepen it, running a hand through her hair.

Gently pushing me away, she says, "You have to go." I nod. Her face is flushed, as is mine.

"Hannah?"

"Yes?"

"Thank you. I...I...think you're pretty amazing. I just want you to know that. If things were different, I'd like to take you on a date."

"A date?" She seems amused by that. And she's right. I'm probably being an ass by thinking it. Do people even do that anymore? It's been a long time since I was single. "You're completely adorable, you know?" Grabbing my cheeks, she gives me another quick kiss, then pushes me away. "Goodbye, Terry Cooper. Remember what I said. Be careful who you trust."

As I get out of the car, I wave at her while she heads off down the road. There's an ache in my chest that shouldn't be there. But it's there all the same.

It's early evening, and I've hardly eaten a thing all day, so I order pizza. My cell screen is a photo of Talissa, the kids, and me—and the realization I've once again become attracted to someone who isn't my wife hits me. I didn't have sex with Hannah, but would I if she'd offered?

I shake my head. It doesn't matter. Detective Hall is gone now, and I'll never see her again. But somehow that makes me feel worse than being separated from Talissa. Which doesn't make sense at all. Talissa is my wife and the love of my life. And

Hannah is... a girl I just met, right? What is it about her that makes me feel so connected that I miss her like this? Is it because she's a cop and protecting me?

I deliberately didn't ask for Hannah's number to avoid any further personal complications. But I'm thinking now that maybe I should have as the disappointment of a missed opportunity settles in.

Fuuuuuck. Why the hell is my life so complicated?

Dialing Talissa's mobile phone, my call goes straight to voicemail. I leave a short message saying I miss her and love her, and to please come home.

Three days in a row I've been involved with three different women, not including my wife. Three different women with different body types, and all of them unique and beautiful in their own way. Even in my prime, I didn't have such luck in the space of three days.

This has to be more than just "getting lucky." I don't understand what's happening to me, but at least BluesGirl88 isn't Lauren or Emily and I don't have a real-life psycho stalking me. Which means the kids and Talissa are safe. At least...I think so. Hannah didn't seem so sure.

But I can't live my life in hiding or worrying about things that might never happen.

I have enough time to shower quickly and put my clothes on before the pizza arrives. Washing the large meal down with a couple of beers, I'm tired but I can't seem to settle. The feeling of peace I had while at Hannah's is gone. In my own house I feel restless and anxious. Is it the emptiness? Is it me? TV is the shithole of vapid nothingness that it usually is.

Damn. I could kick myself right now. I should have gotten Hannah's number before she left. I'm not sure why I didn't. Some kind of loyalty to a crumbling marriage that I've done a really good job of bringing to a rapid end? Or was I afraid of opening myself up to a new possibility, one that might actually be good for me?

I'm not even sure who I am anymore or what I want out of life. All I know is that the few hours I've spent with Hannah today felt more real than I've ever felt in...well, ever. A fact I'm ashamed to admit, given my twelve-year relationship with Talissa—ten of those as husband and wife.

Thinking about it now, maybe a lot of what I feel for Talissa is because it's what I've wanted to feel. I wanted to have that perfect relationship, so I ignored anything that might tell me our marriage isn't everything I always wanted. Beneath the surface of everything we have together, do I really know her? Do I really know me?

If I go on the chat program, will Hannah be there as Erika19? She's been assigned to a different case now, but maybe she'd still look for me on a personal level?

I log into 3DDreamChat and do a quick search. No sign of Erika19, but Babygirlblonde is online and invites me to a private chat.

Brittany the babysitter. Should I, shouldn't I? After a moment, I accept.

She's sitting in a lounge chair by a pool. Her avatar is dressed in a red dress and has long black curly hair, unlike her real-life hair.

Babygirlblonde: "Wow, Mr. Terry. Your avatar looks great."

Terry25: "Thanks. I saw you left your Dreamchat name by my computer. But how did you even know I use it?"

Babygirlblonde: "Your son went into the study and turned the computer on. He didn't do anything on it, but when I saw what he did, I thought I had better turn it off. That's when I saw the computer's desktop, and there was 3DDreamChat."

Damn, I need to make the computer settings changed to password protected.

Terry25: "Okay."

I find I'm struggling to work out how to make conversation with an eighteen-year-old without sounding like a pervert. I mean, what on earth do I have in common with her?

Babygirlblonde: "So, yeah, anyway. I guess I wanted to chat with you because I haven't had a father figure in my life for years. When I was nine, my mother found my father in the shed, a length of rope around his neck. Apparently, it was easier to support his family with a life insurance policy payout than to struggle week to week. Stupid man didn't even realize the policy didn't payout in the case of suicide."

Oh, shit. Why is she telling me this?

Terry25: "So sorry to hear that."

Babygirlblonde: "Thanks. Anyway, I don't care too much for chatting on here. All the guys just wanna fuck, and I'm not really...It's not my thing. You want to hang out tomorrow? I need some fatherly like advice. I need to make some big changes in my life, and I need a second opinion."

Oh, geez. It sounds innocent enough. She wouldn't try to hit on someone twice her age, right? And I'm not interested in anything anyway. But if it's advice she needs, advice I can give. I think for a few more seconds.

Terry25: "Sure, where do you want to meet?"

Babygirlblonde: "Your house. I'll be around in the morning."

Terry25: "I'll cook some brunch then. Do you like bacon and eggs?"

Babygirlblonde: "Who doesn't? I'm not one of those new-age vegan hippy types."

I chuckle out loud. But what have I gotten myself into?

An invite to a chat with BluesGirl88 pops up.

I say goodbye to Babygirlblonde and stare at BluesGirl's invite for a long moment.

I never expected to see her avatar again, knowing the psycho behind it has been arrested. Or at least brought in for questioning. I thought the account would have been deleted or put on hold while the police concluded their investigation.

But that guy had been stealing access to avatars. So maybe this is the real BluesGirl88 now and the police haven't locked her account?

If so, talking with her could tell me if I virtually fucked a guy or if I was with the real BluesGirl88 that night. I'd rather it have been the sexy person I met in that blues bar the first time I was online than a psycho.

I accept, and her infamous mansion scene renders.

BluesGirl88: "It's been a while, Terry. Who were you just talking to? DancerGirl again?"

Interesting. The DancerGirl incident happened the same night BluesGirl and I had virtual sex. So, if she remembers that happening, then maybe I *was* with the real avatar and not the psycho that night. Relief flows through me. But I still want to push it to be sure.

Terry25: "You killed DancerGirl. You chopped off

his head."

BluesGirl88: "In the chat I did, yes. You can't actually kill an avatar. I'm sorry about that though. I got jealous thinking of you with someone else."

Terry25: "None of this is real, you know."

BluesGirl88: "I know."

Terry25: "You've been acting so hot and cold. Why should I bother talking to you?"

BluesGirl88: "Because you can't give me up no matter what you tell yourself, just like I can't give up you. I'm like the drug you inject into your hungry vein, and I take over your whole body and have you under my control. You hate me, you love me, you need me, but you can't have me. Not really. Why do I want you like I do? Same reason you want me. Because I can, no other reason. I'm scared, Terry. Inside, I'm just a scared little girl who needs to be loved, owned, and worshipped. No one has come back to me over and over like you have, Terry."

Oh, holy fuck. She's never shown a vulnerable side before. I can't kick her when she's down. I need to lift her up. And I was right. She's the real BluesGirl and not the psycho I've been dealing with the past few days.

Terry25: "It's true, I do need you, and I don't know why. You scare me sometimes. Other times you excite me. I wish I could hold you and make you feel safe and have you look at me like nothing can hurt you. Let me save you from yourself."

BluesGirl88: "Terry, I wish it was that easy. My life is complicated, and I can't let anyone into my real world. But here, we can be whoever we want to be. We can be together every night and even though we don't exist together in the physical world, we can be here. Just you and me, no one else, nothing else."

Terry25: "Why can't we meet, baby girl? Why can't we give it a shot and talk face to face and see what happens next? There are times when we make love on DreamChat that I can almost feel myself inside you. Do you feel it, too?"

BluesGirl88: "I wish I could, Terry. I touch myself in real life when our avatars fuck, but all I feel is my own touch. I'm lonely, but I'm forced to live in a dream world because the real one just hurts. I don't want to hurt anymore, Terry, but for that to happen, I need to cease existing. My world is black, tormented, and unable to contain anything more than my tortured soul. I wish I could let you in, but I can't. And besides, if I exist in a world that isn't real, nothing can hurt me."

She disappears, and I know I need to get off the computer and get back to the real world before she consumes me with her bizarre ramblings.

What the hell have I gotten myself into?

CHAPTER 8

DAY 7

SUNDAY MORNING SEEMS so unsettled without my Talissa in bed next to me. If I said yesterday had been a strange day, it would be the biggest understatement in history.

I'm showered and have had two cups of coffee already. I'm prepared to face a morning with a breakfast companion.

There are other women on my mind, too. Hannah, who treated me badly and then treated me nicely. The connection had been amazing, and all I want to do is to relive the afternoon we shared at her house. I thought about her last night when I went to bed alone, remembered her physical presence next to mine, and the almost spiritual effect she had on me. Realness, I'm realizing, is addictive in a good way.

And then there's the enigma, BluesGirl88. Is she a depressed loner or just playing the game? I never know what I'm going to get when I log onto the chat with her, and part of me fears maybe I like a woman who takes control and calls the shots. It could be another reason I feel drawn to Hannah. She's a cop who knows how to use a weapon. But unlike every other woman in my life, she didn't take advantage of my weakness.

Is that why I can't get her out of my mind? I should have gotten her goddamn number. There's no listing for Hannah Hall at her address.

Maybe I should swing by her place and see?

There's a knock at the door. I answer it. Brittany is five minutes early. Once again, her height throws me. Wearing sandals, she still stands a couple of inches taller than me.

"Hi Terry, I brought a few things with me," she passes me a bag which I take a peek into and see a six-pack of cider bottles, a couple of CDs, and some folded clothes.

"Are you old enough to drink alcohol?" I ask her.

"Well, I'm twenty-one, so I've been legal for three months now. I know I look young, though. I always get asked for ID when I go to the clubs."

"Come to the kitchen and I'll start cooking." She takes the lead and I follow her. She's wearing tiny denim shorts and a white tank top showing off her midriff. I focus on the eggs and bacon on the counter instead and get my mind back to the business of cooking.

Tension is building inside of me.

I'm at a stage where I can't look at a woman without thinking about what she looks like naked and what type of performer they would be in the bedroom. I haven't been this way since before I met

Talissa, when I was much younger and not attached to a life of responsibility. Back then, the addiction was strong. And I didn't see any reason not to indulge in the booze and sex whenever I wanted. But I've been doing good these last twelve years since settling down. I haven't craved anyone except Talissa until this past week.

So, what's changed?

Brittany offers to assist me, so I have her work on chopping the mushrooms, and she shows pretty decent knife skills.

"Something I should know about you and knives?" I ask her.

"I once stuck a knife in a guy's ball sack and then cut his throat."

Her look is stone cold, and for a second, I'm worried until she smiles and has a big laugh.

"You had me going for a second there," I say to her as I place the bacon in the pan.

"Well, I think you would have been hesitant to leave your kids with me if it were true." She grins as she pulls out a chair and sits at the dining table. "By the way, they're such beautiful little people. You and Talissa must be doing something right."

Talissa, yes—not so sure about myself, though. "Yes, we do love them to pieces, and I have to credit my wife more than myself for that." I crack the eggs and put the mushrooms in a pan with some butter.

"Give yourself more credit, Terry. I bet you're a lot more confident when you're selling a house to someone." She leans on the table, her top falling forward, showing a little cleavage. A tall slim woman like her normally has a small chest, and Brittany's no exception, but she knows how to use what she has.

I force myself to keep my eyes on hers and resist the peek she's giving me. "The professional Terry is ruthless and always striving to make a few more dollars," I say, "but the private Terry is like any normal guy. You haven't even asked where Talissa is."

"Oh. She called me on Friday night, making sure I was okay to work Monday." She shrugs. "I didn't ask why she went away for the weekend without you, though. Figured you would tell me if you felt comfortable enough. I hope you two figure things out."

"So do I," I say, but I'm not so sure anymore. Maybe I'm enjoying the freedom of being separated and exploring where my future might take me.

"I'll do the toast," she says.

I make us each a cup of coffee and join her at the table. She has hers a little sweeter than I do. Every now and then, when she takes a sip, those big eyes of hers linger on mine a little longer than they probably should. Were girls so bold back when I was her age? I don't think so. Maybe it's wrong of me, but I can't help thinking her confidence is refreshing for someone in College.

We make small talk and a few minutes later, brunch is ready. She grabs one of her ciders to wash down the greasy food.

"Wow, it's not even eleven and you've started drinking?" I tease.

"Life's too short, and I don't have to drive." She's

right on both of those points. I didn't see who dropped her off, but I know she didn't drive here today. She raises her glass of cider at me. "Join me?"

I haven't had any alcohol since the beer with Hannah yesterday. Today is Sunday. I don't have to work, no kids to care for. And Talissa won't return any of my calls. I've got no obligations or responsibilities to anyone at the moment. And Brittany is watching me with those big eyes of hers. Youthful innocence and energy. I could use some of that.

"What the hell, you only live once." I stand up to walk to the fridge and grab a beer, but she grins and motions for me to sit.

"I'll get you one." Picking one of her ciders, she pours it in a glass, adds ice, and hands it to me. "Try this."

It's slightly sweet but mellow like beer. I nod. "Very nice."

I can't remember when I last had a drink so early in the day, but I'd say it hasn't been for about fifteen years.

"Geez, I'm a bad influence. You know I don't drink around your kids, right?"

"Hey, I trust you. You came highly recommended according to Talissa, and I always trust her word." Why wouldn't I? I'm the liar of the family. "So why did you come here today? What did you want to talk to me about?"

"Boys my age are so dumb. I want to know how to find a good one."

I sit back in my chair. "Boys get their stupidity

from their fathers. We're born stupid, trust me on this. And we do so much stupid shit you wouldn't believe. I can see why so many women turn into lesbians."

"Oh, no. Not another man who says that. People are either born lesbian or not. If choosing it were the case, then pretty much every female friend I have, including myself, would be lesbian. You men have no fucking idea sometimes."

She has a point. "Sorry, Brittany. Actually, a lot of my ex-girlfriends would be gay if what I said had any truth to it." I need to change the subject. Professionally, I could sell ice to an Inuit, but right now, I'm putting my foot in my mouth with everything I say—so much so, I think my big toe's poking out my ass.

"It's okay, Terry," she says. Leaning across the table, she puts a hand on mine and pats it.

"Truth is, you never know if you've found a good man when you first meet one. They may not be on a date purely for sex, but if they start a date with an itch, you won't get any intelligent conversation out of them all evening."

"Did you date many women before you met your wife?"

'Date' might not be the word I would use. "A few, Brittany—quite a few, in fact. You don't want to know what sort of man I was back in those days."

"Were you a bad boy?" Her hand is resting under her chin as she leans on her elbow. She dons those doe eyes and stares at me.

"Yes, I was, and while it was fun, I'm not

particularly proud of who I was back then. I'd hate for my daughter to one day be used by a guy like me, who used so many women."

"Did it ever occur to you they were using you as much as you were using them? We women have desires, needs, and sometimes, we want it so bad we'll hunt like a vulture to get a bit of action. We just have the advantage. We can be a hunter while appearing as the hunted."

Looking at those eyes and her long body, I can't see how she would have a lot of trouble hunting.

"Why don't we go to the living room? I brought some tunes along for us to listen to," she says.

My glass of cider is empty already. It seems to be hitting me about as fast as the scotch and rum did.

"I'll get us both refills," she says and proceeds to do so before I can protest.

It's not her place, she's the guest. But she bats my argument aside with a flick of her hair and a grin. "I like being helpful," she says as she passes my refilled glass to me.

Maybe it's the cider hitting me now, but I like that she likes helping out and being fun. I follow those artistically sculpted never-ending legs of hers to the living room as she leads the way. She has her second cider in one hand, the CDs in the other, and I see a little bit of butt cheek as those tiny shorts of hers rise even higher. Damn, she's got a tight ass. Perfectly round and perky.

"What sort of music do you like, Terry?"

"Hum? Oh, I like rock, blues, and even a bit of dance music, but don't tell anyone about the last one."

She laughs and makes a beeline to the stereo and turns it on. She ejects the CD from the deck, and I silently hope she's one of those people like me who makes sure the disc goes back into the case, rather than being placed on any rough surface. She doesn't disappoint, and to me, she just passed a test on my checklist of what makes a true music connoisseur.

"Don't you hate it when people just put the discs on the carpet or cabinet where they get the hell scratched out of them?" she asks.

"Yessss!" I nod, as I take a seat on the right side of the three-seater couch. "Only monsters do that."

She giggles and presses play. A sad sounding male voice leads into a song about lost love, which is hardly rare for an opening track to a blues album. I have to say this guy can sing and the slide guitar is smooth. "This is sweet blues," I tell her.

"You really think so?" She smiles, seeming pleased. "People my age don't get my love for the blues. They think hip-hop and dance music is the real deal, but it has no heart."

"You sound like someone my age, Brit."

"Is that a bad thing?" She smiles at me and drains the rest of her cider. "I need another one."

"I'll get it this time," I say to her as my second glass is finished, too. It's not even midday. Once again, she tries to get the refills, but this time I insist on playing host.

Walking to the fridge in the kitchen down the hall, I smile, enjoying the buzz. I'm drinking on a Sunday morning with a six-foot blonde, listening to some kick-ass music without a care in the world. I've done no work all weekend, and I'm not missing it at all. The only thing better would be if I was enjoying this with Hannah. But she's not here. And neither is Talissa. Both of them left me alone.

Except I'm not alone now, am I? I've got Brittany to keep happy.

I get back to the living room with drinks. Brittany is sitting on the couch with a small plastic bag. On closer inspection, it looks like it contains pot. I haven't seen that stuff for years, let alone smoked any.

"Do you mind?" she asks, holding up a joint she takes from the bag. "I would never smoke around the kids, either."

I'll have to make sure I spray a good deal of air freshener before Talissa gets home, but I don't care. It's my house too. And it's my duty as host to make my guest feel welcome and take care of her. "Not at all. Knock yourself out."

She lights it up and takes a big toke on it, holding the smoke in for a few seconds. Her eyes close as if she's enjoying the sensation. The smell of it fills the room. As she exhales, she looks at me and holds out the joint.

I haven't been high in a long time, but I remember how relaxing it was back in College. I walk over to her slowly, accepting the offering.

Youthful energy, here we come.

I hold the joint to my lips, relight it, and breathe in the fumes of the burning dried leaves. I try to hold it in but I'm out of practice, and in seconds I'm coughing up a lung with Brittany laughing.

"You haven't done this before, have you, Terry?"

I try not to laugh, but the muscles in my jaw have taken control. "Not since I was your age."

She takes the joint from me and has another puff before passing it back. My turn again, but this time, I control myself better and draw the smoke back as far as I can. My head feels a little lighter already, and I start to drift like I'm floating. The burn is good. Really good. It mixes with my cider-buzz like milk and honey.

"This shit's strong, hey?" Brittany asks, giggling. We take it in turns until the joint is nothing more than a half-inch butt.

My head is spinning now, but it feels freeing and the only care I have is that the thirst brought on by the smoking needs to be quenched. I drain my third drink and glance at Brittany as she starts dancing to the music. It's as if the sounds of the singing and guitar playing are using her like a puppet. Her arms are above her head as her hips sway to the beats. The movement is mesmerizing. Sinuously beautiful, like a snake being charmed. I can't turn away, and I don't want to. I'd like to see her tight, hot body do this dance naked.

As if reading my mind, she starts wiggling her tight little ass, and her hands move down her body to the front button of her shorts, liberating it from the buttonhole keeping it in place.

I want her to undo her zipper too, but her hands travel to the belt loops on her hips instead, hooking her thumbs through. The song is nearly over, and she winks at me before stepping toward me. Standing right in front of where I'm sitting, she reaches over me and grabs her cider glass.

When the music stops, she drains the contents and looks down at me. "I need another one."

"Okay, Babygirl." I nod and, getting to my feet, I soon realize I'm full-on buzzed. I take my time, putting one foot in front of the other, and head to the kitchen. My lips shape themselves into a messy smile. Brittany is sweet. And hot. And I like taking care of her and how helpful she is. And she likes blues, like me. Who knew?

Only now, the silence is freaking me out. What happened to the music? I need the fucking music.

Barely managing to keep it together, I get myself a beer and another cider for Brittany and weave my way back to the living room, trying hard to not spill anything.

She's changing the CD in the stereo, and grins as she presses play. A simple but catchy bass rift pumps out. Walking toward me to the beat, she dons her cheeky smile again and snatches her drink from my hand. She turns her back to me, takes a long drink, and leans into me, her body making contact with the front of mine. I clutch at her to keep us steady, my hand touching the bare skin of her midriff.

She giggles and bumps my groin with her ass, knocking me backward. "Sit down, mister," she says and takes a couple of steps away from me.

I manage to take a seat on the couch without falling and only slightly spilling my drink.

A smoky female voice belts out an opening line

about wanting the love of a good man.

"Do you like watching me dance?" she asks, seeming almost uncertain as she studies me with her doe eyes wide.

"Yes," I say without hesitation. "Oh, hell yes."

Brittany grins, wiggling her brows. "Good. I like making you happy."

I suppress a groan. She's so damn innocent and sweet. "I like making you happy too," I say, trying not to slur my words. Speaking is getting hard. As is thinking. As is my cock as she tells me to keep watching because she has something special she wants me to see. What am I about to witness? I have the feeling I won't be disappointed.

She turns away from me again and then rotates her head toward me, showing me her pouty lips. I can't see what her hands are doing as she keeps her front turned away from me, but I'm pretty sure she's touching herself in places I'd like to see.

The suspense is driving me insane, but before I reach my breaking point and ask her to turn around and show me, she slides her thumbs through the belt loops again. She leans forward and pushes her bum out toward me. Perky cheeks peek at me from beneath the hem. She pushes her tiny shorts down and then off her hips, letting them fall to her ankles.

Her cute ass is visible in all its glory, her lacy, white G-string barely covering anything. She bends forward, reaching for her ankles, and looks at me upside down from between her mile-long legs.

My cock stirs as I study the wispy bit of

underwear that barely covers what's beneath. Her eyes stare into mine, adding to the intensity of the cannabis-induced euphoria flowing through me.

"You like?" she asks, her voice husky.

"Oh, Babygirl. I love."

"Show me," she says. Her gaze moves to my groin.

I fumble with the button and zipper of my jeans and loosen them, allowing the bulge tenting my boxers more room to rise.

"That's hot," she says. Her gaze trained on my groin, she releases her grip on her ankles and, still upside down, grabs the bottom of her little crop-top. With the assistance of gravity, she slides it off and allows it to fall to the floor. Her white bra is tiny, barely containing her small breasts. Not that I mind. Breasts are beautiful no matter the size. She twists upright again and spins to face me as she rotates her hips to the beat. Signaling for me to stand, she takes a couple of steps toward me and tells me to take off my pants.

Who am I to disobey? I'm a sucker for a woman who knows what she wants. And I want to keep my Babygirl happy, don't I?

Already loose, they fall to the carpet without a struggle. I step out of them and kick them away. She dances and moves my way, making contact with my body and grinding herself against me. Her hands wander up to the bottom of my T-shirt. Grabbing the sides of it, she lifts the fabric up until I take over and pull it over my head.

"Mmm," she says, moving her hands up from my

navel to my chest. "Boys my age either don't have hair or wax it all off. But I find a real man to be so... *sexy!*" She lets go of me and takes a step backward. She puts her hands behind her back and unclasps her bra. Her perky little breasts have pierced nipples, and I am now incredibly hard.

Damn. Fucking damn, she's hot. A hardbody dream.

She walks back to me, and I'm in the unusual position of looking up to meet her as she bends to kiss me. She's so fucking tall and slim.

For the first time, I taste her tongue piercing as she sweeps her tongue against mine. I press my lower body against her, and due to the length of her legs, her pussy rests just above my groin. I've never been with a woman like her before. My erect cock nestles between the gap in her thighs, brushing against her panty-clad pussy.

She withdraws the kiss and we both look down, watching as I tease her with little thrusts, rubbing my cock against the soft fabric barrier between her flesh and mine.

Her face is flushed. She licks her lips. "Terry?"

I tease her with stronger thrusts, clutching her tight ass in my hands, enjoying the sound of her soft, excited breaths and the way it feels for both of us. "Is this what you want?" I ask.

She nods and leans forward and whispers in my ear, "I've never had a guy make me come before."

Shit. Shit shit shit shit. Her words make me so hard I could blow my load right now. I stop thrusting and take a second to find what little cool I have left.

"I might have to fix that," I whisper back, finding her gaze and holding it. "Would you like me to fix that, Babygirl?"

"Yes, please." Her eyes are large and full of need. She's begging. How can I not help out my guest? I'd be a miserable host to deny her what she's been missing and wants most.

I'm so hard, I want to fuck her hot and fast, but that's not what she needs right now. I use what's left of my self-control to gently move my hand downward over her smooth abdomen.

Her eyes widen as I touch the bit of lace between her legs and explore the warmth hidden beneath. She's soft and pliant and I can feel her wetness already, soaking the fabric.

"Do you touch yourself here?" I ask her, holding her gaze while I massage her slowly. Gentle sweeps of my fingers where she wants to be touched most.

"Yes."

"Do you think of me when you do it?"

She bites her bottom lip with her pretty white teeth and sucks in a gasp. "Yes."

"You're a naughty girl, aren't you, Babygirl?"

Her gaze skitters away from mine. "Yes."

"It's okay," I say and rub my finger against the little bump I can feel beneath the fabric covering her pussy. "We all have needs."

Her legs are shaking. She closes her eyes. "Please, Terry."

"Who do you want, Babygirl?"

"You."

"And who am I?"

"A real man."

Fucking hell, I'm so turned on, my hands are shaking slightly as I put my fingers on the sides of her miniature thong and get on my knees. Pulling the garment to the ground, I put my mouth against the smooth, waxed lips between her legs, parting them so I can kiss her deep inside.

She moans softly. Her hands clutch my hair. Within a few minutes, her body shakes, as I become the first man to give her true satisfaction.

* * * * *

I'M WORN OUT. After giving Brittany oral sex, we screw three times within an hour. She makes sure I use a new condom each time. Thinking about the other two women I've had sex with, and the lack of protection used, I hope to hell they were at least on the pill or have an IUD. I don't want to end up with any unexpected children.

Brittany walks to the kitchen to get us each another beer and cider. On her return, I can't take my eyes off her. She's confident and comfortable in her nudity, and why shouldn't she be? She's flawlessly beautiful.

She sits right next to me on the couch, our skin touching, and we each take a long drink. Her gaze strays to my cock as she licks the cold drink from her lips. Grinning, she gets on her knees and straddles my leg, her bare pussy pressing my thigh, and my cock is getting hard again. Is it the pot or the booze or her? I've got the stamina of my twenty-year-old self again.

"Let's get baked before we fuck again," Brittany says and reaches for the table where she put her bag of marijuana and papers. She carefully rolls another joint, smacking my fingers as I fondle her nipple piercings, giggling as I do it.

"I feel kinda creepy now. You're nearly half my age," I say.

"Really? The only reason I came around today was because I wanted to get naughty with you. The first time I saw you I knew you would be able to make me feel like a real woman. It's not that guys my age don't want to perform like a sex god, they just don't have the experience you do."

"Thanks." I touch her left nipple piercing again, gently playing with it, and this time she doesn't stop me. As sweet as she is, there's an edge about her that I find irresistible. "You know it will be awkward now when you come around to babysit the kids in the mornings."

"It'll be okay. But we can never do this again after today. I hope you understand." Brittany lights up the joint and inhales deeply.

I take it from her and take a big puff. A lightness washes over me as I blow out the smoke. I quench the dryness with a big gulp of cold beer, and study all her naked glory. It's like I'm in heaven with the daughter of Satan. We smoke the rest of the joint, and we both have a giggle about nothing in particular.

She rests her hand on my skin just above my semi-aroused cock. Her smile is like pure sin. "Lie back, Terry. I want to return the favor you did for me earlier."

Half-reclined already, I do as ordered, placing my hands behind my head. Scooting backward a bit, she leans over and takes all my length inside her soft, wet mouth. I watch as she does her magic, cupping her head with my hand. Her blonde hair is soft as it slides through my fingers, and that tongue piercing is hitting the exact right places. I want it to last, but it takes just a few minutes before I finish with a loud groan that makes her grin with satisfaction. She licks her lips as she studies me. She's not a spitter. I admire that. And reward her with another pussy-licking on the couch until she arches and moans my name.

With my energy spent, and the booze and pot making the room spin, it doesn't take long before I pass out.

* * * * *

THE SOUND OF the front door slamming wakes me. As I open my eyes, I find Talissa, visibly pissed, staring at me where I lie on the couch—as naked as the day I was born.

I glance around quickly. Brittany is nowhere in sight.

"Kids, go to your rooms," Talissa calls out to them before they step inside and see the mess Brittany and I made of the living room. Talissa waits until she hears the kids' doors close before rounding on me. "Terry...what the *fuck* happened here?"

She never swears, and I sure hope the kids didn't hear from behind the closed doors of their rooms. "I fell asleep." Technically, it isn't a lie.

"No shit, Sherlock! There are empty bottles of beer and glasses all over the place and it smells like," she takes a couple of sniffs, "pot and pussy in here."

Oh, shit. No disguising any of those scents. "I was watching porn and having a little smoke and a few drinks."

"Do you think I'm so stupid I would buy that shit?" She spots something on the carpet near the couch. "Well, then, what the fuck is this?"

Brittany's G-string—irrefutable evidence a female was here. I can't tell her they belong to the babysitter, but it's impossible to deny a woman has visited. "I hired a massage therapist, the type who takes their clothes off while they rub you down. I'm sorry. I've been down, and you wouldn't answer your phone, and I needed some type of release."

"You sick fuck, Terry. I give you what you need, time to yourself to think, and it's still not enough? My mother was right about you."

"I don't care what the stupid bitch says about me. You know she's fucked in the head, right?"

Talissa walks up and slaps my face.

The contact stings like a bee. I did say too much then. I know it, but the effects of the beer and pot are still with me, so I put the blame there to ease my conscience and deny personal responsibility for my words.

"You can sleep in here tonight or your office. I don't care where really, as long as it's not in my bed.

CHRIS HEINICKE

We'll talk about this tomorrow. I don't want to see your face again today, you asshole!"

She storms off and for the first time, I notice it's past six p.m. I've lost so much time over the weekend from falling asleep during the day, but with all my sexual activity from the last few days, it's no surprise I'm so tired. My head is pounding from the effects of the afternoon.

God, what a ride. But what the hell did I do?

I put my clothes on and tiptoe to the kitchen, peeking to see if Talissa is in there. The coast is clear, so I go in and grab some leftover pizza from the fridge. The pots and dishes from the shared brunch are still where I left them, and they will stay there until I know I can stay in the kitchen for a decent amount of time.

I head to the office, seeking the sanctuary of my computer. I turn it on and while it's booting, I close the door to my study.

I don't want the kids to see me like this. Or anyone. Talissa has every right to be pissed with me. I can't seem to get my act straight right now or keep my dick in my pants. When I was younger, I didn't care about who I spent the night with. But I haven't been that guy for years.

So why now?

What the hell changed?

It's like something has taken me over and is trying to ruin my life. Well, if that's the case, then whatever it is, it's winning.

Maybe more booze will kill it? And if not, maybe more booze will kill me. I don't care which at the

Page | 216

moment.

I grab what's left of the bottle of rum and pour it into a glass. I take a short, throat-burning sip as the chat program loads. BluesGirl88 is online, as is Babygirlblonde, RogerU69, and Erika19. My heart lurches at seeing Hannah's chat name.

But RogerU69 invites me into a chat and as the spa scene loads, I see there are four female avatars, one being the babysitter's avatar, Babygirlblonde.

Babygirlblonde: "Hi, Terry."

Terry25: "Hi, Babygirlblonde. I need to chat with you in private."

RogerU69: "You know her?"

His avatar is wearing just a pair of red Speedos and sunglasses that make him appear as if he wants to jump every female in the scene.

I get a private chat request from BluesGirl88 and then a separate one from Erika19. Accepting each one, I soon find myself in four separate chats as Babygirlblonde also accepts my private chat invitation.

Babygirlblonde: "Thanks for today. You were awesome."

Terry25: "You left your panties at my place, and Talissa found them."

Erika19: "Hey, just wanted to make sure you're okay, Terry."

I click through each chat, trying not to get them confused.

Babygirlblonde: "Oh, no. I'm sooooo sorry."

BluesGirl88: "Are you gonna fucking chat or what?"

RogerU69: "Terry? What's going on?"

I can't keep up with it all. No one likes to feel ignored in private chat, so I pick the most volatile.

Terry25 to BluesGirl88: "I'm so busy here, I'm a popular man."

BluesGirl88: "You think I only deserve a little bit of your attention? You think I'm just a virtual vagina for you to bang when you want and then kick me to the curb when you're done?"

Terry25 to BluesGirl88: "They're work colleagues, that's all."

BluesGirl88: "Tomorrow is Monday, right."

Terry25 to BluesGirl88: "Yes, of course it is."

BluesGirl88: "Chat with them tomorrow then. I want your attention on me and me only, or else you're wasting my time."

I quickly type in the chat with Erika19.

Terry25 to Erika19: "I feel so bad. I miss you, Hannah. I felt a spark with you yesterday."

Erika19: "I miss you too, Terry. I feel like, maybe we met in another life, and in this one we remember our magic and each other's soul. But you have your wife and kids now, and I can't break that up."

My vision mists. I know she's right. I need to fix my marriage and forget all about these other women. But Hannah is special, and I don't know why. She just is. Instant connection and I don't want to leave it. I wipe my eyes with the pad of my thumb.

Terry25 to Erika19: "You're right. But I can't just...let go."

RogerU69: "I gotta talk to you, man."

Terry25 to RogerU69: "What is it?"

I really don't need four separate chats going, but none of these can see what I'm typing to any of the others, and that's probably a fortunate thing. And I best ensure I'm in the right window on each occasion I type to someone.

> **BluesGirl88: "I'm getting real tired of this, Terry."**

> **Terry25 to BluesGirl88: "Can you please give me a god-damned minute?"**

> **BluesGirl88: "You always want a god-damned minute, you useless piece of shit."**

I close the chat with her and go back to Roger.

> **RogerU69: "I got a call from Talissa half an hour ago. What the hell have you done?"**

> **Terry25 to RogerU69: "Why didn't you just call me, rather than chat about it here?"**

I can't believe this shit.

> **RogerU69: "You've done something bad, haven't you?"**

> **Terry25 to RogerU69: "It's complicated. Can we talk at work tomorrow?"**

> **RogerU69: "Okay, but promise me you'll try to fix things tonight."**

Terry25 to RogerU69: "I'll try. I want to fix it with her."

It's what I should want, right? If only for the kids.

RogerU69: "This is all my fault for introducing you to this program. I should have known better, Terry, given how you used to be all those years ago when you were single and trying to add 1,000 notches to your belt."

Terry25 to RogerU69: "I'm the one who should be controlling myself. I don't blame anyone, except me. I'll see you at work."

I'm down to two chats now, and I check that Erika19 is still there. Thankfully, she is.

Terry25 to Erika19: "I still think there's something amiss with that avatar BluesGirl88, Hannah. She's still on here. Last night she seemed okay. But now she's unstable and threatening again. Are you sure you got the right guy?"

Erika19: "No, and that's been my concern all along. Please be careful, Terry. I'm not officially allowed to investigate your connection to the case anymore, but I'll keep working on things on my end. My hunch is that we don't have the right guy in custody. I think whoever it is, is using a portable device to chat with over a secure VPN, so she can track us, but we can't track her. Or him."

Dammit!

Terry25 to Erika19: "She won't meet me in real life, either. I mean, I'm pretty sure if she's either Lauren or Emily I've met her in real life already. But she won't admit to it online here or agree to arrange a meeting with me."

Erika19: "That's good. I don't think you should. It would be very risky. I gotta go now, but please...take care."

Terry25 to Erika19: "Wait. Hannah? Can I at least have your number so I can call?"

The private chat closes with my message unseen. Dammit!

Brittany's still online though, sending me smiley emoticons.

Babygirlblonde: "I suck at typing."

I hear a noise through my computer's speakers, "That better?" The babysitter's sweet young voice is barely audible at that volume. I turn up the sound levels and she repeats herself.

Terry25: "Yes, that's better. I'm sorry I don't have a microphone."

Babygirlblonde: "Thanks for today, you were so fucking awesome in so many ways. When I think about what you did with your tongue, mmmm, I close my eyes and lie on the bed. I take my bottoms off and touch myself imagining my finger is your wet, powerful tongue. Can you still taste me, Terry?"

My mouth tastes like ashes, bitter rum, and regret, but I lie. Because why not? I'm getting really good at it.

Terry25: "Yes, your juices still linger on my tongue, but I fear I will never have it on my lips again."

Babygirlblonde: "I hope I find another guy who can do that magic you did today, Terry. The way you made my pussy and entire body..."

At this point, I notice my son standing in the now open doorway. "Go back to bed, Isaac," I say as I unplug the speaker.

"I missed you, Daddy." He comes up and hugs me and then looks at the computer monitor. "That looks like Brittany."

"It's just a cartoon, son." He smiles at me and hugs me, and I pick him up to carry him to his bed. He looks at me with sad puppy dog eyes. "Mommy and Daddy are having some troubles, Isaac. We will work them out. Daddy's not leaving."

"I like it when you and Mommy are happy. I love you so much, Daddy."

I place him on the mattress of his bed and cover him with a blanket. I look at his face and see a glimmer of a smile. Kissing him on the forehead, I say, "I love you too, Isaac."

Walking away, I wipe a tear from my eye and begin to wonder how I can fix everything. Can I even consider myself worthy of keeping the love of the family I've hurt so much? The last twelve years have gone quickly, but it's a long time to be with someone.

Hannah's right. As much as I share an attraction to her, I can't imagine my life being happy without Talissa and especially the kids. And I have to think of them first.

There is nothing I would want more than to climb into bed next to my wife, hold her, and kiss her, and sleep the night away together. Then to see her face first thing in the morning...

It all sounds great, except it's Hannah's face I'm seeing in my mind instead of Talissa's.

I shake my head to clear it and try to push Hannah from my thoughts.

If I truly want to fix things with Talissa, then I need to make her the most important person in my life besides the kids and stop all this running around, chasing other women.

It's the only way to regain her trust.

I know it won't happen tonight, and I know they say time is the best healer, but I don't want too much time to pass before everything is okay again.

Tomorrow starts a new work week. I will bust my balls to get the Pellmont advertising campaign underway and get a sale within a month. I'll put in for time off and take Talissa and the kids away to an island resort somewhere. I need a rest and a bit of time to get my life back on track. I know I have so much to make up for with my wife.

Why did I let my penis make so many stupid decisions this week?

I walk back to the computer and see that Babygirlblonde is now offline, and probably very pissed at me. BluesGirl88 is nowhere to be seen and neither is Erika19. But there's a chat request from a Fiona17 waiting for me. I have absolutely no idea who she is, so I decline and shut down the chat program.

I haven't checked my emails all day, so I go in and have a look. The name I see of the last thirteen emails sends a shiver up my spine.

BluesGirl88.

I can't look at them, so I delete each one of them, and then work through my work-related emails. It takes me a good half hour to read them all and take notes of what I need to work on this coming week. Since it was a long day full of sex, drugs, and booze, I hope the notes make sense when I take them to work tomorrow and go over them in my office.

A new email has arrived while I've been working. It's from BluesGirl88 again. I decide to read it.

"Terry, how many times do you have to be warned? If I can find your email address, do you think it's hard to

find your phone number? And then do you think I can't find where you live? Say goodnight to Isaac and Matilda. I hope they sleep safely."

Against my better judgment, I send off a reply.

"You stay away from my family, you psychotic slut. If you so much as ring my house, I'll have the cops on your ass in a second."

I hear a message come through on my mobile phone a minute later, and I pick it up from my desk and read it.

Unknown Contact: "You didn't say anything about sending a text message."

Shit. I hope the cops still have my house under surveillance and they're monitoring me.

I go back onto the chat and send Erika19 a private message. She's not around, but hopefully she'll see it when she logs in.

Terry25: "Hannah? I think our favorite psycho is stalking me for real. She texted my cell number and mentioned my kids by name in an email. I don't have a good feeling about this."

I drink the rest of the rum in my glass and fold out the sofa bed in the study, leaving the door wide open. I double-check the security system around the perimeter of the house, and then I do a last-minute check on both of my children. If that bitch tries anything tonight, I'll be sure to wake up when the alarm is tripped. Just in case I need it as a weapon, I make sure my favorite golf club is within reach.

Dressed in only my underwear, I lie on the sofa bed, my back feeling like there's an iron bar running down my spine. Tomorrow is sure to be a ten-cup of coffee day.

My mobile phone lights up as another SMS comes through. Once again, it's from Unknown Contact. My hand shakes as I read the words on the screen.

"Prepare for the second-worst day of your life."

CHAPTER 9

DAY 8

THE WORST THING about waking up so tired on a Monday morning is knowing you're going to have a really shit day, especially when your wife forcibly wakes you an hour before you have to be at work. She's still angry, and the day hasn't started well for her.

"Brittany's mother rang and said she hasn't heard from her daughter since yesterday morning. Apparently, she was off to see a boyfriend and hasn't been heard from since," Talissa says.

"Oh, shit. What do we do then?" I ask.

"I've already called in at work. I won't be going in today. I'll call the agency and see if I can line someone up for tomorrow as a backup. Brittany's mother is pretty distraught, though."

"I'm sure she's big enough to look after herself."

"She's only seventeen, Terry. She's still a little girl."

No way! No fucking way. I had sex with an underage girl? Nausea hits me like a punch to the stomach.

"Excuse me." I cover my mouth with my hand and make a run for the toilet, bringing up what little's left in my stomach from yesterday.

Brittany was online yesterday evening, but how can I tell Talissa without bringing attention to the fact I've been in contact with her in a sex chat game? And now I face the knowledge that I'm a pedophile. I feel like vomiting again.

"Something wrong, Terry?" Talissa calls out.

I wipe my mouth and answer, "I drank too much yesterday. It's my own fault. I need a shower."

"I told you to lay off the booze. But you just don't listen, do you?" She pokes her head around the bathroom door and looks at me. What she sees makes her sneer. "I better take you to work then. You look like crap. We still have stuff to talk about, but we'll do it tonight."

She retreats from view. I catch a glance of myself in the bathroom mirror. Bloodshot eyes. A full day's worth of scruff. I'll have to hurry if I want to fix this. I'm looking at being late as it is, but I can't go in smelling and looking like a homeless person on a bender. Even if I feel like one.

* * * * *

WE ALL PACK into the car, and the first stop is Isaac's school. Talissa and I don't say much on the journey as we always ensure we don't argue in front of our children, no matter the circumstances. I battle to stay awake in the car and can't put my finger on how much sleep I got last night, but I know it wasn't much. Maybe two hours of broken sleep.

Matilda is happily singing along with some of the songs on the radio, her mother joining in, too. Once again, I'm reminded of how adorable my wife is, and with so much going on and knowing her husband cheated on her, she can still smile and show joy in front of our children. If I can keep her after all this mess, I won't fuck it up again.

I close my eyes, and I see them all there in my mind looking at me—Emily, Lauren, Hannah, and Brittany. All blonde and beautiful and each of them, except Hannah, have had sex with me. In my dream, they're pointing and laughing at me, as I stand naked before them with nothing to cover my nudity and nowhere to run. A fifth blonde joins them and tells them to stop, and when they don't, she pulls a sword from a scabbard and swings it in a semi-circle, slicing off each of their heads. She looks at me and tells me we can now be together once she takes care of Talissa...

I open my eyes and see the time is eight-fifty a.m., and I'm pretty sure we should make it in fifteen minutes to my workplace. Looking at my wife behind the wheel, I hold back the tears threatening to flow from them. I have to get it together. My colleagues can't see any weakness, not even Roger.

"Why can't you drive today, Daddy?" Matilda asks.

"Daddy didn't sleep well, and when he doesn't sleep well, he could have an accident," Talissa says.

"When is Miss Brittany coming back? I like her,

Mommy. She is so pretty and funny and doesn't even get angry when I ask her why she's on Daddy's computer."

Daddy's computer! What the hell was she doing on there? And when?

"I'm sure she was just checking her emails or social media updates." Talissa glances at me.

"I don't know what that means, Mommy."

Remaining silent on the remainder of the car trip, I breathe a sigh of relief as we stop out front of the real estate branch where I work. Standing out front and watching as we pull up, Emily smokes a cigarette.

"Is that the woman you drove home the other day?" my wife asks.

"Yes, that's Emily."

"And you fucked her in *our* living room yesterday?"

"No. And don't we watch our language in front of our kids?"

"What does fuck mean?" Matilda asks.

I point at Talissa. "See what you did?"

"Just get out and go to work, you *prick*," my wife screams at me.

I do as she says and see that our little girl has started to cry. Things continue snowballing, and I try to wave to Matilda before Talissa drives away.

"Rough start to the day?" Emily calls out.

I turn to her. *Fucking bitch.* Standing there like nothing's happened and she's innocent. "Long story, Em. I didn't get much sleep last night, and I've used up those pills you gave me." I'm never touching them again, but I want to see what she'll say.

She puts out her cigarette. "Come see me after morning brief, and I'll fix you up some more—for a price that is. I have a proposition for you, too. Would be good for both of us."

"If 'proposition' means what I think it means, I don't need more trouble. I had fun the other day, I'll admit, but I've fucked up my marriage so badly. We can't do it again."

I open the door to the building for her. She pauses before walking through. "I understand, Terry, but what I have in mind doesn't involve sex with each other. Please, just hear me out when I tell you later."

Her hand touches mine for a brief second as she grabs the door near me. She smiles at me then looks ahead as we make our way to the morning brief. When we reach the closed door of the staff room, she pushes ahead of me. As we enter, Roger, Kate, George, and Phelps turn to us.

"Nice of you to greet us with your presence, you two. Grab a coffee and take a seat. Then we'll start the Monday briefing," Phelps says. It's a lucky thing Emily walked in late with me or else Phelps would probably tear me a new one.

"Sorry boss, car trouble. The wife had to drive me in," I offer my excuse.

"Monday induced CBF," Emily says.

"What?" Phelps asks.

"'Couldn't Be Fucked'. I'm no good on a Monday until midday."

Phelps opens his mouth but offers no direct

comeback. Emily and I go about making our coffees as everyone else gets ready for what will probably be a boring half-hour listening to Phelps's drabble. I fill two mugs of coffee, attracting a few stares and then look at the table to see the only vacant spots are next to either Kate or Phelps. Picking the lesser of the two evils, I sit next to Kate, who offers a sad smile seeing the state I'm in.

The meeting starts with Phelps talking about sales targets for the upcoming month, then Kate's auction success on Saturday with a property achieving a twenty-thousand-dollar higher than expected purchase price, and then his request for me to follow up with the Pellmont property.

"I met with her on Friday. I can say it all went well. I'll be dropping over some paperwork later," I say.

Phelps nods and continues with the meeting. I tune out, and Emily, sitting opposite me, catches my eye. She has a pen resting on the edge of the table, and I see her nudge it off with her elbow, trying to make it look like an accident. It rolls on the floor and ends up closer to me than her.

"Oops," she says.

"I'll get it," I say, and I bend down to retrieve it from the floor. Emily has her legs apart and a hand pulling her skirt up far enough for me to see that she's wearing nothing underneath. I look away as quickly as I can and hit my head on the edge of the table. The throbbing pain from the collision is instantaneous, as if my head weren't already aching from lack of sleep and overconsumption of alcohol and pot from the day before.

Emily flashes me a wicked grin. This bitch is pure sin. How the hell can I rid myself of this devil in a non-lethal way? I don't want to have to deal with her at work anymore. I need to talk to Roger before I visit her in her office.

"Are you okay?" Kate asks me.

"Yeah, just a little *smack* to the head."

Phelps carries on with the rest of his spiel, and I just want this day to end so I can get some sleep. I've already drained the first coffee, so I take a sip from the second. Maybe I could suffer a sudden heart attack and be taken to the hospital. It might also earn some sympathetic love from Talissa, and her inquest to what I did on Sunday may come to a sudden end. My mind spins some weird shit when I'm tired, and I should shut it off before it fucks me over.

Phelps asks Roger about his upcoming clients— a middle-aged couple selling a family home in the western suburbs who want to downsize. He has the potential to not only sell a house for the couple, but also a chance to line them up with a viable selection of our properties for sale. The boss is impressed with him, which is hardly surprising, but I don't begrudge my friend for that.

The meeting finally comes to an end, and I refill my empty mugs with more coffee. Roger taps me on the shoulder, and this, I know, means he wants to have a chat. I need to do this.

I follow him and he pulls the door shut behind us. He takes his usual seat, and I sit opposite the desk from him. "I did it again, Roger—two times, in fact."

"You fucked Emily another two times? When did this happen?"

"Not Emily, another two women. There was Lauren Pellmont on Friday, and the babysitter yesterday. Multiple times too, each of them."

Roger's jaw drops. He tries several times to say something, and finally, just shakes his head.

"Yes, I know, Roger. I'm going to hell for this, especially the babysitter—she's just seventeen-years-old apparently. She told me twenty-one, but I could go to jail for that, Rog." I stand up, waving my arms to emphasize what I'm saying.

"Calm down, Terry. You can get through this." Then he frowns. "Did you say Lauren Pellmont?"

"Yeah, she seduced me in her bedroom. I passed out, and several hours later I had to rush out of there because Talissa had rung the office to try to find me and gotten hold of Phelps, who told her where I was."

"Terry, excuse me, but did you say you had sex with Lauren Pellmont?"

"Yes, that's what I said. Please, try and keep up."

"Geez, you are desperate to sell that place—she's like seventy years old."

What the hell is he talking about? "She was only twenty-six years old, and one hell of a hottie, Rog. I'm sure you would do her in a heartbeat."

"There must be some mistake. The widow Lauren Pellmont is seventy years old, or close to it. There was a whole news article dedicated to her late husband, given his philanthropy and heroics back in his firefighting days. Go look it up."

"But her file said..." Or maybe it didn't say. Maybe I didn't read it right and thought I had? My head spins quicker than when I was buzzed yesterday. If the woman I had sex with isn't the widow Pellmont, then what the hell have I done? Before I can get off my chair, Phelps bursts into the office. "Terry, my office, *NOW!*"

He turns around and heads back out before I can offer any kind of response. Roger looks at me. "Good luck, buddy."

"Thanks." My legs take my unwilling body down the hall to Phelps's office, and I think I know what could be on the agenda for our discussion.

"Close the fucking door behind you," Phelps says without looking up from a piece of paper, "and don't bother sitting down."

"What is it?"

Phelps looks up from his desk. His little grey eyes bore into me like bullets from a pissed-off, middle-aged, male-pattern-balding gun. "We have a serious problem. I just got off the phone with Mrs. Pellmont, who has been away from her place for the last two weeks, only getting back home yesterday. So, can you imagine her surprise when she finds brochures and a business card on her kitchen counter from our branch?"

"Sorry, boss. There's been a big misunderstanding. I went there on Friday and this young woman said she was some sort of trophy wife for the old bugger. I took her around the house and..."

He cuts me off. "Do you not ever read the fucking news? Mr. Pellmont was often seen with his dear old wife at charity events."

"Well, I thought he'd remarried or something. How the hell should I know? And how the hell did this blonde woman get in the house? This must be your fault as much as mine, if not more. Who arranged the meeting with you?"

"It doesn't matter. Mrs. Pellmont said her bedroom was all messed up and smelled bad like people had been having sex. She's gone so far as to threaten to get her bedsheets DNA tested."

"I'll make it up to her."

"No, you won't. She doesn't want you anywhere near the house ever again. The only reason my branch still has the selling rights to it is because her late husband and I attended several events together, and also because I've assured her I'm giving George the property."

"I don't know what to say. I made the appointment to see her through her personal assistant." I feel deflated.

"This is your last warning, Terry. Now get out and go do something useful for me."

I breathe deeply and win the battle against my rising anger, making sure not to slam the door on the way out. There must be a way to get to the bottom of this. I've been set up. I'm pretty sure of it. And I'm starting to think I know who did it.

Emily could gain a permanent position here by making me look like an idiot and getting me fired.

She also has access to everyone's office and files, including my own. It wouldn't take much to alter the Pellmont one for me. The woman pretending to be Lauren was probably her friend. And how hard would it have been to slip one of those little white pills of Emily's into my drink that day at the mansion and knock me flying? The little white pills that Emily did me a 'favor' by fixing me up with, keeping me horny and going for hours until I crash and burn...

Shit. It all makes sense. The bitch set me up from the start. I clench and unclench my hands, letting the tension and anger bleed away as I struggle to keep a cool head.

Miss I-don't-need-to-wear-panties thinks she can play me, eh? Well, I'll show her a thing or two about being a player.

Emily's office isn't far, so I walk to it and tap on her window. She tells me to come in. I find her behind her desk, which is mostly empty.

"What the hell do you actually do here?" I ask, my attention directed toward her barely used desk.

"I don't need to make a mess in order to look active. My work is up here and in there." She points to her head and then her computer. "Is that why you're here?"

"No, I need another one of those pills, remember? I got shit for sleep last night, and I don't think I'll make it through the day unless I receive some sort of miracle."

"So, you like to know me when you need me to be your whore and pharmacist? You think you can just come here, in my office, for all the sex and drugs

CHRIS HEINICKE

you need?"

"Please, Emily. I'll pay you for a damn pill if I have to. I'm not interested in sex, though. I'm already in enough trouble because of your panties left in my car."

She gets up from her swivel chair and walks my way. "You need me..." She laughs. "That's really cute, Terry. Okay, I'll give you the pill. Think of it as an 'I'm sorry' gift." Picking up her handbag from the floor, she smiles as she lowers herself in such a way that her skirt rides up her thighs. She opens her legs slightly, showing me she's still wearing no panties.

"Why are you doing that?" I ask her.

"Oh, come on, Terry. Most men want to see it and here you are complaining." She stands and walks over to me, grabs one of my hands, and places a white pill on my palm.

I pick it up with the forefinger and thumb of my other hand and stare at the little pill. "Got any water?" I ask her.

"Really? You're such a needy bitch today." She turns to her desk, reaching for the pitcher of filtered water she keeps there.

As soon as her gaze is off me, I quickly put my hand in my pocket and let the pill drop there. "Don't worry about it," I say and make my throat move, pretending I swallowed the pill. "Wow, that's better already. What the hell is in these things?"

"It's probably better you don't know." She walks past me and closes the blinds, then returns to her chair. "Please sit, Terry. I have a proposition for you, one that could benefit the two of us."

Reluctantly, I take my seat. "I'm curious, but if it means you and me having..."

"Get over yourself, Terry. I could go out there and get sex whenever I want. I don't have to rely on your nearly forty-year-old body to get it. I'm talking about a business deal—you and me going out on our own." She undoes the top button of her blouse. "You know, with my looks and your brains for business, we could do very well. You must have a list of contacts as long as your arm, and could you see male clients not wanting to work with me?" She lets her hair down to hang free, and I have to agree, any straight man with a heartbeat would probably sign her up within seconds.

"It's a big thing to leave the security of working for someone else, Em. I guess a free spirit like you doesn't have as much to risk as I do. Do you have a plan on paper or is this just a light bulb shining in your head?"

"Do you have to be so blunt? I'm picking you over any guy I know to take this chance. My gut tells me you're the guy with the balls for this type of thing. Will you at least think about it?"

"I can do that, Em, but I can't promise much more. I lost the Pellmont property to George, in case you haven't already heard."

"I hadn't heard that. What happened?"

I study her. She seems so sincere. And yet, I know that she knows exactly what happened since she's the one who set me up to lose the contract. "It's complicated," I say.

"I'm sorry. But...I could make you feel better,

Terry." She gets to her feet and starts unbuttoning her blouse from the bottom.

"What are you doing?" I ask.

"Celebrating the potential start of a great partnership. I know I said I could go out and get sex with whoever I want whenever I want, but why do that when we can do it in our office?"

"Sometimes, I think you must have some sort of split personality. I'm trying to fix my marriage and having sex with you is not a good start." I get up from my chair and head for the door.

"Oh, no, you don't!" she says and moves to block my path.

Standing between me and the door, she stares me down as she rips off her shirt. As I take a step to go around her, she jumps at me. Even with her small frame, there's enough weight thrown on top of me to knock me over onto my back. Nearly every bone in my body, especially my spine, feels the collision with the floor. Luckily, I prevent my head from smacking the tile, although I can't imagine my headache being any worse.

"Please, I just want to get out," I plead as I try to push her off me and sit up.

"I want you in me, Terry. Stop fighting," she slaps me on the side of the face.

I need to get away from her without hurting her physically. My cheek feels like someone hit it with a book. She straddles my waist and her hands go for my belt, and as I try to push them away, she slaps my other cheek.

"Let me go, you crazy bitch."

"You're supposed to want me, Terry. Stop fighting it." Keeping me pinned with her thighs, she lifts her skirt up over her hips, leaving her naked from the waist down. I buck sideways, trying to roll and knock her off, but she clings to me, using all that aerobic fitness she possesses.

And I can't seem to focus and gain an inch here no matter which way I turn. Maybe I did hit my head. My ears are ringing and vision slightly blurred.

"If you'll just get off of me, I'll do what you want," I say hoping she'll believe me.

Her fingers are undoing my belt and zipper. "Nice try, but...no." She squeezes my abdomen with her thighs, making me almost blackout.

"Why the fuck aren't you hard?" she asks as she puts her hand down the front of my briefs.

"Because I'm not fucking psycho like you. I don't get off on violence. *No means goddamn no!*"

Emily lets me go and stands. Pointing down at me, in only her bra and shoes, with her skirt hiked up around her waist, I can almost see her vomiting up her anger.

"So that's how it's going to be? Fine. You had your chance."

She turns away from me and dives at the window, pulling on the cord to open the blinds and deliberately smacking her head into the glass. I stand up as quickly as I can and pull up my pants.

Through the window, Phelps and George look straight at us.

"Emily, are you okay?" Phelps yells.

She bangs her fists on the window and cries out

loud, and I head for the door, not wanting to see what she's trying to do to herself. I grab the doorknob and find Roger standing in the doorway.

"What's going on?" Roger asks. His gaze takes in the scene: me doing up my pants and Emily's bare ass as she turns to Roger and tries to cover her nudity with her hands.

"That prick tried to force himself on me."

"Terry?" Roger stares at me as I hastily secure my belt and try to tuck in the ends of my shirt.

"The bitch is crazy, she—" Phelps and George come in, cutting me off.

"Are you okay, Emily?" George asks. He picks up her shirt and passes it to her.

Tears flow from her eyes. This bitch is a great actress, I'll give her that. But judging by the horrified looks the others are giving me, I'm in real trouble of them believing her act. "I managed to fight him off me, but he ripped my shirt and my panties."

"Lying slut! You weren't wearing any panties and you ripped your own shirt."

Roger puts a hand on my shoulder. "Calm down, Terry."

"No, I will not calm down, she's lying. She's set me up from the start."

"Dirty creepy *prick*. You tried to rape me." Emily points at me. She covers her face with her hands and sags against George, sobbing.

"You have ten minutes to pack your stuff and get out of here," Phelps says to me. His tone is icy cold and decisive.

"*What?* You're just gonna fire me without an

investigation or anything? This is bullshit."

"I know what I saw, Terry, and I wouldn't blame Emily for laying criminal charges. Now get the fuck out of here." Phelps points to the door.

Rage fills me like an overblown balloon. After the last few days of stress, my crumbling marriage, and now this...the unfairness of Emily getting away with her game because Phelps is a useless prick, I snap.

I swing my left fist around. It connects with Phelps's nose, hard. I grin as he staggers back, clutching his face.

Roger grabs me by the arms and pulls me from the office. My only regret is allowing him to do so before I can follow up with another punch to Phelps.

I'm laughing as we head down the hallway, aware it sounds a bit hysterical. I'm beyond caring what anyone thinks. They won't believe me anyway.

That bitch set me up good and now Phelps has got his wish to get rid of me. What a fucking perfect day.

"Terry, what have you done?" Roger lets me go as we reach my office.

"Emily did this, the conniving skank. The morning briefing when she dropped her pen and I picked it up, she had no panties on and proudly showed me. Then, when I came to her office, she tried to have her way with me. And when I turned her down, she attacked me. She says I'm the one trying to force sex on her, but it's the other way around, Rog. She's fucking crazy."

"Terry, what's in your back pocket?" Roger asks

me as I open my office door.

"What?" I feel both my rear pockets and locate something soft. Pulling it out of my pocket, I stare in disbelief. "You've got to be shitting me." *A pair of ripped women's underwear?* I drop the panties to the ground as if I've been burned.

"I didn't do this." I look at Roger, willing him to believe me. "Honest to God, I didn't do this. She planted them on me. Maybe when she was on top of me. I think I hit my head and blacked out for a second. I don't know."

I touch the back of my head and it feels tender enough I wince, but I can see by the look on his face that my best friend thinks I've lost it.

"I'm outta here, Terry. I can't get involved." Roger turns his back and charges down the hall, and I'm left alone to pack up my personal items.

Fuck that bitch. Fuck her all to hell.

I turn on the computer because I'll be damned if I'm not taking my client network with me. Opening my drawer, I find a USB stick to back everything up on.

My pens, pencils, and the dragon paperweight are first in the cardboard box I keep around for carrying files. There's a coffee mug with a laser printed photo of my kids on it from when Matilda was a newborn, a few books on salesmanship, and lastly, there's the wedding photo of Talissa and me.

The edges of the frame dig into the clamp-like grip of my hands as I stare into the eyes of a younger version of myself and my new bride. When I get home tonight, if I can capture just a fraction of the love sparkling in this snapshot of our magic day, I'll feel like my life can be rebuilt from the mess it is today.

Tears stream down my cheeks because deep down I know I've done damage to my marriage that would take a miracle to be forgiven, but never truly erased from our memories.

Phelps storms in. "You have two minutes, asshole." His gaze falls on the USB drive plugged into my computer. He lunges for the power cord and yanks it from the back of the desktop unit. "I don't think so, Terry."

I clench my fists to keep me from swinging them at him again. "I built this branch into the powerhouse it is today, you outdated pencil dick. You just watch me because one day, you'll be hearing my name out there, and you will rue this day."

He shakes his head. "Rue this day? You people crack me up when you say that."

I pick up my box and walk out of the office I've spent the last fifteen years working in—and I don't look back. I can feel everyone's eyes on me as I walk through the hall and then out the front door. I'm not sure what hurts more, the fact Emily got away with her game or the fact that the people I've worked closely with for so many years would so easily believe her.

I take a left and head toward the train station and home.

What the hell do I tell my wife?

* * * * *

SITTING ON THE train, going nowhere fast. The seats are filled with a myriad of faces, uniquely different, but all bearing the same dull gaze from the weight of living a life of mundane existence.

A sagging posture, a frown, a blank look. Are any of us truly happy with our lives, going to and from unfulfilling jobs just to make enough money to live in houses we'll spend our whole working life to pay off? And what about those who work hard in jobs that pay shit who'll never own anything? How many of us love what we do and do what we love?

Not many.

I think people do a lot of pretending.

Pretending to be happy. Pretending to be in love. Pretending to be normal, and real, and good.

Work hard and toe the line and you'll be successful in life.

What a crock of shit.

It's the liars that win, isn't it? The people who learn early on how to manipulate the system to give them what they want.

The rest of us are just fools for their game.

Fuuuuuck. I need to shut my brain off for a while. The more tired I am, the more my mind spins and I dwell on things that aren't helpful to be thinking.

The reality is my life is pretty fucked up right now and the blame lies fully with me. And turning off my brain won't escape it.

I look out the window as the train enters a dark tunnel. In the reflection behind mine is a woman sitting across the aisle. Her hair is long and blonde and as she turns to me and her eyes catch mine, an evil grin spreads across her lips.

Heart racing, I spin my head to the left and search the seats...but there is no sign of her. My mind's playing tricks on me. Seeing things that aren't there. Invisible fears I'm ill-equipped at this moment to battle.

I close my eyes and lean my head against the seat, allowing the random images I can't filter out to dance in my mud-clouded mind. My body aches from Emily's beating, and my sore knuckles are screaming that they haven't had a fistfight since my teens, and with good reason.

The train jolts and jiggles in its endless rhythm, and, for a moment, I manage to sleep.

* * * * *

IT'S ONLY EARLY in the afternoon when the train reaches the end of the line, and a random stranger wakes me. Although I've slept, I don't remember any dreams, which is probably a mercy. My watch indicates that two hours have passed since I first boarded this train.

The box is still tucked under my right arm on the seat and nothing has fallen out or been stolen. I head for the nearest door, and on doing so, I glimpse familiar buildings only a half-hour walk to my home.

A police car drives by, reminding me of Hannah, and I wonder if she's seen the message I left for her in the chat program.

I check my phone for calls from Talissa and find a text message from an unknown sender that reads, 'Bad day at the office?'

The details say it was sent an hour ago, so there's no wonder I didn't hear it as I slept on the train.

"Time to use your balls," I say aloud to myself, and from the list of options, I click on 'call.' Within a second, a beep repeats, which tells me I won't be getting through to the caller.

The trip to my house is long, but the walk has been good. I could have taken a cab, but the air has helped clear my head.

Talissa's car is out front. I have no choice but to face the music now. I steel myself as I make my way up the path to the front door and fish through my pocket for the key. The door opens before I can even put it into the lock.

Talissa stares at me, her hand on the doorknob. "What the hell happened today?"

I suck in a deep breath. "It's complicated. I'm tired, and my life is screwed. If someone offered to drive over me in a truck, I'd lie on the road in front of them. I've messed up badly, Talissa, in more ways than you can fathom, but I need you in my life. I need to see your face each day when I wake in the morning and to hear the kids laughing at the table each breakfast and dinner. I need to feel that long black hair of yours through my fingers, your soft mouth on mine, and your beautiful womanly curves curled against me. My body aches to get close to you again, to be inside you, and to be one with your soul."

Talissa stares at me in silence, her pale face

stricken, and for the first time since she got home yesterday, I see a tear gather in her eye. It spills over her lashes and down her cheek.

I reach to wipe it away for her.

She smacks my hand and walks away from me.

I feel like a stranger. As if I'm further away from her than I was before we even met.

Could anybody blame her? She doesn't know the full truth yet, but she may as well. If she's going to go on hating me, she needs to know why. I'm shaking at the thought of spilling it all out. But she deserves the truth.

"Talissa," I call out, heading for the kitchen. If it's like any other day, she's probably already preparing the night's meal.

"What, Terry?" She looks up at me as her knife continues slicing at the chicken breasts. A few small bowls of various ingredients line the counter, filling the kitchen with the aroma of garlic and other herbs.

"You need to know everything I've done. I'm not proud of it, and if you tell me to get out, I will. Not because I want to, but because you deserve more than this. I have been unfaithful."

"That's not exactly a breaking news headline, is it, Terry?"

I shake my head. "The first woman was the blonde I work with, Emily, the one who left her panties in my car. We hadn't done it at that point, yet, and I think she left them there on purpose so you would find them. The next day, Friday, I slept with a woman who I thought was Lauren Pellmont."

She snorts. "If you ever kept up with what was

going on in this city you would know the real Mrs. Pellmont is twice your age."

"So, I've heard but it doesn't take away the fact I was unfaithful with a woman and I have no clue as to who she even is."

"Is that all?"

"No. On Saturday, I was arrested here and taken away by the police handcuffed and nearly naked."

"Yes, Mrs. Harris next door asked what the hell happened and smiled at me when discussing how you were only in your briefs. That was kinda disgusting."

"Well, I saw the lady cop's tits, too. I didn't have sex with her though." *Even though I wanted to.*

"Geez, Terry. Is there anyone you haven't had sex with, besides the babysitter?"

"Well, that was Sunday..."

"*Oh, my God.* No wonder she hasn't been back." She slams the knife down on the cutting board and slaps me in the face. "You realize she's only seventeen, don't you?"

"Yes, you told me that yesterday and I threw up. Talissa, she told me she was twenty-one."

She slaps my other cheek. "And you thought that was a green light to have sex with her? I guess she brought the pot around?"

"And the ciders. How could she have them if she's underage?"

"A pretty girl like her? Anyone would happily buy them for her. Or a fake ID. Surely, you had a way to get booze before you turned eighteen."

"And today I got fired because of Emily. She

tried to force me to have sex with her, and when I didn't comply, she started hitting me then opened the blinds to the office and made it look like I had attacked her. Phelps saw what he needed to see and told me to pack my stuff. And then I punched him. I'm unemployed, I've lied and cheated on you numerous times, and pretty much the whole neighborhood has seen me nearly naked. I'm a ruined man."

"Terry, you're not a ruined man, you're a cu—"

Isaac walks in, cutting her off. "Mommy, Daddy, please stop fighting."

Talissa glares at me, then turns back to our son and embraces him.

* * * * *

I SHUT MYSELF in the study and turn the computer on. First thing I do is check my emails. I filter through the ones I don't intend to read and delete them instantly. There's one from Phelps Brothers Real Estate saying an official notice of separation will be sent by courier ASAP. Then there are a couple from my brother and one from my sister talking about getting together with Mom and Dad.

But the one that gets my attention is the one posted a minute ago from BluesGirl88.

'I need to see you online ASAP.'

The last thing I want is a squabble with her, but if it gets me closer to a resolution with what's going on, I need to do it. I load the chat program and there she is waiting for me, inviting me to a private chat before I can even think to do anything else. Accepting, I take a quick peek at my other contacts—none of them are online, and Hannah hasn't seen the message I left yet, but then it is only three p.m. and she's probably busy doing cop things.

The blues club scene loads where I first met BluesGirl.

BluesGirl88: "So here we are, where it all began nearly a week ago."

Terry25: "If I knew then what I know now, I never would have gone into this chat program. I've lost my job and I've lost my wife, and come tomorrow, I'm going for a long drive to do the world a favor and end it all."

BluesGirl88: "If you want my sympathy it's not going to happen. If you want me to say 'no, don't do it' then you'll be sorely disappointed. You're the one who took it too far, who thought he could take what he did in 3DDreamChat into the real world and go fucking everyone without consequence. You had it all, Terry—the beautiful wife, two beautiful children, and a successful career—and you squandered it all. You can sit there and blame me, but you know it's all your fault."

Terry25: "Yes, it is my fault, but why the hell have you been stalking me?"

BluesGirl88: "I thought if I could keep you occupied on DreamChat, you'd be too occupied to have sex with real women who aren't your wife."

I feel like every time I chat with her I'm talking to someone different. I repeat those two words over and over—*someone different.*
Holy shit!

Terry25: "I've worked it out, BluesGirl. You're a multi-operated avatar. That's why you can't be tracked down, because you move between locations when someone else takes over you. You're four people in one, and you're all in this together to fuck me up."

BluesGirl88: "I'm not sure I like what you're suggesting, Terry."

Terry25: "So, who are you now? Are you Emily? Or Lauren? Or Brittany?"

Or even Hannah, I add mentally. I don't like that thought, and the way it makes my heart twist, but my dealings with her have been unusual too. And she kept telling me to not trust anyone. Maybe she means even her.

BluesGirl88: "You couldn't be any more wrong if you tried, Terry. I know those women you speak of, and how you fucked each and every one of them, but none of them are me. I would love to tell you who I am, just to see the look on your face."

Terry25: "Why not, then? Why can't we meet somewhere public and have a real face to face discussion? Why come on here each day and play around when we could have something real and fantastic and possibly have a future together? Don't you want to take that plunge?"

BluesGirl88: "I don't think we'll ever be ready for that, Terry."

Terry25: "I need to know how you know so much about me, while I know nothing about the real you. You have me by the balls, BluesGirl, and I'm helpless."

BluesGirl88: "You need to get away, Terry. Come tomorrow, you won't be safe where you are, and neither are your wife and kids."

I stare at the threatening message, icy fear running down my spine.

Terry25: "Who's after me, BluesGirl?"

BluesGirl88: "The most dangerous bitch on the planet, and if you're anywhere near as smart as you think you are, you'll work it out soon before it's too late. It's been great, Terry, but we can never communicate again. **Please be safe, and in my own weird way, I love you."**

And with that, she's gone. I should feel relieved she's ended our online connection, but I'm not.

Can I be sure it really is over? If she has my email address and phone number, how can I ever feel a hundred percent secure she will leave me alone?

There's a sex chat psycho murdering people on the internet. I'm in danger. And if it's not BluesGirl88 after me, then who the hell would it be?

Emily, the bitch who leaves her undies where other people can find them, rather than wear them herself? She's hot for me one minute, then a cold, calculating psycho the next. And I'm pretty sure she's been setting me up to sabotage my career since the day we met.

Or maybe Lauren, or whatever the hell her real name is. Why impersonate a widow to have sex with me? Emily must have paid her well for that gig. Unless someone else was behind it.

Or Hannah—the cute policewoman who I feel inexplicably drawn to, but who insists I should watch who I trust.

And then there's Brittany, the lying little skank who told me she's four years older than she really is. She also seemed quite competent with a kitchen knife.

Could be any of them, or all. Or someone else completely different. How the hell am I supposed to know what's real and what isn't anymore? My life stopped making sense a week ago.

Talissa and I need to put our problems aside, go to the police together, and get protection. If it's me that some psycho wants, I can find a remote place to wait out the storm, while my wife and kids seek refuge at her family's place under surveillance.

I leave the study in search of Talissa, only to find her heading my way down the hall. Given her scowl, she isn't any less angry than before she sent me from the kitchen, maybe even more.

"I just got off the phone with the police. They'll be around in the morning. They haven't told me why, but they want us to all stay put here for the time being. What's going on, Terry?"

"I think it has a lot to do with those women I told you about. I know it sounds crazy, but I think they're working together to set me up and hurt me pretty bad, and perhaps you and the kids. I hope not, but I can't be sure. I was warned to not trust anybody. I'm not even sure I can trust the police right now. Do you still have your gun?"

"Yes, and I can still hit a tin can from a hundred yards."

Talissa had once been a champion sports shooter in her early twenties, and I know, if she needs to, she'll use it. I tell her about the chats I've had with BluesGirl88, the whole lot, including the animated sex and violence and the threats she's made.

"Gee, Terry, you really know how to pick them, don't you? You'd better never go near a computer ever again." She looks down at her feet and shakes her head, then puts her hands on her hips and looks me in the eye. "This is what we're going to do... I will sleep on the floor outside the bedroom after we put the kids in the bed. I want you in the middle of them and you better not leave the bedroom unless I tell you it's safe, because I'll be sleeping with the damn gun under my pillow and will use it on anything in the dark that moves. Someone needs to protect our family." The look in her eyes is withering and full of the accusation and resentment in her tone. "You really think someone's out to get you, even the police?"

"Yes, I do." I'm not sure about the police, but the rest fits, and I wish I could tell her something different.

"Let's just get through tonight then. Tomorrow we'll figure out what to do next."

As I watch her walk away toward the kitchen, I wish I could rewrite the whole past week. I might deserve whatever punishment is coming, but my family is innocent and doesn't deserve the mess we're all in.

What kind of a father am I to have brought this onto them?

CHAPTER 10

DAY 9

IT'S THE EARLY hours of the morning, and my son and daughter are fast asleep on either side of me. Despite my extreme tiredness, I haven't been able to close my eyes, let alone get a wink of sleep. Every sound I hear puts me on edge, be it a moth hitting the window screen or a car driving by. Sometimes, I think I hear voices outside: Emily, Lauren or Brittany, or even Hannah. But it's just my imagination, tricks my mind is playing on me brought on by the last few days' madness.

The bedroom door creaks open.

My heart nearly jumps out of my chest before I recognize the familiar silhouette of Talissa. She silently signals for me to come out of the room with her.

I maneuver out of bed like a soldier stepping through a minefield, one wrong move or a single touch of an unseen limb and I'll set off a child to immediately awaken.

Once I'm upright, and out of the wake-up danger

zone, I pad across the carpet and through the open door.

Closing it behind me, Talissa grabs my hand and guides me through the dark to the living room where she has set herself up in a makeshift bed constructed of quilts, blankets, and a few pillows.

"You haven't slept at all either, have you?" I ask her.

"No. Not a wink. I don't think I can tonight."

She looks like an angel in the darkness in her white tee and white panties, albeit an angel built to sin like the devil. A she-devil. Her pistol is strapped to a holster on her thigh. She's ready to do anything to protect her family, and at this moment, I've never seen anything sexier.

She unstraps her gun and places it onto a nearby lamp table. "I want you to know I don't hate you for what you've done. I don't love you for it, and I wish you'd been stronger and not done it. But I don't hate you."

"You don't?" I stare at her, my heart racing. I'm not sure if I deserve her forgiveness in any way shape or form. *I* hate me right now for the harm I've brought our family. And she definitely should not only hate me right now, she should also be tossing my ass out the door and letting me suffer whatever consequences come my way.

Instead, here she is in the uncertain light of the lounge, telling me she doesn't hate me in the room where I repeatedly had sex with the babysitter not even forty-eight hours earlier.

"I don't deserve this," I whisper.

"We've all done things we're not proud of. No one is innocent." She looks down at the floor and shakes her head. After a moment, she looks at me again. "But you're the father of my children and a good one at that. At least you are when your attention is on them rather than blonde sluts who want to fuck you for reasons only known to them and me right now." I don't need to see her frown to know it's there. I can hear her disapproval loud and clear, and I don't blame her. "I don't know what's going to happen now. We could all be on the run tomorrow, or you could be in jail or...or even killed. And I don't want to leave it like this." She touches my cheek with her fingers. "I want you to fuck me, Terry. Like you fucked those other girls. You gave them what belonged to me and I want it back right now. Not just for old times' sake, but because you owe it to me. It might not make sense to you or anyone else, but I need this. I need you. And I want you to fuck me like I'm the only woman you've ever loved or wanted."

"Talissa..."

"Don't speak," she lifts her shirt over her head, and those big breasts of hers stare back at me like a pair of long-lost friends. She pulls her panties down to her knees and gravity does the rest, allowing them to hit the floor as she wriggles out of them, which, of course, makes her breasts sway.

God, she's beautiful. Fit and lush. Pointy nipples. Strong thighs. Closing the gap between us, she pulls my boxer shorts down to the ground, and kisses me like it's the last kiss we'll ever share. There is no hesitancy. She's almost rough as her lips press against mine, demanding what she needs from me.

The hunger in me rises, and it doesn't take long before we're on the makeshift bed, touching each other, so desperate to get close to each other we're shaking. And within a few minutes, we're screwing like we've overdosed on Emily's little white pills.

* * * * *

I WAKE FEELING more rested than I have in weeks. The sleep I fell into after we had sex felt incredible, even though I've only squeezed in four hours of it. I'm still tired, but there's no time for a sleep-in as the early rays of the morning sun glare through the living room windows.

We're covered only with a sheet, so I pat around the floor looking for my boxers. Talissa stirs and soon sits up, searching the floor for her bra and panties. Looking at the closed expression on her face, I can't help feeling things are back to how they were before we had sex in the early hours of the morning. Did she mean it? Or does she truly hate me?

"We should check on the kids," she says, as she locates her items of clothing and promptly puts them on.

"We should head to my parents' place for a few days until this thing blows over."

"I'm not running, Terry. I'm staying here with the kids. If Emily really is coming for you, why should I feel unsafe? You go to your parents' place." She straps her gun in place. "I can take care of myself and my children."

There's a hardness in her tone that sounds very final. *Herself and her children...but not me.* I frown. I'm thinking now that last night was just a goodbye fuck or something and the positivity I woke with is quickly changing into a sourness I can taste. "But what if she uses all of you to get to me? If anything happens to any of you, how bad do you think I'll feel?"

Matilda comes bursting into the living room. "Is Brittany coming today? I miss her."

I put my arms out and allow her to dive into my embrace. "I'm sorry. I don't think she's coming back." I fight back a tear and tighten my embrace.

"I love you, Daddy," she says. Now I've lost the fight against the tears. Talissa leaves the room, and a couple of minutes later, I can hear the water of the shower running. Matilda still hasn't let go, and I don't want her to. Then she looks at my face. "Why are you crying, Daddy?"

There are too many reasons to name them all to her, but I have to pick something. "Daddy has to go for a drive, and he might...be gone a long time. But don't forget I'll always love you and your brother, and you can carry that in your heart."

"But why, Daddy?" Her eyes water and I don't think I can take any more of this.

"Daddy has to get dressed, sweetheart. I won't be long. And then we'll make some of your favorite pancakes for breakfast."

Matilda nods, seeming happy with that idea, and relaxes her embrace on me. I walk to the bedroom and find some clothes to change into after I take a shower. Talissa is quick as always in the shower, and the water is turned off already. Isaac is still in a deep slumber, and as usual, no amount of noise wakes him until he's ready to be woken.

Walking into our little bathroom, I find Talissa wrapped in a towel, standing outside the shower cubicle, but she doesn't smile at me as I strip off next to her and get under the showerhead. I guess the sex hasn't repaired much of the bad feelings she has for me after all.

"Don't be long," she says, walking away from the bathroom, leaving me to bask under the massaging jets of water hitting my back. Barely a minute passes when I hear the doorbell.

I turn the water off and try to dry myself with a towel in world record time, but the water doesn't seem to want to leave my body as quickly as I would like. Hanging the towel on the hook, I grab the clothes I threw on the bed next to the sleeping figure of my son and start to dress.

"The police are here, Terry," Talissa says. "They want to speak to you urgently."

"Okay," I answer, and she's gone before I get the second syllable out. I throw on the rest of my clothes and walk to the front door. Hannah and Ed are there, waiting for me.

I can't help staring at Hannah. I hadn't expected to see her again after she'd been transferred to a different case. But here she is with her hair pulled back and her police cap and uniform on that tells me she's Officer Hall not Detective Hall at the moment.

Her expression is serious as she studies me for a quick second and glances furtively around the room.

"Terry, can you step outside with us please?" It sounds like a question, but Ed's tone leaves no room for choice.

With a glance toward the kitchen where I can hear my family organizing breakfast, I follow the officers outside onto my front landing and close the door behind me.

"What's going on?" I fold my arms across my chest and study Hannah and Ed, trying to read their poker-faced stares. I can't imagine it's anything good if they are here in person, especially after the last time they graced my door like this with their questioning. "Have you caught the online killer?"

Ed frowns. "The situation has become serious. Your boss, Harold Phelps, has been found dead in his home. A knife, which we presume to be the weapon used to inflict the fatal wound, was left at the scene for us to find. No prints. We know you argued with him and were recently dismissed from your job. However, given the timeline of events, and the fact surveillance reports you were at home with your family at the time of death, we do not believe you are involved." Ed shows me a photo of the brutal murder, which halts the glib comment that's forming in my mind to ask if they found any panties by the body.

I grimace at the sight of Phelps' face with his eye still open and blood surrounding the protruding weapon. It takes me a moment to form any words. "Is this normal to show a non-suspect this sort of thing?"

"There's something else," Hannah says and passes me another photo. It's a picture of Brittany lying face-up on the side of the road with a bullet hole in her chest, wearing the same clothes she wore at my place on Sunday.

My stomach threatens to rise. And then it stops threatening and lurches upward. "Oh, shit." I cover my mouth and barely make it to the bushes on the left of the garden path. I empty the contents of my stomach for a good couple of minutes, but I can't empty the images from my mind. Brittany, so young and beautiful...now dead. Phelps, dead.

Who's next?

I wash my face under the garden hose and try to regain some composure before turning back to talk to the cops. They haven't moved from their spots, and Hannah is doing a great job of treating me like a stranger today.

"Sorry for the disturbing images, but you need to know what you're up against, Terry," Ed says, "and why it's imperative we move you to safety immediately."

"What about my family?"

"They will be protected as well, but we believe it best for you to go to separate safe houses for now."

I nod. If I'm about to die by some crazy online stalker, I don't want my family anywhere around. The image of Talissa with her gun last night, ready to do whatever it takes to protect her family settles in my mind. She shouldn't need to do that. It's my fault that this has happened. And it should be me to end it.

I suck in a long breath. "I have somewhere I can go that's remote. My family's farm. It's a good open spot to draw out the stalker if that's what you want. I'll be bait. Just make sure you catch this bastard."

Hannah lets out a sound like a choked gasp, but when I look at her, her expression is a blank mask. No safe house with her this time. I need to do this my way.

"You need to be aware of the danger you're placing yourself in. This killer means business and is intending to win," Ed says.

"I understand."

Ed nods. "We'll track your movements by your phone and follow you from a safe distance. You won't be alone."

I nod.

"We'll have a squad in place to cover you as well as your family, in case the killer tries to harm either you or them. The important thing is that everyone will be kept safe. But remember, don't trust anyone," Hannah adds.

The warning lingers in the air as I glance at the house. "Talissa knows where I'm going, but I don't want her coming out to the farm with the kids. I have to do this myself. Please tell Talissa I love her." I turn and run to my car. If I see my kids right now, leaving will be even harder. I'll call them all later once I've reached the farm. I don't want them to worry, but I can't risk them trying to stop me from going now.

Ed follows me and I pause just outside my vehicle.

CHRIS HEINICKE

"Put this tracker on your phone. It will allow us to monitor your calls as well." He holds out a small device that looks like a memory card.

As I do as asked, I glance at Hannah, who stares straight back at me with that same blank expression that shows nothing of what she might be feeling.

Then, with one last look at the house, I get inside the car and drive away.

* * * * *

THE TRIP TO Salinas Valley takes me a little under two hours until I arrive at the turn-off for my parents' old farm. Growing up here, I used to complain about it being five miles to the nearest neighbor and an hour from the outskirts of the city. But I know the place like the back of my hand, having lived here until my late teens, and the remote location is the perfect place to draw my stalker to and away from my wife and kids. If it comes to a confrontation here that the police can't handle, at least the only casualty will be me. The house itself hasn't been lived in for a few years since my parents decided to downsize, but the property and farmland is still maintained due to my parents leasing it out.

Croplands fill the horizon as far as the eye can see. A bird's eye view would be breathtaking given the patchwork of colors from the various fruits and vegetables growing in the supple earth. The driveway consists of crushed gravel and stretches for a half mile from the road, and as I drive along it toward the house, hearing the familiar crunch of stones as the tires pass over it, I feel like I am coming home.

The old brick house stands solid as if untouched by time; a tribute to the strength of the building itself, and in our family unit, too. But, turning past the front of the house, I nearly slam on the breaks. Three vehicles are parked in the driveway. I immediately recognize my father's old station wagon, but there is also a crimson-colored sedan and a charcoal grey SUV.

What the hell?

I find a patch of lawn to park in and hurriedly get out and head to the front door.

"Dad?" I call out as I ascend the wooden steps. My mother, father, brother, and sister appear at the top of the landing a second later. I smile, feeling both surprised and annoyed to see them here, and they seem just as annoyed to see me.

"Terry, what the hell have you done, boy?" my father asks in the tone I know from childhood means I'm in for an ass-whooping.

I freeze mid-step and stare at each of them, trying to process their angry expressions, and why the hell are they here now? As I turn to my mother, she slaps my face.

"What was that for?" I ask, touching my fingers to my stinging cheek and taking a step back.

"Talissa is the nicest woman you could meet and what do you do? You break her heart," Mom says.

"You went back to your old ways, Terry?" my brother, Joe, asks.

"Hey, look, I didn't come here for some kind of

damned intervention or whatever the hell this is. There's a dangerous psycho after me. I thought this place would be empty. I don't know why you chose today for this reunion, but you really need to go."

"Yes, we were told that by the police. But whether you're a dick or not, we stick together no matter what." My sister, Janet, holds a pump-action shotgun by the barrel and raises it into the air for me to see. I know she knows how to use it. Rifles and shotguns are common on the farm. We quite often used them to scare birds and rodents away from the crops that were the financial blood of our lives. None of us were crack shots, but we could scare the crap out of anything that moved with a single shot in the air.

"The police called you?"

"And Talissa," Mom says.

"You really screwed things up, Terry," Joe says. "Why didn't you tell us you were in trouble?"

I glance at my family, each of them angry and disappointed in me, but family just the same. "You really came here to help me?"

Joe shakes his head. "Yeah. Kinda wondering why now that I'm staring at your stupid face."

I ignore his barb. "If any of you get hurt, I'll never forgive myself. Please, just go, or at least stay hidden. The police are sending a squad to take care of things."

"What about Talissa and the kids?" Mom asks.

"The cops are keeping watch on our place until this blows over."

Dad nods. "Is it really that serious, son?" He may

be in his seventies, but he's as wiry and sharp as ever.
I'd hate to be on the receiving end of a rifle pointed
at me if it's in his hands.

"Yes."

He nods decisively. "Then we're staying."

I don't know if I should feel happy or sad about
that, but I know that it's impossible to argue with my
dad once he's used that stubborn Aussie, end-of-
discussion tone.

My phone beeps, indicating an incoming
message. When I grew up here, there were no such
things as mobile phones or the internet, and as far
as I know, the cell reception is still spotty at best. I
pull out my phone and see several text messages
from various people. One stands out from a number
neither my phone nor I recognize, and as I open it,
the hairs on the back of my neck stand up.

**Unknown Caller: Dear Terry, please tell Talissa I'm
ok and can babysit again tomorrow. I miss you and your
beautiful cock.**

I stare at the message, trying to make sense of it.
Is it a joke? Is someone messing with me? If it's a
prank, it's a sick one. The tone of the message
sounds very like Brittany. Who else would know she
liked my cock? But geez, if Brittany's alive, who the
hell was in that photo the cops showed me?

"You okay, son?" my dad asks.

"This doesn't make sense," I murmur under my
breath, ignoring everyone else. I turn my back on my
family and walk back down the steps. I need to call

my wife and see if she's heard from Brittany as well. I take the tracking chip out of my phone and try the number to our home. I pace back and forth by the steps while it rings several times before my wife picks up.

"Talissa. I know this isn't going to make any sense, but have you heard from Brittany today?"

"What? No. After you left, those two cops told me she'd been found shot dead. Thanks for leaving without a goodbye, by the way."

I ignore the irritation in her voice. I don't have time for arguing about things. "I just got a message from Brittany. I think she's alive. And I think those two cops lied to me." If the photo of Brittany was fake, then I've been set up. "I'm not sure who to trust anymore, but something isn't right. You need to get the kids out of there now and come to the farm." Nowhere is safe anymore, but the only way I can be sure to protect them now is if all my family are together.

"Oh, my goodness. I thought there was something up with that bitchy blonde cop. She seemed very insistent that I stay here instead of contacting you about it. Okay, Terry, I'll try to find a way. Stay safe."

It was a short and sharp call, but long enough to get things moving. Why the photo of someone who's not the babysitter? It's looking more certain that Hannah's the dangerous person I've been warned about, along with her partner, Ed.

"Son, is everything okay?" Mom asks.

"For now, yes. Maybe. Okay, not really. But I

need to do some things on my phone, find out some things." I look at the ring of faces watching me, now filled with concern. "Just be prepared for anything. I'm not sure I trust the police. And I don't know what might be coming."

My mother nods. "Okay, son. No matter what has happened, you know we still love you." She comes over and gives me a big hug. I hold on for a few seconds longer than normal. Despite the obvious danger it puts them in, I'm glad they're here.

My sister pats the barrel of her shotgun and nods at me before following my mother inside. They've got my back, no matter what. And considering the circumstances, I'm beyond glad.

The speed of the internet on my phone out here on the farm is pretty slow, but the first search I type in is of Hannah's name. I wait the required several seconds for the results to load. There're a few matches on her name, mostly web page articles about her being a spokeswoman on behalf of the police force on domestic violence. There's her social media profile and a police cadet recruitment video advertisement showing her and a few other young cadets her age. So, it looks like she's a real cop, at least.

I go to her profile page on the social media site and put in a friend request to her. Progress is so slow out here when trying to navigate the internet on my mobile phone, especially compared to the fast connection I have in my home in the suburbs. But given it's all just a waiting game now, it doesn't really matter, and there's nothing I can do but have faith that Talissa can get away with the kids.

I could call the police station and check if what Ed and Hannah have been telling me is the truth. But if corruption exists, how deep does it go? Calling the station could be more risk than it's worth until I know more.

Reading web pages isn't the easiest task to do on a phone either, and the small screen makes me wonder if I'm getting to the age of requiring reading glasses. But as I go through each article about Hannah, there's nothing to help me learn more about her than I already know. A couple of the clippings have her pretty, smiling face in them, and once again, I'm reminded of the afternoon spent together when I saw more than her face. Just looking at her picture makes me feel the safe closeness between us that I thought was so real. Can I have been so wrong about Hannah? Can she be the psycho killer? Are my instincts that off?

I'm hoping not, but something doesn't seem right about everything that's been happening for the past week or so.

How did my life get so damn crazy?

My family goes about preparing a cooked lunch. Nothing ever gets in the way of food when it comes to this lot; it's always been that way. When things go wrong, they cook. When things go well, they cook. Everything centers around a family meal and my mother's cooking, no matter what. Should we be figuring out possible defense strategies in case the psycho stalker shows up? Most definitely. But I don't even bother suggesting it, knowing exactly how offended my mother will be if we don't have her 'dinner fixings' first. Going into battle on an empty stomach just isn't in the game plan, ever.

"You're spending an awfully long time on that phone, son. Everything will be alright. We've got this," Dad calls out to me from the porch.

I smile at the reassuring sound of his voice. Even after all these years of living in America he still has a faint Australian accent, but I wish I shared his confidence right now. "Just doing some more research on a possible threat. I won't be much longer."

He takes a seat right next to me on the steps. "I know how it feels to do wrong," he practically whispers down my ear, "the male of a species wants to spread his seed far and wide, and it's a natural part of our gender. The one thing separating us from the animals though is that we know right from wrong and putting value in our relationships." He glances at the closed door of the house then studies me. "Back when you were only a few months old, and we decided you were the last of the children we would have, I was on a business trip with a couple of other work colleagues. They were both single, and instead of just having dinner with these two crazy men like I would any other trip, I went out for drinks with them afterward."

This is a revelation. "I thought you were always a farmer, Dad. Didn't you and mum buy this place when you moved from Australia?"

"I'll get to that." He keeps his voice low. "So, I'm hanging with these guys and we start on beer, then progress to heavier stuff like scotch and bourbon, and then a few tequila slammers. By this stage, we're all pretty much charged up and out of control. Then into the bar walks these three beautiful women—one blonde, one redhead, and the finest one of all had jet black hair. My head kept telling me to go back to the room and get to bed, but my *you-know-what* had other ideas. The woman with black hair had her eye on me as all six of us were up on the dance floor, and before I knew her name, she danced right up close to me. An hour later, I parked my car in a garage it shouldn't have been parked in."

"Oh, shit. Really?"

"Hey, your brother and sister don't know, but the guilt tore me to bits until I told your mother, and then she nearly tore me to bits. She should have left me, but she stuck it out with me. We haven't looked back since, and I haven't so much as looked at another woman." He pats me on the shoulder. "And after that experience, I quit my job as a buyer for the property development group I was working for and bought this here farm."

"Well, I don't know what to say, Dad, but what I did was worse."

"The principle's the same, son. We both did wrong and regret what we did. If Talissa can see the man you truly are, then she'll take you back. She won't ever trust you again, but she'll still love you."

"So Talissa told you and Mom everything that happened?"

"Yes. Well, she spoke to your mother last night anyway, and from what I could make out, it was quite a lengthy chat. I can't say we weren't disappointed in you, but we were able to empathize with her, from both sides of the sins you committed."

I close my eyes. It's nice to know they can forgive me, but I can't forgive myself. "Thanks, Dad. I hope you're right."

He gets up from his chair and joins the others. It has been about a half a year since we were all together and in the same room. The house hasn't had a tenant in a year or so, but the electricity and water are still hooked up thanks to the generator, and it's been kept up. And it still holds many memories.

I watch them for a few minutes, having a dig at each other and laughing and smiling as they smack each other with the dust shrouds they pull off the furnishings. I think I am the odd one out in my family. I want them to leave. They shouldn't be here if the stalker arrives. None of them are responsible for my sins. But with guns at the ready, we can get through this together.

I continue my research, putting the name Emily Philips through the search engine. The connection speed is so slow I wait a whole minute just to be presented with 'no results match your inquiry.'

Really? No Emily Philips, *at all*? How is that even possible? Maybe the connection is so bad it timed out before finding anything. I type in the name Lauren Pellmont, and after the same slow waiting time, I'm presented with a heap of results about the old widow. There's no need to click on a single one of them. I learned yesterday, the blonde I had sex with is not the woman she told me she was.

This just leaves Brittany the babysitter who may or may not be alive, and not remembering her last name or wanting to trouble Talissa for it, I don't even begin to try to search for her. I can't work out what the deal is with the photo of her the cops showed me. Seeing the text message from her just throws everything up in the air again. Maybe she is dead, and the murderer took her phone and contacted me. That makes sense. It probably was the stalker.

But how am I supposed to know what's truth and a lie anymore?

Mom walks over to me, the loving smile I've sought comfort in many times as a boy beaming from her face. And now I feel like that young, scared boy again, lying awake at night and frightened by the strange sounds coming from the fields surrounding us. She would always tell me everything was okay, and I could sleep in peace and not have to be afraid.

"I'm sorry, Mom. I've done so much bad in the last week."

She puts her arm around me. "I don't like what you've done, but you're still my baby boy. I could never stop loving you. You will sort this out with your wife. It might not happen in a day, or even a week or month, but you have the rest of your life to fix this as best as you can. I love you, Terence."

Damn it, I can't stop the tears from falling. My mother pulls me in close, and I soon feel her tears on me. The room is quiet except for the others serving the midday meal onto plates. It smells great—roast chicken with baked vegetables. Then to top it off, the overwhelming smells of my brother's secret recipe gravy. I look at the time and realize I've spent the best part of two hours on my phone, and it's running out of charge.

"Come and get it!" Dad yells out.

I walk toward the dining table, and we all pause as the hum of a car engine and the sound of the stone driveway crunching beneath rolling tires becomes audible. Dad, my brother, and sister scuttle around and grab their weapons, while my mother and I get down low and seek the solid protection of the brick wall below the bottom of a large window.

The crunching sound of stone gets closer, and with its approach, I recognize the familiar car motor as it nears. "It's just Talissa, everyone," I call out. I stand and watch through the window, relieved to see the face of my dear wife behind the wheel of the white sedan. The car parks near the front of the house. The others stand down and relax again as I run outside to greet my wife.

The kids get out of the car a few seconds before Talissa and run up with outstretched arms toward me. "Dad!" they both shout in unison.

I get down to my knees and accept their embraces, hugging each of them tightly as if they are my lifeline, which they are. I'm shaking with relief to see them. Talissa slides out the driver's seat. She's neither smiling nor looking angry as she makes her way toward me and the kids.

"Talissa, how did you make the slip?"

"I didn't need to. They let me go and said they'd follow me out here. They kept their distance, but I don't think they'll be far away."

"I don't trust them. So much of this doesn't feel right. I think Hannah's in on something with Emily, the fake Lauren Pellmont, and Brittany. They all seduced me for a reason, but I can't work out why the hell they would all do this."

"Well, Terry, you're the one who fucked those women. So, if you believe they're after you, then it's your fault. But I wasn't about to let you come out here by yourself without protection, so I called your folks last night. They needed to know the whole story, and despite everything that's happened, I don't want them to think less of their son."

"Come inside. Mom has made her usual meal and we're about to eat." I place my hand on her arm to guide her, but she shakes me off.

"No, Terry, I don't think so. I'm waiting to be picked up, actually. I'll be leaving for a few days. I just wanted to drop Matilda and Isaac off. They are your responsibility for the next few days, possibly weeks, while I go away and think about what I want to do."

"You're leaving?" I stare at her for a long second. "I can't blame you for wanting to leave me, but how can you leave the kids when it's not safe?" This is a far cry from the Talissa who slept with a gun at the ready last night, waiting to kill whoever might harm her family.

"Terry, nothing is going to happen while your gun-happy family is here. And if whoever is stalking you does show up, it's you they are after, not the children." She presses her hands together in front of her.

"Isaac, Matilda, please run inside and say hi to Grandma and Grandpa," I say to them. I watch them run up the steps to my waiting parents, then I turn back to my wife. "You're really going?"

"Yes."

"Do the kids know?"

"No. That's for you to explain."

She's acting so cold, I'm not sure I even know her now. But I can't leave it without saying how I feel.

"Okay. I'll respect your wishes. I won't try to stop you if this is what will make you happy, even though I don't think it's safe for you to leave right now. Just...don't forget that I will always love you."

Her expression darkens then grows as rigid as her posture. "You should have thought about that before you started banging other women. My ride will be here soon. Do what you want with my car." She looks down the driveway and starts to walk away.

I let her go and stand there watching, a lead weight burning a hole in my chest. I know she needs time to digest everything that's happened, and I need to accept she might not come back, but damn this hurts to see her walking away without once turning back.

Another car is heading up the driveway. Due to the dust cloud spun up from the tires moving rapidly on the loose gravel, it's hard to tell exactly what make.

Shit. Is that Talissa's ride, the cops, or the

internet stalker come to finish me off?

"Talissa!" I shout, but she keeps walking down the driveway as if completely unconcerned, and as the car draws nearer and begins to slow, I start to make out the details of it—a dark shade of grey and low to the ground. If I didn't know better, I would say it's Roger's sports car.

Roger?

Wait, *Roger* is her ride? He's the person she called to pick her up? Roger, my best friend who never called me to tell me about Talissa's plan to leave me and the kids?

Over my dead body.

I start jogging down the side of the stony track, rage flooding over me and tightening my hands into fists. Fucking Roger. Stabbing me in the back when the chips are down. Was this what he wanted all along? He's always been jealous I married Talissa.

It doesn't take long to catch up with my wife, but she ignores my presence even as I plead with her.

"You can't go with Roger. He won't ever love you for the person you are. He's always wanted to fuck you, nothing else. This is why he wanted me to go on that stupid chat program—to get me to cheat so he could get you."

She stops and turns around and stares straight through me. "I don't care about that right now, Terry. I just need someone to hang out with. Maybe he might be dynamite in bed. Maybe I might find out, maybe I might not, but either way it's none of your fucking business anymore. Just let me go."

Her words sting as if I've been slapped. I stop as

she turns away and continues toward the car. If it's a revenge fuck she's after, she's picked the right guy. I can make out Roger's sleazy silhouette through the tinted windshield of his car. My own best friend here to run off with my wife and go to fuck knows where. The rage flooding my body and making me shake is turning to nausea.

Roger pulls to a stop a few feet away from Talissa and lowers his window. He looks straight at me. His sunglasses hide his eyes, but I catch the full meaning of his grin.

Fuck this shit.

"Terry, no," Talissa says as I race past her and head straight for the driver's side of the car. Roger presses down on the door lock. Fucking coward.

I reach the car and bang on his window as he raises it up. "Get out the car, Roger—you little chicken shit!"

"Terry, leave him alone," Talissa shouts behind me. "I rang him, not the other way round."

"I don't care."

I grind my teeth as I stare down my so-called best friend through the window. "You'll have to unlock the car at some point to let your new girlfriend in."

Something hard connects with my lower back, knocking me off balance, and for the first time ever, I know how it feels to be the recipient of Talissa's martial arts abilities. I fall forward from the unexpected blow and hit my head on the roof of Roger's car. Blood drips from my nose as I stagger sideways away from the car and somehow manage to keep my footing.

I blink, my vision a haze of pain caused by the collision of my head and the metal car frame. As I press my fingers to my nose to stop the bleeding, Talissa walks around to the passenger side of the car. Roger pops the door lock so she can get in.

I make a lunge for Roger's door and pull the handle. He grabs it from the inside and resists my attempt to open it while Talissa climbs in. I've always been stronger than my friend, but he puts up a struggle for half a minute, holding the door mostly shut. He can't hold on forever, so he puts his car in reverse, forcing me to release my grip before I get dragged along with him.

Hands on my knees and bent forward wheezing, I try to catch my breath as Roger speeds about twenty yards away and then breaks to a hard stop. I don't bother pursuing any longer. Within a few seconds, all I'll see is the dust they leave behind as they take off together.

The car engine revs, stone pebbles flying behind and landing a few feet in front of me as the car does a U-turn. A loud clap fills the air, followed by glass smashing a split second later. Instead of bolting forward down the drive, the car veers off the gravel track and into a fencepost.

What the hell?

I run toward it, heading for Talissa's side of the car, but she's out the door and running at me before I can get far.

"*Run, Terry!*" Talissa screams and it's that panicked kind of scream that makes the hairs on my neck stand to attention.

I skid to a halt and nearly fall sideways as a loud pop ignites the gravel near me with a burst of dust and stone shards.

What the fuck?

I scramble to reverse course and get out of the way as it happens again a second later.

Bullets? Someone is shooting at me?

Shit. Shit, shit, shit.

Following Talissa's lead, I turn blindly with my sights set on the old farmhouse and the safety of its brick walls as we run from an unseen enemy. The air is filled with the sound of bullets being fired. I can hear dull thuds as they hit the ground and miss both of us. I haven't had to run like this since I used to play football, and the stakes were nowhere near as high, despite how much value people put on sports.

Talissa is much quicker than me, especially when she's wearing tennis shoes like she is today. I don't see the bullets hitting the ground close to her, and I dare not turn back to see how close to me they are landing. The house is only a few more seconds of running ahead of me. Talissa springs up the porch steps and disappears from view into the front entrance.

At least the mother of my children is safe. Just a foot from the steps myself, I indulge in a smile as I leap to safety. Like thunder shaking the sky and ground, the shooting erupts around me. Sharp pain bursts in my lower leg as a small lead projectile rips through the flesh and hits the steps on its exit. I crash onto the landing, unable to stop a scream escaping.

Bullets rain down near me, sending splinters flying from the wooden porch and hitting too close to my body for my liking. In seconds, I'm going to die if I stay here like a sitting duck.

A hand grabs me by the collar, and I glance up to find the grim face of my brother looking down at me. I slide against the timber structure, hitting my ribs on the jagged surface as he tries to pull me up. As I struggle to help, my brother stands tall, using all his strength to drag me through the doorway and into the safety of the brick house. Then he staggers back, his hold on me abruptly severed by a shot to his forehead.

It's a clean shot, blooming red with blood.

I stare at his eyes, still open but now lifeless.

"Joe! Oh, God, no. Joe!"

My mother's screams shake me from my frozen state. I put a hand up as she starts racing toward Joe.

"Mom, stay away." I force myself along the floor as quickly as possible and out of the line of fire. I need to shut the door, but its partially blocked by Joe's body. My sister is there, rifle in hand, eyes wide as she stares at Joe, then me, then the window she's got open a crack and I realize that the thunder has stopped booming outside.

The shooting has stopped?

In the sudden silence, I stare at Talissa, who is hiding near my father below a windowsill. "Is this real enough for you now?"

My leg should be hurting like a son-of-a-bitch, but I can barely feel it through the pounding of blood through my veins.

She glares back at me. "Yes, Terry, you were right. Happy now?"

I glance at the open door. My brother remains slumped lifelessly on his side. Things have changed so rapidly, it's hard to keep up. I'm numb in mind and body.

"Roger?" I ask Talissa.

"What do you think?" Her voice is hard. Cold.

I think he's lying in his car dead with a bullet wound to the head like Joe.

Who's going to be next? I close my eyes to block out the ugly visions my mind is feeding me of my entire family dead because of me.

My leg is bleeding. I know it is. I do my best to put pressure on it. Mom can't stop crying about Joe, but it's as if her pain has to travel through a thick fog to reach me. My kids are hiding together under a table, eyes wide, too shocked to cry yet, maybe. The others are silent, staring at the windows, guns at the ready, wondering when the bullets will rain down outside again.

I don't have a gun, and I'm a shitty shot anyway, but I need to do something to try to save my family. I grab my cell and fumble in my pockets for the tracker I took out of the phone earlier. If Hannah's on my side, maybe she can help. If not, and it's her out there shooting, then at least things can't get any worse. The search of my pockets turns up empty, however. I can't find the tracker chip. Maybe it fell out while I was running around being shot at? Maybe it doesn't matter since we're all about to die anyway.

Above the sound of my mother's sobbing, I hear a sing-song female voice shout from outside, "Terrrrry... Talisssssa... Anyone else—respond if you can hear me?"

I look at the frightened faces of my wife, father, mother, sister, and children. Talissa shakes her head at me vehemently, but I know I can end this right now by walking outside.

"Give me a minute," I yell.

"Make it half a minute, Terry, or we start shooting again."

I'm pretty certain it's not Hannah talking. It sounds more like Emily's voice. But 'we'? She's not alone? How many people are out there? *Shit.*

"Terry, no," my sister says, her hushed voice sounding like a hiss. "We'll shoot whoever it is if they try to come in here. No need to go out there like an idiot target."

I shake my head. "It's me she wants. Save your bullets for protecting you if I can't talk us all out of this." I look at my children with my sister standing over them to keep them as safe as she can. "Isaac, Matilda, Daddy has to go now, and I might not be coming back. Be nice to your mother, and don't forget I love you both very, very much."

They bolt from the table and cling to me. Matilda is crying and Jacob trying hard not to, but the fear is real for all of us. Tears squeeze from my eyes. What if this is it? I can't remember the last time I cried, prior to the last couple of days, but I know the recent events have caused me to make up for it now.

They won't let go, and I urge Talissa to peel them off me so I can face my fate. She does as I ask, the look in her eyes full of sadness as I pull myself to my feet and hobble back through the door again. The effort makes me dizzy, but I manage to keep upright as I drag my wounded leg without putting any weight on it.

"I'm coming, Emily."

She laughs. "At least you're telling me this time, unlike that day on my desk." A couple more voices outside join in her laughter.

I pull myself along, past Joe's lifeless eyes staring wide in my direction, until I'm at the top of the stairs.

The three of them are standing behind Talissa's car—the athletic Emily, the leggy Brittany, and the voluptuous Lauren—or whatever the hell her real name is. Or whatever the hell any of their real names are. They've clearly all been in this together and taking me for a ride.

I feel simultaneously vindicated for being right all along and like I want to scream at the insanity.

"Why?" I ask as I look at their faces in turn.

They keep their pistols trained on me as they move in unison toward the veranda. They're dressed in matching black leather pants with sleeveless leather shirts like a blonde-only version of *Charlie's Angels*. If it wasn't for the fact they're here to kill me, I would be thinking that it's kind of funny.

Emily takes point position for the trio and calls out so everyone inside the house can hear. "If anyone takes a shot at any of us girls, Terry gets a bullet to the head, and then we shoot you all, even the kids."

"Why the hell are you doing this?" I ask again. My hands are raised. I've got no weapon and I'm already wounded. I'm completely defenseless. "What do you want from me?"

"We get paid to do this, simple as that," Emily says as she draws nearer to me. "It's nothing personal. You're just a job, a paycheck. You should be happy you got to live this long. We normally get paid to kill quickly, but the person who hired us paid extra to have you brought down slowly."

"Who the hell are you people?"

"Have you ever heard of a praying mantis?" asks Lauren.

"Yes." I stare at the three of them, standing a couple of feet away with guns pointed at my head. "It's an insect. The female kills its mate after sex. And eats it."

"You're a smart man, Terry," says Emily. "We don't eat our prey, but we do kill them once we've had our way with them." She gestures to the two women beside her with a nod. "Welcome to the Praying Mantassassins." A grin splits her lips. "You like that name, Terry?"

"Creative." I nod in agreement. "But once again, why me?" I've been wracking my brain, trying to think of what I might have done to have a group of hired killers after me, while simultaneously wondering if these people are as insane as they seem to be. *Praying Mantassassins?*

Brittany laughs. "You'll find out when the time

is right."

I focus on her as a wave of pain makes nausea tighten my stomach. I grip the railing to keep from falling. "Don't get me started on you, you lying bitch. Do you have any idea how creepy I feel for having sex with a seventeen-year-old?"

She purses her lips. "If you've fucked a seventeen-year-old, that's on you, not me."

"You're not seventeen?"

"Like you said, I'm a liar. I lied about my age. But good to know you'd fuck a teen girl like the dirty perve you really are, Terry." Her eyes widen and her expression changes to the innocent, blue-eyed babysitter I know all too well. "Oh, Terry," she says in a sing-song voice. "I've never been touched before. I'm so innocent and horny. Show me how a real man does it."

The other two women laugh, the sound echoing as if from a distance as Brittany's words burn through me. Knowing what I've done, knowing how stupid I've been. Knowing my family has heard it all. There is no escaping the judgment. The humility. If they want to shoot me right now, I'm ready to go.

Another car is approaching up the driveway, lights flashing. This siren makes my pulse race. I can only hope it's the police coming to save the day, and that there is more than one vehicle coming down the track. I don't doubt for one second these crazy bitches will open fire on any approaching cops.

The three women run up the steps. Emily and Lauren each grab my arms and drag me with them as Brittany enters the house first, followed by the rest of us. She looks at my well-armed family and orders them to drop their weapons.

"You're going to kill Terry anyway, aren't you?" my father asks.

"Not if you do as we say. All of you, drop your weapons. Now." Emily's tone is no-nonsense as she pushes the long barrel of her pistol into the back of my head. I've never been into guns so I can't tell one make from another, but I'm pretty sure that when there's one poking me in the back of my skull, size doesn't make any difference to the mess it will make of my head.

My father and sister both lower their shotguns. Mom had never picked hers up again once Joe was shot. I see the terror in the eyes of my children, and I don't know who's most scared, but I need to say something.

"Ladies, please let the children leave the room. They don't need to see this."

"I agree," says Brittany. She looks at my mother. "Take them away, stay with them, and don't dare leave unless you have our permission."

"I understand," Mom says. She reaches out and asks my children to each grab a hand and walk with her. They hurriedly leave the room, my mom soothing Matilda's whimpers with soft shushes, and I can't help feeling relieved that at least they won't witness whatever happens next.

"Oh, dear, two cops. You'd think they would have brought some type of backup," Lauren says nonchalantly as the police car comes into view through the open doorway.

I catch a glimpse of a mass of blonde hair from the driver behind the steering wheel. *Hannah!* Whilst the passenger is blocked from my view, I assume it's Ed. I want to call out to warn them, but the pressure of the gun against my head makes me pause. "Don't any of you dare make a noise," Emily warns. She tells me to get to the floor, the gun still pressed against my skull. Talissa is looking my way, but from the direction of her eyes, she seems more interested in the blonde women surrounding me.

Car doors open and shut, and then a male voice blasts through what sounds like a megaphone. "We know you're in there, and we know you have hostages. Maybe as a sign of good faith you might release two hostages to me. Do that and we can talk."

"Come on, please, let the women go. Pick Talissa and Janet," I say to Lauren.

"Janet and your father," she says back to me without any audible pause. She calls out to them, "You two, go to the entrance. Walk, don't run."

They stand as instructed and keep their worried gaze on me as they silently make their way to the place where Joe met his end. All I can do is hope they don't join him and that these women keep their word. Hands raised in the air, their steps are slow but steady, and I'm sure they can feel everyone's eyes upon them. I hold my breath as they descend the porch stairs. With only a few feet left for them to reach the police car, I see Hannah—it's definitely Hannah—peel away from her partner to meet the released hostages.

Ed pulls a pistol from his holster and then two

shots ring out. Hannah stops in her tracks as if surprised, and then falls forward, hitting the ground face down. Time seems to stop as Ed darts a look my way and smiles, then fires another two shots that take down my unsuspecting sister and father before they can even turn to run.

I open my mouth, but I can't seem to suck in any breath. I've seen three family members shot in one day. "No!" I scream. This can't be happening.

Ed walks toward me, his smug smile deepening.

"Weren't expecting that, were you, Terry?" He shifts his gaze to the Mantassassins surrounding me. "You started the party without me."

"But you did so well, jumping right in." Emily laughs her husky laugh as she bends toward my ear. "Meet the fourth member of our squad, also known in chat circles as DancerGirl."

I study the cop or Mantassassassin or whatever the hell occupation he is as he walks through the entranceway. Ed? *Ed* is DancerGirl? "But I thought DancerGirl was dead."

Ed shakes his head. "That's only because *we* told you he was. Did you hear a news report or see proof that he died? No, you didn't. That's because Hannah and I made it up when Hannah mistakenly assumed she had infiltrated our group." Ed turns his head toward her face-down body that's sprawled on the lawn near the driveway. "Looks like that didn't go so well for her."

I squeeze my eyes shut tight. I don't want to see more. Hear more. But I can't shut off my ears.

"Aww, poor, Terry. You really liked her, didn't

you? Did you want to fuck her too? I bet you did. But you want to know what's really sad? She actually wanted to fuck you too, but didn't, unlike the rest of us," Lauren says.

"That's how we knew her heart wasn't into being a Mantassassin," Emily says.

"It's such a shame. You're actually a pretty decent fuck. I'm sure she would have liked it. I mean, you know your way around a woman's body, and I didn't regret that afternoon with you," Brittany says. "You did take me where no other man has before, so thanks for that."

"Yeah, I'd score you a nine out of ten, maybe a couple more inches and you'd be a ten," Emily says with a giggle.

"You and your need of big cocks, Em—you're as bad as Ed," Lauren says.

The four of them laugh.

"I don't find this amusing," Talissa says.

"Oh, yes—your cheating husband who slept with three different women, as well as you, in the space of four days. Maybe we should let *you* shoot him," Ed says.

"Well, he wasn't exactly in control of his hormones, though, was he?" Emily says, sounding smug.

"You drugged me on purpose?" The realization hits me like a hammer.

"Well, to be fair, you did take the pills willingly. But the other stuff in your drinks...that was for added excitement."

Emily shifts the pistol against my skull. "The

first pill was an upper, which did what it was designed to do, but the side effects include impotence. Then the next pill, well, as you know, kind of did the opposite and sent your hormones nuts, pardon the pun." I don't need to see her face to know she's enjoying this moment of confession.

"And then there was your scotch. And the ciders. I wasn't sure what the pills would do when mixed with alcohol like that, but the results were...arousing," Brittany says. Her gaze runs down my body and settles on my groin. "You truly lost your mind just to have sex."

"It's a shame we can't have a go with him now," Lauren says, looking me up and down. "Give him some pills and all have a turn, one last time together. I bet he'd even enjoy Ed having a go if we get him worked up and stoned out."

Icy prickles of fear run down my spine with renewed vigor as the image passes through my throbbing head of what the last few moments before I die might be.

Ed gives the three female Mantassassins a hard scowl. "Stop it. You know what the client's orders are. This is a paid job, not a fun house at a carnival. Did you even stake out the place and make sure it's secure? I don't like surprises." Without waiting for an answer, he strides across the room and makes a turn opposite to the kitchen. His route takes him toward the bedrooms, and I assume he'll follow the flow of the house and check each space. I hope he leaves my mother and the kids alone, wherever they are right now.

Brittany rolls her eyes at Lauren. "I think your brother, or step-brother, whatever the hell he is, needs a time out." She gives me a little shrug. "Sorry, Terry. I guess you're just not Ed's type. But honestly, he doesn't know what he's missing."

I feel like I could vomit any second. "If you've been hired to kill me, then just do it. What are you waiting for?" I glance at Joe's lifeless body. I don't want to die, but after everything that's happened, I don't know how much more I can endure.

"5PM," Lauren says.

"You're waiting until five p.m.? Why?"

"No, not the time. The *person*."

I stare at her for a long second. "It's a code!" Understanding shoots through my brain like the impending bullet from Emily's gun. "Praying Mantassassins—PM." I point at each of them in turn. "You're 1Pm, 2PM, 3PM and Ed is 4PM. So 5PM is...." I glance around the room as if I might find some clue as to who the fifth Mantassassin might be, but all I see is Talissa, staring at me in silence. "5PM is the big boss? The person who hired you?"

"So much potential." Emily pats my ass with her hand. "Shame you aren't smarter though. Well...a shame for you, that is." She leans down closer to me until her breath tickles my ear. "You call us sluts, bitches, skanks, and names like that, Terry, and we don't like it. Why is it that you men think it's okay to bang anything with a heartbeat, but when women do the same, they're all those bad things you call us?" She makes a tsk-tsk sound of disapproval and shifts position. "Women, as well as men, have needs, and

CHRIS HEINICKE

part of our assignment included having sex with you. Coercing you into it. Seducing you. Tipping you over the edge. You loved it. Well, I know you did when you fucked me on my work desk. I bet you loved the thought that we could have been caught, didn't you? Put sex and danger together, the result is something ...explosive."

"My wife doesn't need to hear—"

"What, that you had sex in someone's mansion?" Lauren says. "You probably wonder how I got into the Pellmont house and then convinced your office that I wanted *you* to see me at the appointment. You're fully aware of my charms. I used them to gain access to poor Mrs. Pellmont's security codes. She thinks she's giving money to cancer research each month now."

"Did you kill her husband?"

"Only with... love." There's a smile in her voice that makes an icy chill go down my spine.

"At least, I didn't get that task," Brittany says with an exaggerated shudder.

"And my wife trusted you with our children after the recommendations of the agency."

"What agency? Anyone with my smile and beauty can get a babysitting gig, especially if the client specifically chooses me for the job."

"What? But why would she purposely—"

"Think about it, Terry," Talissa says. She gets to her feet and walks toward me. "You said it yourself...5PM."

"What?" I stare at her for a long minute where the world seems to stop moving and I can't breathe, let alone think, because what's she's saying isn't making any sense and I'm pretty sure I'm misfiring under all the stress. "What?"

She sighs and runs her hand through her long dark hair. Her gaze flicks to Emily, and with a nod at the blonde Mantassassin, the pressure of the gun against my head eases.

While keeping my gaze fixed on Talissa, I rub the spot on my scalp where the barrel had been pressed.

Talissa. My wife, Talissa. The woman I've been married to for ten years. Talissa is an assassin? I feel sick. There's no way it could be possible. "You? You're the fifth member? You're 5PM? The big boss?"

"Not the boss, Terry, no. But, yes, I am 5PM." She shrugs, looking for all the world like this is an everyday conversation we're having and not that she's just admitted to being a secret killer-for-hire.

A sudden laugh escapes me, and I slap the floor with my palm. "You had me going, you really did. This is all a set-up, right? A joke? And you're all in it." I glance at the other women who are silently watching me. "Joe's not really dead and—"

Talissa shakes her head, her serious expression cutting me off more effectively than her words. "It's not a joke, Terry. I'm 5PM. I'm part of this team. And the bullets are real."

Tears squeeze from my eyes as the ache in my chest I've been keeping wrapped in numbness explodes in a painful breath. "*Why?*"

She shrugs again. "I was an active assassin a long time before I met you. I had been on a mission that went pear-shaped. I couldn't be responsible for bringing the organization down, so I had to go into hibernation. The best way to hide, they say, is in plain sight. I needed to find a husband and a regular job as a cover and neither proved hard. When I saw you at the club that night, and you were hot for me, I knew you had the potential to fit what I needed."

"So...these past twelve years have been a lie?" I brush at the wetness on my cheeks as anger starts to take the place of disbelief. I don't want to believe it, I don't. It's outrageous. A scam of some sort. Payback for me fucking these other girls. She's trying to do my head in and teach me a lesson for being an unfaithful idiot.

But a part of me nods as all the little inconsistencies I've pushed aside over the years begin to link together and form a certainty I'm still not ready to accept. Because it JUST. CAN'T. BE.

Except it is.

"Don't think of it like that, Terry. We had many good times, and until this last week, you made me feel like a princess. I knew the day would come when I would be recalled into service, but I never thought it would be because of you. I'm so sorry—"

"We had two children together, a house, and a solid future. Why are you doing this?" I sit up as straight as my damaged leg will allow and face her. Maybe, if we can just get back to where we were five minutes ago, we can get out of this mess now and deal with the details later. "Forget your previous life. Come back to me. I still love you—that hasn't changed. Think of the kids."

"I am thinking of the kids. If I don't do what they want, they'll kill the kids right in front of me. Then they'll kill you slowly. And then I'm dead. I'm bound to this contract. If I complete it, only you have to die." She lets out a heavy sigh. "It's not personal, my love, but you have to understand I have no choice. I've never had a choice."

I stare at her for a long second. "Wait... How long have you been in on this hit to get me? From the start? Or did they add you to the team later?"

The look in her eyes is steady and calm, but she lowers her gaze, unable to keep mine any longer. The action tells me everything I need to know but don't want to believe. She does that light shrug again. "I'm 5PM, Terry. I have to do what they want."

I grab my hair with my hands and tug it while I squeeze my eyes tight. The scream that escapes me is muffled only slightly by my clenched teeth. When I open my eyes again, I point an accusing finger at her. "This whole time I've been fucking all these other women, you were in on it? You were actually fucking in on it? Drugging me? Setting me up? Watching me go out of my mind? And to think I thought I was the bad guy. The one who betrayed our marriage. The guilt I've carried..." I shake my head, barely able to speak over the rage boiling through my veins. "Everything. Everything has been a lie. Every moment of the last twelve years. Our marriage. Our entire fucking relationship. And you not only knew, you were okay with it all. *Fuck*. Why, Talissa? *Why?*"

"Don't do this, Terry. Please don't make this any harder than it already is." She stops and kneels next to me.

I look around the room, seeking answers that aren't there. "What have I done to deserve all this?"

Talissa's expression hardens. "You did something very bad a long time ago, Terry. So did Roger and your boss. I didn't want to believe it when they first came to me, but facts are facts, and you're a very bad man. And if you truly loved me, even with the power of those drugs we gave you, you wouldn't have strayed from your marriage vows."

"*What?* Tell me what I did. What was it? Tell me what was so bad that I deserved this?" I glance at my brother's lifeless body. "Or Joe. Or my dad. Or Janet. Or even Hannah? *Why the hell did they deserve this?*"

A tear is running down her cheek. Despite everything, part of me wants to give in to my instinct to wipe it away and comfort her. But the stony expression on her face stops me. As does my growing disgust for everything she is and has done.

"She can't tell you, Terry, and if you don't shut up about it, I'll shut you up myself," Emily says.

"Really?" I bark out a laugh. "You're gonna kill me anyway, so what's it matter?"

My right leg won't move on its own. I shift position by placing my palms on the floor and use my good leg to help me move closer to her. Talissa's handbag is less than a foot away from me and I'm betting she has a gun in it. She probably has one hidden on her body too, but she'd carry one in her bag. I stare into her eyes. "Can I have just one last kiss, for old time's sake?"

Laurel breaks out in scoffing laughter.

"Geez, I think I'm going to puke," Brittany says.

Emily gives me a disgusted glare. "You really are a piece of work, Terry."

Talissa stares at me and I can't tell what she's thinking with that schooled expression she has in place. I move closer to her and she doesn't back away.

"A goodbye kiss," I whisper.

I put one hand on the floor for balance and the other through her hair. She stays stock still as I slowly cover her mouth with my own, tasting her tongue and kissing her deeply like we did the other night by the lake. She's stiff for only a second, then moans as her body relaxes.

As I pull back from her after a long minute, I hold her gaze. "Please tell the kids I was brave to the end."

I dart my hand into Talissa's handbag and find her gun immediately. I grasp the weapon with a firm grip and have only a split second to pull it free and fire blindly before Talissa is reaching for it, eyes wide.

The shot hits Lauren in the chest, and as I squeeze the trigger again, I hear a clicking sound but no bang. Emily and Brittany aim their weapons at me, and I can't be sure which of them fires the bullet that rips through my shoulder. I scream as I squeeze my eyes shut tight and fall sideways, expecting any second to feel the shot that will permanently end the pain burning through me.

But as I lie there clutching my shoulder, Brittany

says. "You shot Lauren."

I open my eyes and find Emily glaring at Talissa, and Lauren slumped on the floor with Brittany bent down, peering at her.

"I thought you said your husband couldn't shoot an elephant in a hallway," Emily says.

Talissa reclaims her weapon from where I've dropped it. Her eyes narrow as she glares at me. "Lucky I had just the one bullet loaded in my spare. Terry, what were you thinking?"

Thinking? *Thinking???* All I can think about is pain. Lauren is writhing on the floor, blood spurting from the chest wound I gave her. But it seems distant and slowed down, like a scene from a movie. My mind isn't ready to absorb the fact I've shot someone.

"What the fuck's going on?" Ed storms into view, his pistol drawn. He catches sight of the woman on the floor. "*Lauren!*"

Brittany is kneeling beside her, trying to stop the flow of blood pouring from her chest with a tablecloth. "Oh, shit, she's dying."

Lauren looks over at me, blood now frothing and gurgling in her mouth. Even in her dying moments, I fear she's trying to get to me, but her spastic jerky movements are uncoordinated and more painful than the burning in my shoulder to watch.

"I can't let her suffer," Brittany says as she shoots Lauren through the head.

Ed races toward me and points his pistol at my face. "I don't care who's paying us. This asshole is dead."

"*No!*" Emily catches him by the arm, pulling him back. "You can't do this. Terry's not going anywhere. He can't walk and his right arm is useless to him now."

"He killed *my sister!*"

"And this is why we don't like hiring siblings, albeit of the step kind. You need to separate your emotions from this, Ed. There's a big payday coming if we leave him for the boss as instructed." Emily glares in my direction. "There is another way you can hurt him." She gives Brittany a nod. "Go get the kids."

"No! Leave them out of it," Talissa pleads.

"What did you think was going to happen after all this?" The look Emily gives her is filled with disgust. "You can't come back to being a Praying Mantassassin and cart those two little brats around."

"Do you people have a heart at all?" I shout, exuding as much hate as possible through gritted teeth as my weakening body will allow.

"Of course." Emily arches an eyebrow at me. "I love all sorts of things, like money, nice clothes, and hot sex with well-hung, inked-up biker boys. But most of all, I like killing people. I'm the true embodiment of the praying mantis. I've even shot a man dead while he was coming inside me, and— needless to say—I exploded from the rush as his dead body squeezed out the last of his jizz in me."

I stare at her as she closes her eyes and does a little excited shudder. How the hell could I have ever found her attractive? "You're sick."

"You say sick—I say I'm a rich genius who

anyone in their right mind doesn't mess with." She looks past the kitchen to the hallway. "Brittany, would you hurry up?"

"Please, Em. Don't make them pay just to upset Terry," Talissa says.

"You've gone soft, haven't you? All those stories I've heard about how great you were at your job years ago? I have to say, I'm disappointed to see what you've become. I might need to call this in."

"Maybe we should shoot her, tell the boss she died in the crossfire. They don't need to know what really happened." Ed points his weapon at my wife.

"Mommy! Daddy!" I hear Matilda's high-pitched voice scream out.

"Are you okay?" Isaac asks his mother and runs over to her as Brittany releases him and Matilda.

Talissa looks over at me. "Yes Isaac, everything will be okay."

"Daddy?" Matilda says. Her eyes widen as she stares at me and the blood soaking my shirt and pants. "What's wrong with Daddy?" Her voice is nearly hysterical.

"Hush, baby," Talissa says and wraps one arm around both kids while keeping the gun in her other hand. Did she reload it? I don't remember.

I notice Ed smirking at my crying family, and if it weren't for my busted shoulder and leg, I would put every ounce of energy into taking him down. I wondered if Hannah had been the bad cop; I could never have been more wrong.

"I know what you're thinking, Terry, and I don't blame you, but this is a serious business," he says. "I can't kill you, but I can kill the family you love *soooo* dearly that you were ready to throw them away for a fuck." He gives Brittany a sharp nod. "Bring the girl to me."

"Don't you fucking do this, Ed," I yell.

Brittany pulls Matilda from Talissa's grasp and stands my screaming daughter a couple of feet in front of Ed, facing away from him. My ex-babysitter's voice is smug as she turns her head to me. "Make sure you watch this, Terry. Remember, you're a real man."

Tears cloud my vision. I can't watch this, but I can't turn away either. I try to shift along the floor to intervene, but I'm nowhere close enough to save my daughter as Ed lowers his gun and brings his aim down low in line with the back of her sweet, innocent head. Her screaming turns into a wail of tears. Pain shoots through me as I try to rise to my feet. During the split second I close my eyes to clear my head, a gunshot rings out.

"You bitch!" Brittany screams.

I open my eyes and find Matilda shoved my way unharmed and Ed lying on his back, not moving. Brittany jumps at Talissa and launches an attack that knocks my wife's gun from her hand.

I cradle Matilda and use my body as a shield, protecting my little girl from Emily. Isaac has taken the initiative and is running out the door and down the steps.

Talissa flips Brittany off of her back and slams her long body onto the floorboards. She turns to Emily and pivots on her back foot, swinging her leg

CHRIS HEINICKE

up and kicking the blonde assassin's weapon from her hands.

"I don't need a gun to beat you," Emily says and stands in a defensive position, bouncing on the balls of her feet, ready to take on Talissa. "I've got this, Brit. Go get that boy."

"*Run, Isaac.* Go to that hiding place," Talissa yells as Brittany leaves the fight to race after him.

"You traitor." Emily sneers and throws a punch at Talissa. "I always knew you were weak."

Talissa ducks her head and Emily's swinging fist travels above her. Throwing a counterpunch of her own, she hits Emily in the ribs, drawing a groan from her target. I want to help Talissa, but I'm doing all I can to shield Matilda and soothe her tears, even as the blood leaking from my shoulder wound starts to discolor my daughter's light brown hair.

I'm hoping I don't pass out from lack of blood before I can get medical attention. But I'm hoping even more that we make it through this alive together.

The two women continue to trade blows, each blocking and attacking with agile skill. Although Talissa has a few years on Emily, they seem well matched physically.

"I agreed to come back, and I agreed to turn Terry over, but I never agreed to have my children killed, you psychotic bitch."

Talissa takes a step back and lowers herself. Spinning on her front foot, she swings her rear leg around and hits Emily in the ribs, bringing her to the ground.

A single gunshot rings outside, making Matilda flinch and begin crying all over again. I fear the worst for little Isaac. Did he make it to the cubby house my father built for me and my siblings when we were children? Or does that shot mean Brittany has found him?

Emily takes advantage of Talissa's split-second distraction and kicks upwards, striking her between the legs and bringing her to her knees. The blonde woman rolls over, regains possession of her pistol, and stands over her opponent, aiming at her head. "You had your chance, Talissa."

Talissa slides sideways, reaching behind her back to her holster. A double shot rings out a second later, but instead of Talissa falling to the ground, a bullet wound blooms in the middle of Emily's forehead. She falls to the floor and lies still.

I glance at Talissa and the smoking gun she holds in her hand, searching her eyes for any sign of anything that might make sense anymore. Damn she's a fast shot.

She gets to her feet, kicks Emily's discarded weapon out of my reach, and aims her own at me.

"*What?* You're still going to kill me?" I shake my head in disbelief. "Why? We're okay now. Help me up before Brittany comes back. We can get through this if we just work together."

"I'm sorry, Terry." She shakes her head and there seems real sadness in her expression. "It's too late. It's better this way. For you. For me. For the kids. I can end this quickly instead of letting it play out the way I was paid to."

"Mommy? What are you doing?" Matilda asks. She wriggles out of my grasp and walks toward Talissa. "Mommy?" She pulls at her mother's hand, trying to get her attention.

Talissa's eyes are trained on mine, however, full of all the things that tears are made of—sorrow, regret, pain, but above all, icy determination.

I shift my gaze to my daughter. "Daddy's been a very bad man, and he has to go away and not come back. Isn't that right, Mommy?" I look Talissa in the eyes again.

A tear escapes down her cheek, even as she nods in agreement with me.

"Matilda, make sure Mommy always has your love, no matter what happens." I keep my gaze trained on my wife, the woman I have loved for twelve years, but have never really known.

"Mommy will always love you, Matilda. Please turn away now." Talissa holds our daughter tight against her and covers her eyes with an arm while keeping her gun directed at me. "It will be quicker this way, Terry."

"I just want to know who sent you."

Talissa shakes her head. "It doesn't matter." Her finger tenses as she pulls back on the trigger.

The gunshot cracks through the air, and I flinch, expecting to feel the impact. But as a bullet passes through Talissa's wrist and immediately draws blood, the gun drops from her hand. Her shot goes wide, hitting the floor beside me instead.

She gasps and grabs the wound with her free hand. Isaac comes running through the door, drawing all of our attention. "Mommy, Daddy! Are you okay?"

Before either of us can answer, Detective Hannah Hall follows him into the room, her gun pointed at Talissa and ready to shoot again if necessary. "Are you okay, Terry?" Her voice is soft and full of concern, mirroring the look in her eyes as she glances at me, making note of my wounds.

I nod, despite the pain, as relief rushes through me, making my breath shake in my chest. "I thought you were dead."

"I have a bullet-proof vest on. I expected trouble today. He got me in the shoulder though and knocked me out." She nods toward her left shoulder where blood has been covered by a quick dressing. "I'm just glad I didn't take a headshot."

She turns her attention to Talissa, her gun's aim never wavering. "Shauna Logan, you are under arrest for multiple counts of homicide between the years 1998 to 2002. You have the right to remain silent..."

Shauna Logan? What? Even her name was a lie.

"Kids, go to your father." Talissa's expression is set in stone.

The children do as told, and the three of us watch in silence as the mother of my children is restrained in handcuffs and led outside, blood dripping from her wound.

"Daddy? What's going on?" Isaac asks.

"Mommy's going to take a ride in a police car," I say. "That sounds like fun, doesn't it?"

Isaac nods and Matilda shakes her head and

---

pouts, and I can only imagine the years of therapy this is going to take to work through if we can ever get out of here alive.

"Talissa, is there anyone else coming?" I ask her just as she disappears out the door.

"No, Terry. The threat has been neutralized," she calls out. Hannah turns and looks at me before she follows her new prisoner outside. "I'll be back in a moment," she says.

Both of my children are clinging to me as tightly as if they haven't seen me for days.

"Is Grandma okay?" I ask Isaac.

"I think so, Daddy. Brittany hit her though and made her fall down in the bedroom."

"Can you please go and tell her it's all okay now?"

Isaac nods, and, taking Matilda by the hand, both children leave the room. My body feels heavier than lead and I feel more tired than I ever have in my life. I could probably crawl to the wall and lean against it but lying on the floor and looking at the cracks in the ceiling seems to be far more interesting at the moment. I blame the two gunshot wounds, lack of sleep, and extreme adrenaline overload for my dire condition.

Hannah returns and looks down at me with a sympathetic smile. "Sorry for not telling you more before today, but I couldn't risk the chance you might blow the operation if I mentioned your wife was a suspect."

"It's okay," I say as she kneels beside me and rummages through a first aid kit. "I wouldn't have believed you anyway."

Her lips pull into a thin frown as she creates a bandage for my shoulder, pressing on the wound to stop the blood flow before wrapping it. "This might hurt," she says.

"I noticed," I say with a wince.

"Oh, now you're just whining." She flashes that cheeky grin that makes my heart feel at ease despite the intense circumstances. She tilts her head as she works, and her expression slides back into seriousness again. "Some time ago, I infiltrated the Praying Mantassassin group. My objective was to gain their trust, then let them work out that I was still on the side of the law, in order to force their hand. It was important that I let Ed think I was his junior. But it's not true. I'm a senior detective, Terry. I've been doing undercover operations for a few years."

She's beautiful, with the way stray strands of blonde hair have escaped from beneath her cap, falling forward to frame her face. "You look like a twenty-five-year-old."

"You've lost a lot of blood, haven't you?" She winks at me her smile lighting her eyes. With a tight gauze wrap on my leg, she finishes up with my wounds. "I've called for an ambulance as well as the local Sheriff for backup. They shouldn't be long, but this is a rural property and that might mean half an hour or so."

Isaac, Matilda, and my mother walk into the room, each child holding one of their grandma's hands. She looks pale and shaken and a bit unsteady, but she cries out as she sees me lying on the floor. *"Terry!* Oh, my God."

"Are you okay, Mom?"

She nods as she hurries to my side and touches my face with her gentle hands. "Thank God you're alive."

"Thank Hannah that I'm alive. We have a lot to talk about, but I want you to go with the kids and Hannah while I wait for the ambulance."

"Terry, I can't just leave you here," Hannah says.

"Yes, you can. I need you to get my mother and the kids out of here before anything else happens." I look meaningfully at the dead bodies of Emily, Lauren, Ed, and Joe.

The threat has been neutralized. Talissa's words echo through my exhausted brain. If she's been lying to me for ten years, can I trust what she says now?

"I have both Talissa and Brittany handcuffed in the squad car. I get what you're saying, but I don't want to leave you like this, and I can't fit everyone in the car." Hannah looks at my family.

"Take my car then. Leave Talissa and Brittany locked up in yours and take my car. Just, please, get my mom and kids out of here."

"Terry, it's highly irregular to leave a crime scene before backup arrives—"

"Irregular? Tell me what's been regular about any of this?" I switch tactics. "Mom, please take the children outside. You can wait in my car for Hannah. The keys are in my pocket."

My mother stares at me for a second.

"Please!" I practically beg.

"You'll always be my baby, Terry." Grim-faced, she reaches for my children. "Come now. Daddy will meet us later. Right, Daddy?" She gives me a hard look.

"Yes. It will be okay." I give the kids a reassuring smile and fish my car keys from my pocket. I hand them to my mother. "The ambulance is coming for me in a few minutes. You'll be safe with Hannah."

Detective Hall gives my mother a curt nod. I can tell neither woman likes this decision, but my mother ushers the kids outside without another word. The kids' safety is the most important thing at the moment and I'm grateful they understand that.

When they disappear from view, Hannah leans toward me. "I know a lot has happened today, and you need to digest what's happened with Talissa and that she isn't the woman you thought she was all these years. But I hope in time you'll come to realize that none of this was your fault and that you are worthy of so much more." She bends down and gives me a kiss on my forehead that as shocking as it's everything I need right now. I catch her as she pulls back and place my lips against hers. It's a quick kiss, and completely misplaced considering everything that's happened and everything I've been through, but it feels like the absolute best thing I've done all day, and I don't want her to end the kiss when she pulls back after a too-short minute.

"Hold on, Terry." She strokes my cheek with a soft touch of her fingers that's mirrored in the look in her eyes. "The paramedics and back-up will be here soon, and those two bitches in my cop car aren't going anywhere except to jail for everything they've done to you and your family. We've got time."

Maybe, but there's a sense of urgency lodged in my chest that is telling me that time isn't on my side today. "Please. Just get my kids and my mom away from here. I can't relax until I know they are safe. They've been through too much already."

She shakes her head. "But Terry—"

"Please, Hannah. You're the only person I trust." And I do trust her. I realize how true the words are as soon as they leave my mouth. Maybe I'm wrong to trust anyone ever again after everything that's happened. But of all the women in my life recently, she's the only one who's not wanted to screw me over. Literally and figuratively.

She lets out a heavy sigh. "Okay. I don't like leaving you alone like this, but I'll take your mom and kids to a safe house, and I'll stay with them for as long as they need."

"Thanks, Hannah. For everything." I do my best to pull off a smile, despite the growing agony my body is in and the tears that threaten to leak from my eyes.

"Just...be okay. Please," she says.

And with that, she's gone out the door. Bittersweet relief rushes through me with the knowledge that my kids will be okay even though I'm pretty sure I won't be. I'm certain the threat is not, in fact, neutralized and I will most probably never see those four people again, but I'm okay with that as long as they are safe and unharmed.

As I hear the familiar sound of my car's motor

start and then slowly dissipate down the driveway, the exhaustion and pain that's been hovering like a cloud takes me into sweet unconsciousness.

* * * * *

WHETHER IT'S THE insistent buzzing in my pocket that wakes me or something else, I'm not sure, but I blink open my eyes to find time seems to have stood still and nothing has changed. Bodies still litter the floor around me. I'm still in pain. And alone. And alive.

The buzzing in my pocket happens again. I pull out my phone. The text message reads:

'Let's play a game of hide and seek, Terry.'

I don't need to see the sender's name to know it says 'Unknown'. I know who it is anyway. This is the stalker who's been haunting me for weeks, setting up the final game in this charade.

Are they here already? Watching me? I glance around the room, but it's filled with the stillness of death and nothing more.

How long have I been out for? Only moments, perhaps. The cops aren't here, and neither are the paramedics.

I push upwards and try to stand, but the lack of strength in my left leg from the wound prevents me from getting to my feet easily.

Using my one good arm, I pull myself to the table, and, shaking with the effort, manage to stand.

Shuffling as quickly as possible, I lean on the wall for support as I head for the room I slept in as a child. There's no point in trying to call Hannah. I want my mother and children far away from here if the stalker is coming to get me. The ambulance and police should be here any second. All I need to do is hide somewhere safe until then.

Hide and seek.

The going is slow, and with each dragging action, my good arm and leg quickly tire from the demands of the workload. But I keep moving. If I don't, there is no hope for me. Before I discovered Talissa's true identity, I would have been quite happy to meet my end today—but my children need a parent despite my thoughts a few minutes ago of being okay with dying.

I push forward toward my childhood bedroom with renewed strength.

CHAPTER 11

SO HERE I am, lying in the gap between the concrete foundations of this house and the wooden floorboards of my bedroom.

As a teenager, I discovered this section of the floor could be lifted and made into a secret place to hide things in, most notably the nudey magazines Joe used to buy me. But now it's me hiding beneath the trapdoor, flat on my back and trying not to sneeze, which is hard with the dust in the air tickling my nostrils each shallow in-drawn breath that I take.

And Joe... Damn, why'd he have to die? He'd probably be laughing at me being holed up where the porno stash had been hidden, except he's dead. And it's my fault. All of it.

Dying like this is what I deserve after all the pain and death I've caused today. Would my kids' lives be better without me? My mother would take care of them. Probably do a better job than me, since I can't seem to even tell when a person is a lying bitch assassin, not even after being married to them for ten damn years.

CHRIS HEINICKE

Knowing my marriage was nothing but a lie doesn't ease my conscious about my sins from the last few days. When I committed those acts, I was still in what I thought of as a normal marriage. The fact I was being drugged so I could perform like a trained monkey on a leash doesn't change the fact that at the time I was doing it, I enjoyed the rush it gave me.

I deserve this death that stalks me.

Boot heels click and clunk on the timber flooring throughout the old house, the echoes carving through the deathly silence and making my heart race.

I can barely move, and as soon as this stalker finds me, my life will be over. Whoever it is has planned well if their goal is to make me suffer before killing me. What I might have done to necessitate the hiring of a group of professional assassins to shatter my world into shards of pain, I have no idea.

Maybe I'll find out before I die. Maybe they will just kill me without ever telling me. I want to pass out and be done with it, but the movement of footsteps advancing my way jerks me to alertness. For a split second, the noise stops, and without the ability to see what's around me, I can't be sure where this person is standing right now. Above me. Somewhere in the room above me.

The clunking resumes, and with each heel tap on the wooden floor, I fear the end is near. Clunk. Clunk. Clunk. The steps continue until the noise stops so close that I can hear the person breathing.

Oh, shit. *Shit!*

As the trapdoor creaks open, sunlight pierces through the woolen blanket, now the only thing hiding me from view. The loud thud of the door crashing against the floor makes me jerk involuntarily.

Pain is of no concern now. As the blanket is lifted off me, and I squint through the late afternoon sun shining into my childhood room, I know this is it—the moment of truth.

It takes me a few heartbeats to form words as the shock of who has been stalking me takes its toll on my over-stressed mind.

"Kate?"

She watches me with the quiet calm of a successful predator, while I squirm with the discomfort of seeing my redheaded workmate aim a long-barreled pistol at my face.

"Surprise." Her voice is that same bland tone I've always hated, but now it sends a ripple of fear through me.

Kate is the stalker? *Kate?* The woman who always seemed to have the personality of a pasty, white pancake. I lick my dry lips and taste dust and fear. "Why?"

She shifts position and bends down on one knee.

"You're a piece of shit, Terry. A fucking misogynistic piece of shit. And you deserve to pay for it."

She's dressed in all-black just like the Praying Mantassassins, except on her it's a skirt and top, the tight leather looks like the casing of a stuffed sausage.

"I don't understand."

"Of course, you don't. You think you're a nice guy. Guys like you always do. But you're not. You use women, and you hurt them, and then you laugh at the fun you've had and forget them. That's probably the worst part. The way you use people and then don't even remember, as if they mean nothing." Her lip curls into a sneer. "Well, it means something now, doesn't it?"

"Did I...did I do something to hurt you?" I'm wracking my brain for whatever it is that I might have done to Kate, but in all the time I've worked with her, we've never shared more than a coffee at the office. Is all this because I wasn't interested and turned her down? "Whatever it is, I'm—"

She thrusts the gun at me. "Don't. Don't you dare insult me with fake words. I know you aren't sorry. You don't even remember who the hell I am."

I stare at her in silence, afraid to speak in case it's the wrong thing and she pulls the trigger.

"Even after all these years of working together, you still don't recognize me from the day we first met. The day you fucked my sister when she was drunk and high." The gun is quivering slightly in her hand as she glares at me with all the pent-up fury of a moment in time I can't recall ever happening.

"You don't remember her, do you? Just like you don't remember me."

"I—"

"*Don't lie!*"

"No. I don't remember," I admit.

"You're such a piece of shit," she says. "You and

Roger drank with her, and when you went to the can, Roger got her high on coke. Did you know she was so high when you were banging her senseless? Did you like it when you saw me walk in on you when you were doing her doggie style in her bed? My beautiful half-sister, who took care of me from the age of fifteen when my parents died in a car accident. You drugged her, and fucked her, and forced her to sign the forms to sell the family house that was our only means of security. But you didn't care, did you? As long as you and Roger got those jobs with our now-deceased boss, you had no reason to give a shit."

Pieces of the puzzle fall into place and begin to form a picture of a time in my life that I've tried very hard to forget. Before Talissa, before I knew my limits. Back when booze and addiction ruled my life, and the excitement of fucking a hot one-night-stand was almost as good as scoring a real estate sale for Phelps. And if what Kate is saying is what I think she's saying, she's right. I am a piece of shit.

"Leonie Crocker ...You're Leonie's little sister?" The connection smacks my forehead like a mallet. Leonie's name on the title deed to her family home. It had been the last obstacle in Phelps's quest to sell all five properties that needed to be demolished to make way for a major apartment development worth millions of dollars. The word on the street had been Phelps had also been on the receiving end of a cash settlement if he could keep the total outlay below a certain figure.

Roger had known enough about Leonie to be able to get her to drink with us at our usual Friday afternoon drinking spot, and back then, he had the occasional intake of the white powdered nose candy. But had I known he'd drugged Leonie that night? No. And I hadn't been high either. I refused to ever try it, on account of my tendency to fall victim to any type of addiction. I was already hooked on sex and alcohol. But did I fuck Leonie? Yes. Just like I'd fucked a hundred other girls back then and been too drunk to even remember if I'd enjoyed it.

I study Kate. "I don't remember you coming into the bedroom."

"Really? You came pretty quick when you saw me watching. But it doesn't matter. You got what you wanted then. And I'm going to get what I want now."

"And what is that? To kill me? And to think that all this time, I thought you wanted to fuck me."

She nods her head. "Oh, yes, I'm gonna fuck you, but most of all, I've been waiting for this day to fuck you over. Did you know my sister was the only person I had left in this world after my parents died? And did you know she slit her wrists a month later once she realized she'd signed the fucking form you put in front of her when she was in no state to sign a damn thing?"

I close my eyes as the memory plays through my mind. Leonie, looking pale and hungover. Roger laughing about how easy it had been. The newspaper clipping about the death in the obituaries. But I hadn't pieced it together that she'd killed herself because of what we'd done. Was that because I hadn't wanted to know? Had I bothered to even check?

Guilt lodges in my chest as painful as the bullets that riddle me. "I'm so sorry, Kate. I had no idea back then about anything but getting myself in the hottest real estate firm in the city. But I'm not like that now."

"You, stupid prick. That doesn't bring Leonie back, does it?"

I shake my head.

"But it's okay now, Terry. After I've fucked you like you fucked my sister, you'll get to join her, Roger and Phelps. And once I'm done with you, I'll put a bullet in Talissa's head, too. You don't think I saw her sitting there in the back of the cop car next to that tall blonde skank just waiting for me to shoot them both?"

"You've had this all planned for a long time, haven't you?"

Kate smiles and nods.

"So why didn't you just kill me? You had so many opportunities over the years," I ask.

"I had to make you suffer. I had to make you think you had done the worst thing ever to your wife by sleeping with those three skanks I hired. I wanted you so cozy in your marriage that you'd feel like killing yourself when you realized what you're really like deep down inside."

I stare at her as she shows a grin full of teeth like a predator about to eat.

"You'll fuck anything, won't you, Terry? You'll fuck anything with tits. You like the power and the excitement, even if it means it makes you a piece of shit."

"I'm different now than I was back then. You had

to drug me to get me to break my vows and do what you wanted."

"No, you aren't. You haven't changed, and the guilt's the same, isn't it? It's been twisting you up for days. You cheated on your wife and you enjoyed doing it, didn't you? It's been tormenting your mind, just like signing our house away tormented Leonie."

"I didn't know she would kill herself."

"It doesn't matter anymore. You took away everything from me, and now I've done the same to you. Your marriage, your job, your kids. Everything you loved is gone. All because you're a piece of shit who can't keep his dick in his pants. I could kill you right now, but I want you to die knowing what it feels like to be truly fucked over like you did to my sister..." she aims the gun low at my groin. "Unzip your pants."

"What?"

"You heard me." She gestures with her gun at my crotch. "Unzip your pants."

I close my eyes. I can't think of anything more revolting than Kate having a go with me right now. Or any time. But right now, it's not even physically possible. "Look at me. I'm wounded and bleeding. How do you expect me to perform in my condition?"

Kate takes a hand away from her pistol to dig through her skirt pocket. Pulling out a coin purse, not unlike the one Emily had, she smiles. "You're familiar with what these pills can do. Once you take one, it won't matter if you can't move. You'll do whatever I want with your cock." She pulls a pill from the little purse.

"Did you kill Phelps?" I try to change the subject to deflect her attention and buy myself time to think of a way out of this. If I don't do what she wants, she will kill me. If I do what she wants she will kill me anyway, but maybe if I play her game, I can find a moment of advantage for me.

Kate shakes her head. "Emily's work. My only demand was that I would be the one to kill *you*!"

"And it's quite a clever plan. I'm impressed. But there's something you need to know." I lick my lips and try to gauge her reaction to my compliments.

"And?" she prompts as the pause lingers.

"And I wasn't sure how to tell you this before. But I wanted you, Kate. In fact, I think I always have—ever since I saw your sweet, innocent face watching me pumping your sister. I didn't realize it then. Didn't make the connection. I've been hiding it for so long, even from myself, but in truth, I've always wanted to bend you over your desk, smack that big ass of yours, and fuck you from behind until you scream my name. You've been giving me those signals for years, and I can't believe it's taken us this long to act on our urges."

The lie is so thick, I'm surprised the words come out without me choking on them, and I'm half expecting her to just shoot me now. But her cool expression doesn't change as she bends down into the hiding space and holds the pill above my face. "Open your mouth."

I keep my eyes trained carefully on hers as I obey and let the pill fall into my parched mouth. I try not to cough as it starts to dissolve before even traveling

CHRIS HEINICKE

down my throat. The results are predictably fast. Even in my weakened state, I feel a stirring inside my pants as the drug rushes through my veins, just like the other times I've taken this pill with Emily, except now it seems even more intense. Is it a higher dose? Or is my heightened state of anxiety exaggerating the effect? Either way, with any luck the rush of energy will give me a chance to grab that gun while she's distracted with trying to fuck me.

I close my eyes as the euphoria of the upper flows through me in almost orgasmic levels already. *Damn.* The buzz feels so good, I've almost missed the electric feeling of being alive that it causes. "You should take one too," I say. "These things are fucking great."

I open my eyes. The gun's still pointed at me but her gaze keeps flicking from my face to the pronounced bulge in my pants.

I grin and thrust my hips in her direction, ignoring the pain in my leg and shoulder that the movement causes. "Come on, Kate. Let's get this show on the road. You wanted to fuck me. Well, now's your chance to ride me like the naughty slut you truly are." I touch my cock, feeling the hardness through my pants, and yeah, okay, it is a turn-on that she's watching. "I want to be inside you, filling you with my big, hard dick while I fill my hands with those big fucking tits of yours. Hurry up and rip your skirt off, Kate, and your shirt, too. I'm injured. I don't know how long this pill will last."

"I'm calling the shots, remember?" she says as she starts to unbutton her blouse with one hand.

"It's hard to forget when you have a gun pointed at my head."

I unbutton my shirt, an almost mirror image of her actions as she stares straight at me, the look on her face blank. Her hands move as if she's in a trance. My body aches, and although the bleeding is slow from both wounds thanks to Hannah's bandages, I feel the stickiness of my blood as I move my good arm.

Both my shirt and hers are fully unbuttoned, and she moves her weapon from one hand to the other as she drops her shirt sleeves down one arm at a time and lets her top fall to the floor beside her. Her black bra, designed for practical use rather than visual appeal, does a great job of supporting the twins that are proportionately sized for her body.

She could fuck me without getting undressed, but for whatever reason, she wants me to see her naked. Does she want to be admired? If someone would have told me two weeks ago that I'd be having sex with the frumpy redhead from work, I would have died of laughter.

But she's showing her weakness by taking the time to remove all her clothes. Unless it's part of her plan to further make me suffer. But I don't have a choice except to roll with it in the hopes I might have a chance to wrestle the gun from her.

With my strength only slightly revitalized, I lift my hips and pull my pants down to my knees. The pill's effect keeps the excitement building inside my boxers as she releases her skirt from her hips and stands on the floor above me in her matching underwear.

Except for the sounds of our breathing, the room remains silent. The blaring call of sirens still hasn't arrived, heralding salvation. It's up to me and me alone, broken and bleeding, to save me. And if I'm going to go out, it will be with a bang.

The irony of the statement makes me giggle involuntarily.

Kate pauses as her bra falls down her arms, and those big saggy breasts stare at me in their full pale glory. "You find this funny?"

"Not really, no."

Her eyes narrow into a glare. "Remove your boxers." Her pistol is shaking as she points it at my cock.

She's pasty and pale and saggy instead of curvy, and not to mention a complete psycho, but with the drug flooding my body, my cock doesn't care about anything other than she's female and nearly naked. As I pull my boxers down to my knees, my excitement is fully exposed to her prying eyes. I was right—she has always wanted me. The eyes don't lie, and the hunger I see in hers could consume me in one bite.

She removes her panties and steps down into the opened hiding space, standing beside me in just her heels. Keeping the pistol pointed at my head, she places a leg on either side of me and then gets down on her knees.

Her hand reaches down and grabs my hard cock, guiding it inside of her as she lowers herself to my crotch. The experience is unsettling. My cock wants to enjoy it, but with a gun pressed to my forehead and the fact that I find her repulsive on a level that goes far beyond the physical, not to mention that I'm moments away from imminent death, I'm caught somewhere between wanting to cum and vomit.

But if I can get her to lose control, I'll have a chance to grab the gun before she can fire it. Which means I need to focus on being in the moment and giving her what she wants.

I close my eyes and it's Hannah I see straddling me, which should feel wrong given I've been married to Talissa for ten years, but doesn't. I feel the tight wetness and there's no denying how good Kate feels. But it's Hannah I'm imagining, Hannah I'm seeing as she bounces up and down quickly. The gun's still pressed to my head, despite her fast breaths and movement, and as I rub her gently, she responds with a deep moan. I've been told before I must have a compass in my finger with how I seem to touch just the right place, and by the way she moans louder with each bounce and rub, I know I have her getting close to the edge.

Opening my eyes, I see she has her head tilted back, her spine arched, and those huge tits look as if they'll hit me in the face. The gun is no longer pointed directly at me. If I'm going to make a move, it needs to be now. She starts to scream and her head tilts down as she looks into my eyes. Her body's shaking, and as she tightens, I know I'm about to shoot my load into her. I reach for her gun-hand as she achieves her climax, but the weapon is pressed to my forehead in a split second.

She stops moving and grins at me as my body continues to shake from the reflex of completing the need to spill my seed. It's far from pleasurable to release like this. But my body has other ideas. Watching me closely, she tightens her hot wetness around me, and I'm lost, gritting my teeth against the moan that spills from inside me.

"There you go, there you go," she coos. Her satisfied grin is the last thing I want to see, but I can't look away with the gun pressed to my head. "Fuck, that feels good, doesn't it?" she says. "I'm better than all those other bitches. The real Praying Mantassassin." With her free hand, she touches my lips, tracing the curve of them, and I taste the pungent scent of Kate whether I want to or not. "I'd keep you around to play with, but I'm afraid that this is it for you." She pulls back and tightens her finger on the trigger. "It's time to die now, Terry."

"Do it," I whisper. I don't care anymore. I'm too tired to fight any longer. I can barely lift my hand let alone wrestle a gun from her. The energy I felt after I took the pill has already drained.

My chance at salvation has come and gone. Already, I can feel myself fading.

"They'll find you like this, with your pants down around your ankles, and jizz drying on your limp dick." She uses the hem of my shirt to wipe down the gun and press it into my hand. I want to turn it against her, but my trembling fingers won't do what I ask. That wasn't a normal upper she gave me. I realize that now. That was a different drug entirely.

She helps me place the gun to my temple. "How

does it feel, Terry? To go out with a bang? To know that everyone will think you took your life, just like Leonie took hers? How does it feel to be truly fucked over and used? Is it humiliating?"

A tear trickles from the corner of my eye.

"I thought so." She smiles at me, and all I can do is stare at her gloating face. I can't even blink now or turn away. My breath comes in a shallow gasp.

Then a thundering gunshot fills the confined space of the bedroom and the world goes black.

CHAPTER 12

5 YEARS LATER

THERE ARE STILL times when I shut my eyes and think of that day five years ago when my brother, father, and two of the assassins hired to kill me all lost their lives, and my wife was arrested for murder.

The ambulance did eventually arrive for me, but due to my body going into shock paralysis from the drug Kate gave me, I missed everything in between climaxing inside her and waking up two days later in a hospital with my mother, sister, children, and Detective Hannah Hall watching as I opened my eyes.

My sister, Janet, had been hit by a bullet in the abdomen that day and passed out for some time. When she woke, she grabbed a shotgun, and once she eventually found where I was, she blew Kate's head off her shoulders.

My sister saved me from the revenge that Kate thought would avenge her own sister's death.

It's a lesson in irony that's never been lost on me

a day since. Family is everything. And I've made sure to make that the focus of my life now.

Talissa was charged with twenty-one counts of first-degree murder, enough to sentence her to death by lethal injection. But having made a plea bargain deal, she was sentenced to life in prison instead. I take the kids to see their mother once a month, and although we are civil with each other, we agreed to a divorce. Not only because what we had was based on a lie, but because, as it turned out, I fell in love with someone else.

Detective Hannah Hall and I became a romantic item a few months after I was released from the hospital. We haven't married yet, but that suits us fine as we live happily in a log cabin near Seattle, far away from the bustling San Francisco life we used to endure.

As for the Phelps Brothers Real Estate Empire, they went into involuntary dissolution, and as the sole surviving employee at the Frisco branch, George soon found himself out of work.

Knowing he's a solid agent, when I started my own real estate business, I asked him to be a partner. Part of our new approach is to get in and help the sellers as best we can by lending money to them to renovate their homes, which they can pay back interest-free when we sell their property. We also source quality tradesmen to do any of the jobs required to help improve the property for a quick and profitable sale. Our business does very well for itself and we donate ten percent of our net profits to help fund local schools and the women and children's hospital. It's the least I can do to give back after all the years I spent being a ruthless agent and for what I did to Kate's sister.

Hannah did a lot of digging on the members of the Praying Mantassassins, found their real names and backgrounds, and matched up many unsolved murders with some help from DNA samples taken from the bodies of Emily, Lauren, and Ed. Brittany didn't fare as well as Talissa and remains on death row for her involvement in multiple homicides.

But even with the fear that there are more members of the Mantassassins out there that haven't been discovered yet, at least the financier of the team hired to go after me is dead. Kate probably saved most of her last ten years' worth of earnings to pay for the hit she took out on my head.

Kate took it hard when her sister committed suicide, which worsened what I suspect may have been a lifelong struggle with depression. She never dated and rarely went out. Inspection of her computer records found a string of notes typed up with names and methods to kill said people, as well as short stories of working as an assassin for hire. She also kept an online journal, which confirmed that she fantasized about joining a well-known killer for hire organization. Her chat history also brought up her strange conversations on 3DDreamChat and threats of murder to multiple chat users, but none of them had been killed in real life.

She also had several prescription medicine bottles on her premises, including anti-depressants, uppers, and downers. But unlike the assumed stereotype given to women who live alone, she didn't own a single cat. Overall, the knowledge of her solitary existence saddened me, but realistically, I couldn't have done a thing to help her.

Out here at the cabin, we have everything we need, and my children have been given the chance to grow close to nature. It's been a good place for Isaac and Matilda to recover from their ordeal. Their therapist feels that in time, they will no longer be afraid of anything bad happening to Daddy or that people with guns will run in the door and start firing.

Each year, the nightmares have been less and less, and for that I'm grateful. If I could go back in time and save my children from the trauma they experienced at the hands of the Mantassassins, I would do so in a heartbeat. The guilt over what happened to them weighs heavy on me, but as I watch them grow in their new life with smiles and laughter and love for Hannah, I'm grateful for the resilience of children.

There's a great fishing lake here a couple of hundred meters down a hiking track, and forests of pine trees as tall as city skyscrapers surround our home. The snowfalls during winter make this place we call home a photographer's dream, but we get to live it. We have electricity and running water, but no internet or mobile phone coverage, and we intend to keep it that way. The landline phone is sufficient to conduct business and keep us in touch with those we want to stay in touch with. We have two phone lines just in case Hannah needs to be contacted by the criminal intelligence investigations unit she now works for.

Love and laughter flow through our home. But if I thought that having a sex life would be easier now we are away from the busy city life, with all of us being home most of the time, the challenge has risen to a new level. Saying that though, each moment we have together is one I am grateful for. I should be dead right now. But thanks to my family standing by me in my darkest moment, I'm very much alive.

Life is good, and I intend to keep it that way.

As I walk down the driveway to the mailbox, enjoying the scent of the trees and fresh air, I'm grateful for everything I have. Today I'm working from home while coordinating a new property development for a company that works with one hundred percent clean energy. Yes, I've become a Dudley Do-Right, but that's probably what happens when death stares you in the face. I'm a changed man, and my sex and alcohol addiction has been curbed, thanks to the monthly meetings I attend.

Opening the hatch to the mailbox, I find several envelopes, junk mail, and a postcard. One envelope looks suspiciously like a power bill. I'm tempted to toss that one, but I tuck it behind the other envelopes in my hand instead. Another one is an opportunity to purchase raffle tickets to win a mansion in a city I don't want to live in, and a third is a letter addressed to Isaac from a pen pal. The junk mail goes straight to the recycling bin I keep at the end of the drive for that purpose. I tuck the bill and the letter to Isaac under my arm and study the postcard. The front of it displays a full-color photo of a band playing to a small crowd. The print at the bottom says, *'Greetings from House of Blues, Las Vegas.'*

My brow furrows as I try to think of anyone I know who lives in or is visiting Vegas, but no one comes to mind. As I flip the card over to read who it's from, my head spins and my stomach threatens to rise into my throat.

I blink for a moment, not wanting to understand, but the words are written in bold, hand-printed blue ink, conveying their message clearly.

Miss me, Terry?
Love, BluesGirl88 xxx.

THE END

7PM - THE BOX SET: 6 TALES OF SEX, MURDER AND REVENGE

Thank you for reading *5PM*. I hope you enjoyed Terry's journey and the interesting twists and turns it takes. The story continues in *7PM—The Box Set: 6 tales of Sex, Murder, and Revenge*.

In the cut-throat world of assassins, The Praying Mantassassins is a mysterious organization. Basing their technique on the mating habits of the praying mantis, the group utilizes the skills of seductive beautiful women and men to make their kills...for a premium price.

Brittany, Ed, Hannah, Talissa, and Emily, from 5PM, and two new characters, Jack and Bjorn, each tell their stories of sex, murder and revenge as their lives crisscross across six short tales. Who will escape the organization? Who will stay? And how will their lives as bounty hunters affect those around them?
Available at www.legacyhunter.space

ABOUT THE AUTHOR

Chris Heinicke is a multi-genre Australian author, most notable for the internationally best-selling Legacy Hunter series, co-written with Canadian author, Kate Reedwood.

His published works include The Man in Black, a science fiction criminal investigation story, as well as his debut novel, 5PM, a suspenseful romantic thriller, and the spin-off 7PM assassins series.

Chris Heinicke's stories feature strong female leads and plots that take the reader on a journey full of twists and turns, often through time and space, where the good guys (usually) win.

While writing, Chris Heinicke listens to classic rock, especially Queen, drinks vast amounts of coffee to fuel his robust imagination, and is inspired by stories such as Game of Thrones, Back to the Future and Star Wars. He enjoys creating new worlds with Kate Reedwood, as well as his solo works, and is most often seen at his laptop, writing.

Chris loves to hear from his readers, so please leave him a review at the vendor of your choice. You can also email him directly at: **KCBooks@legacyhunter.space**

For up to date information on Chris Heinicke's books, including upcoming releases and giveaways, please visit the KC Stories website at: **www.legacyhunter.space** where you can also sign up for the KC Stories newsletter and join Chris

Heinicke's Facebook reader group The Legacy Hunter Guild.

SCIENCE FICTION
ROMANCE SUSPENSE
URBAN FANTASY

Find our exciting stories at:
www.Legacyhunter.space

BOOKS BY FELICITY KATES

LITTLE MISS KICK-ASS SERIES
Sizzling contemporary romance with a aranormal twist
Cosplay
Secret Identity

THE NEW EARTH SERIES
Sexually-charged post-apocalyptic sci-fi romance

Project Hell Parts 1-5
Project Hell the complete novel

BOOKS BY CHRIS HEINICKE

THE PM SERIES
Psychological thriller with a sexy dark side.

5 PM
7 PM – Brittany
7 PM – Jack
7 PM – Ed and Hannah
7 PM – Talissa
7 PM – Emily
7 PM – Bjorn
7 PM -- Boxed Set

THE MAN IN BLACK
Out-of-this-world investigative sci-fi

The Man In Black

COMING SOON…THE ZODIAC SYNDICATE
Urban Fantasy in a MC world
12 book series

BOOKS BY CHRIS HEINICKE AND KATE REEDWOOD

THE LEGACY HUNTER SERIES
Science Fiction Adventure

Queen Killer
Star Keeper
Dark Horizon
Fatal Fortress
Phoenix Rising
Core Shifter (coming soon)
Lost Legacy (coming soon)

COMING SOON...THE GALACTIC MISFITS SERIES
Time travel science fiction adventure set in the Legacy Hunter universe. Featuring Shiznit from the Legacy Hunter series.

Book 1 – *Microscopic Mayhem* available as part of the ***UNKNOWN REALMS*** anthology.
Buy it now at **www.legacyhunter.space**